Johann

Vampire's Mate, Book Four

Grae Bryan

Content warnings: Erotic blood play, moderate violence, descriptions of past emotional abuse.

Contents

Prologue

Jay

If Jay sat very still and concentrated really, really hard, he could hear the yelling.

It was pretty faint, and honestly more confusing than illuminating, but he couldn't help trying anyway. This wasn't the first time the den had needed to hunt down a feral member, but it was definitely the most emotionally fraught instance he could remember.

Silas was old, and thus quite strong, and also one of the den's original founders. The de facto leader, really. He'd been over to Vee's home a million or more times, and Jay had obediently served him booze or blood or whatever else he requested. And true, lately Silas's behavior—never all that nice to begin with, in Jay's unasked-for opinion—had been erratic. And his scent had taken on a sickly rotting edge. But anytime Jay had brought it up with Vee, she'd told him to shut his mouth and threatened to send him to his room, so he'd stopped mentioning it.

Maybe he should have kept mentioning it.

It wasn't like Jay even liked Silas. He'd always been cruel to most everyone, mocking Jay at every turn for being weak and silly and nothing like what vampires were supposed to be. But that didn't change the fact that in the end, he was...family.

Was that the word for it?

Jay supposed it must be. Because that was what family was, right? At least for vampires. Family meant the terrible creatures you were stuck with because you had nowhere else to go.

And now a member of Jay's family was going to be put down like a dog. That should make Jay sad. It really should. But Jay was finding it kind of hard to muster up the emotion. He was telling himself it was because he was too worried for Vee to manage it.

He rose from the couch and paced the sitting room some more, sat back down for a while, careful to keep the lines of his suit neat, and then considered whether he had the focus to pick up a book.

But then he heard it, surprisingly clear among the distant shouts and scuffling.

Johann.

Jay paused where he stood, worrying at his lip with his teeth. Vee was calling for him. He needed to go to her.

But he didn't want to go. The thought of what he might find out there had his heart racing, his mouth horribly dry. Feral vampires always frightened him. But the punishment Vee would enact for disobeying her frightened him too. The isolation. The lost hours of time. Vee would know, somehow. She'd know he'd heard her and chosen not to listen.

She always knew.

So Jay walked out the front door, his legs stiff and his knees locking every other step. The air outside was crisp, the forest's leaves changing beautifully with the turn of the season. But Jay wasn't able to stop to enjoy it.

Instead, he ran.

It took him less than five minutes to reach the scene of the fighting, a clearing in the midst of their den's large forest acreage. Jay paused there, uncertain and scared, the metallic, musky scent of vampire blood flooding his nose.

Anton lay on the ground, neck twisted all the way around. He certainly wouldn't be up for a while. Out of the corner of his eye, Jay could see the mangled legs of someone up in a tree, but they weren't moving, so they must have had worse injuries than that keeping them out of the fray. Wolfe was at the edge of the clearing, his right arm—clearly broken—dangling at his side and an ax in his left hand.

And Vee, in Silas's hold, her long neck all torn to bits, from either teeth or sharp nails. She was only barely holding him off, one hand clutched to Silas's forehead and one to his jaw, clearly trying to keep those fangs off her at any cost.

She sensed Jay immediately, as she always did, turning her head slightly to catch his eye. "Johann," she gasped. "Come. I need your help."

Jay—his stomach a horrible, knotted mess—moved forward one shaky step on instinct, but then Silas let out a guttural snarl, and Jay's momentum faltered.

He didn't know what to do. He wasn't good at fighting, and he wasn't exceptionally strong. Especially not compared to Silas, who was so much older, even without the extra edge his feral state gave him. Jay tore his gaze from Vee to look to Wolfe, who arched a brow at him as if to say, *What are you gonna do now?*

Jay licked dry lips. "I—"

"*Johann.*" Vee's nostrils flared, her voice a cold, sharp blade. She was angry with him. So angry.

Jay took another step forward. This was his duty as her companion, right? To die for her if she asked. It didn't matter if he was frightened.

He wished desperately for his beastie to take over, to give him courage, but it was staying deep within him, unmoved by Vee's plight, indifferent to her rage.

Jay's feet faltered again as Wolfe stepped toward Silas, his ax raised slightly. Jay flinched in place.

"Johann," Vee snarled. "I swear to God—"

But Jay didn't get to hear what Vee wanted to swear to God because in the next moment, Silas stopped trying to knock off Vee's hands and went for her throat with his nails instead, digging into the wound on her neck and just....tearing.

The awful sound of Vee's decapitation was unlike anything Jay had ever heard. Wet skin and muscle, the snap of bone, the last gurgle of her attempt to call Jay's name.

Vee's head, when it rolled to his feet, was frozen in a mask of rage. Rage at Jay, who'd done nothing to stop this. Who'd disappointed her yet again.

Jay didn't wait to see the rest.

He didn't help Wolfe, didn't stay to see what would win in the battle between sharp ax and feral vampire strength.

He ran.

He ran faster than he ever had, through the woods and all the way back home. He ran up the stairs to his room, tore apart the covers on the neatly made bed (*no excuse for slovenliness, Johann*), and hid beneath them.

He didn't come out for a very long time.

One

Jay

J ay bounced on his toes, looking in delight at the white powder covering the streets in front of him. It had snowed again last night, and the fresh blankets of it made everything look so lovely in the afternoon light. So pretty, so glittery and magical.

Even if the brightness *did* hurt his eyes a bit.

Oh well. A little discomfort never hurt anybody. Or...Jay bit at his lip, pondering. He supposed it *did* hurt by definition. But maybe what he meant was it didn't harm? What was the difference between the two again?

He made a note to himself to look it up later.

What would be really nice right now would be to dive right in on the snow-covered lawn, maybe even make a snow angel. He'd never made one of those before. He smiled to himself at the thought but ultimately stayed standing upright. He didn't want to get messy before work. That wouldn't do.

You're too pure, Johann. Filth has no place around you.

"Off to work, Jay?"

Jay turned from where he was standing at the end of the drive to look back at the little duplex building behind him. Mr. Sumner was standing at his front door, dressed in a robe, with a steaming mug in his hand. He'd told Jay once that since he was retired, he was allowed to wear robes well into the late afternoon. Jay thought that was lovely for him.

Jay waved at his landlord. "Yes, sir. I'm the closer today."

He made sure to always call Mr. Sumner "sir." It was polite to address elders that way, even though Jay had been living in the upper apartment for over six months now and even though Mr. Sumner was technically younger than Jay by close to two centuries. It was more about how it seemed than how it actually was. Soren was always telling Jay to be mindful of appearances when trying to blend in with human society.

Which was why Jay was so pleased he'd remembered to wear his winter coat today. The cold may not have bothered him, but snow outside was a pretty good indicator it would have bothered him were he human.

See? Jay was great at blending in.

Mr. Sumner raised his coffee cup in salute. "Have a good day, then. Make sure those customers treat you right."

"Will do, Mr. Sumner."

Not that Jay had to worry about that. His customers were the nicest people in the world. And even when sometimes they weren't, it never lasted long. His coworker Alicia said that was because Jay had a way with people. Which was, in Jay's opinion, a super nice thing to say.

He'd told her so, and she'd patted him on the head, which had also been nice.

The walk to the café took nine and a half minutes, and by the time the bell chimed above Jay's head at Death by Coffee's door—Jay loved that little bell, its little dinging welcome—he had a bit of a headache from all the brightness of the sun reflecting off the snow. It was his fault for not wearing sunglasses, but he liked being able to see everything around him clearly, without dark lenses in the way.

He apologized mentally to the vampire part of himself—the little bit of his being that didn't like the bright light—for irritating its senses. *I'm sorry, little beastie.*

Alicia was at the counter, her red hair up in a high ponytail, with pretty blue eyeshadow on her eyelids. She always looked so nice.

She would be lovely to paint sometime. But maybe sitting for a painting was a weird thing to ask of a modern-day coworker? Jay would have to think it over, maybe ask Soren the proper etiquette.

Alicia tilted her head and eyed Jay critically as he approached the counter. "Oh, Jay, honey. You really need to let me take you shopping."

People were always calling Jay "honey" and "sweetie" like that. Jay supposed it had something to do with his looks: he was petite, his facial features were maybe kind of doll-like, and he knew people thought of him as cute. He supposed that made them want to call him pet names. He didn't mind it though—in truth, it warmed his chest when people called him nice things. It made him feel wanted, even if all it really meant was that he was nonthreatening.

"Soren always says that too," he told Alicia, hanging up his coat—which was bright orange and padded and hung all the way down past his knees—on the peg by the counter and glancing down at his outfit, one he'd picked out at the thrift store the other week. "I like my clothes though."

And he did. His fleece pants were the prettiest baby blue, so cozy, and his T-shirt was so fun; how could anyone not like it? Lime-green tie-dye? Amazing!

"His clothes are fine," Colin called out in a monotone from the office. "Leave him alone."

Jay smiled in the direction of the office, even though Colin couldn't see him. His manager was always so nice to him, never mean or overly stern like the managers on Jay's TV shows. He was always patient and kept his voice calm and level, even when Jay made mistakes.

Although, to be fair, Jay didn't make very many mistakes anymore. He was a fast learner and good at following directions, especially if they were clear and concise like the ones Colin gave him. A good worker bee, one might say.

My Johann. You were born to serve.

Jay made his way around the counter as Alicia huffed at Colin's words. "I'm just saying...he's such a cute little thing."

See? Jay was cute! Alicia shot him a wink when he grinned at her. "With the right outfit, we could have the girls all over you."

At Jay's wrinkled nose, Alicia raised an eyebrow. "Or...boys?" she corrected hesitantly.

"Alicia!" Colin stood in the doorway of his office now, glaring out at them. Ooh, he'd changed his hair from its former purple to blue, and switched out his sparkling eyebrow jewelry to match. Would Jay look good with a piercing or two? Or would his accelerated healing just...push it out of his skin? He should ask Soren.

Colin pointed an accusatory finger at Alicia. "Stop trying to surreptitiously find out Jay's sexuality. It's against the company rule book."

"Please." Alicia rolled her eyes, tossing her ponytail over her shoulder. "Like you've read the company rulebook."

"It's against common decency, then."

Alicia turned to Jay, her voice full of exaggerated sweetness. "Does it make you uncomfortable, honey?"

Jay had to take a moment to focus on an answer. He'd gotten distracted feeling out the word *surreptitiously* under his breath—it was so rarely used in everyday conversation that it was nice to taste it out loud. "I don't mind. I didn't realize you wanted to know. I like guys. I just don't have a lot of experience with them."

That felt safe to say out loud here. Alicia didn't know his real age, so she didn't know just how unusual the lack of experience on Jay's part was. And Colin wouldn't judge him for it, for reasons of his own.

Alicia gave a little shout of triumph, which was nice for her but also a little confusing for Jay. He hadn't had any idea she even wanted to know what kind of person he was attracted to—he would have told her, if she'd asked him outright.

But that was all okay. Because Jay was hit just then, not for the first time, by how nice it all was: to have human coworkers and engage in human conversation. Everything was soft and easy, and no one tried to bite or tear or snarl at anyone else. They argued sometimes—Alicia and Colin, at least—but they always did it...gently.

"Just get to work," Colin grumbled, turning back into his office.

"Right on it, Colin," Jay chirped, tugging on his apron and taking a moment to breathe in all the yummy, swirling scents of the café.

He'd liked the place since the very first time he'd set foot in it. Jay had never held a job before—that was *definitely* not allowed back at the den—but he'd seen the help wanted sign and realized working there would give him a reason to come back again and again without being a bother to anyone.

It had felt like fate.

He liked making the drinks—he liked how each one had very specific, easy-to-follow instructions. He liked making his customers happy, liked watching the humans sip their coffees, the little smiles they got on their faces when they were treating themselves to something nice.

He liked it all.

As he and Alicia switched out the register so Jay could start manning it, Alicia cleared her throat. "Um, Jay, honey? Can I ask you a favor?"

"Of course!" Jay loved a chance to do a favor for a friend.

"I'm trying to take a pottery class at the community college, but the only available one is in the mornings. Would you be willing to switch shifts for a while? You'd have to open the café, come in at five a.m. I get it if that's too early for you."

"Oh, I don't mind early. I don't sleep very late anyway." Or much at all, but he didn't want to worry her by saying so. She wouldn't understand her body had different needs than his was all.

She gave him a relieved smile, tightening her ponytail. "Okay, awesome. I'll train you to start. I already talked it over with Colin."

"No pressure, Jay!" Colin called from the office. "You can tell her no."

But Jay didn't want to tell her no. A chance to do a friend a favor? To see new customers and learn new ways to make the café run smoothly? Jay was all for it.

He hummed happily, closing the register drawer. "I'll switch with you, Alicia."

Alicia hugged him then, her body warm and soft against Jay's. It felt nice. He missed being touched this way. His friends here were all bonded mates, and none of them seemed to want to provoke jealousy in their partners, so Jay wasn't getting a lot of cuddles these days.

Vee hadn't always been the warmest person in the world, but sometimes she would hug him, if he really, really needed it.

But Jay wasn't going to let sad thoughts bring him down. Because he *was* getting a hug. And a new job to do. And there was still sparkly snow on the ground outside.

Coming to Hyde Park was the best thing Jay had ever done.

His only wish was that it could last.

Jay's apartment was quiet after the bustle of the café at closing time. Much, much quieter than he would have liked. Which was silly because Jay loved quiet. Really, he did. Or at least...sometimes he did. When he was reading, or when he was drawing. He loved a good, old-fashioned peaceful afternoon.

But it was more what the quiet *meant*, ever since he'd left the den. Solitude.

Jay rubbed at his belly as he hung up his coat. A familiar itchy sensation was building under his skin, settling in the pit of his stomach. It was still subtle enough to bear, but he'd definitely need to feed in a few days. He made a note in his head to make arrangements as he fussed with the couch cushions, trying to get them just right.

The little one-bedroom had come already furnished, which Jay was grateful for, because he didn't really know how to decorate a place by himself. Vee had always chosen their home furnishings. She had impeccable taste, according to her.

She wouldn't have liked this place at all—not one bit—but Jay did. He liked the soft beige couch, with its fluffy cushions, and the scratched little coffee table in front of it. He liked the big TV—garish, she would have called it—he could watch his favorite shows on. He liked the little kitchen he no longer attempted to cook in.

He'd even been adding a few things here and there—mostly a multitude of cozy blankets he'd found at different shops around town. And also a big, ornate chest for his art supplies. That was the one *ostentatious* thing he'd allowed himself.

We're not ostentatious people, Johann. We're above all that. Don't let me catch you flaunting our wealth.

Oh Lord. Jay rubbed at his forehead, resisting the urge to knock at it with his palm. Vee's voice in his head was super strong today. It just wouldn't quit. He wished it were possible to shake it out—like, physically shake his head until the old admonishments stopped coming—but that had never worked before. So instead he sang softly to himself as he puttered around, straightening the various blankets, trying to fill his head with music rather than harsh words.

Then for a while he just...stood still.

For a very long while, actually. Jay wasn't sure exactly *how* long he was standing there in the living room, but when he blinked back to awareness, it was fully dark outside.

Oops. Sometimes Jay lost time like that, when he was alone. A bad habit left over from Vee's old punishments.

He took a seat on the couch and cleared his throat, trying out some words. "I don't like being alone," he declared, his voice ringing in the silent apartment.

There, he'd admitted it. He'd voiced it out loud.

At least...he didn't like it as much as he'd thought he would, when he'd left the den. Sure, there were lots of good parts to his new independence—working at the café, family dinner nights at Danny and Roman's house. Jay had even gotten to take a trip to Tucson and rescue a scared woman from a feral vampire and take her to the hospital, where the police asked him lots of questions and Soren had to eventually come in and compel everyone to forget Jay's face.

That had been exciting, right?

But Jay didn't like the long hours at night when he was all by himself, just him and Vee's harsh voice in his head.

He used to hang out at the hospital some nights, just to have a place to be. But eventually Danny's friend Chloe had asked about his sick family member and Jay had to lie to her about it, and then he'd never gone back after that.

Jay sat stiffly on the couch, trying to figure out what to do next. He supposed he could call Soren or Danny. But he tried not to be too much of a bother. They had their mates to keep them company. And, despite what some people may think, Jay wasn't stupid. He knew Soren hadn't really meant his invitation last spring, when he'd told Jay he could come to Hyde Park. Soren hadn't really expected Jay to show up at his doorstep.

But Jay had seen a chance—one last chance—and he'd taken it.

And everyone had been so lovely to him, really. Danny called him "sweetie" all the time and had taught him how to drive. Sometimes Jay and Soren got together for classic movie nights. It wasn't *their* fault Jay didn't have anyone else.

Someone just for him.

In Jay's old life, at the end of the day, when all his chores had been done, Vee would often sit with him while he amused himself. As long as he was neat and quiet and polite and she didn't have anything better to do, she'd stay with him and keep him company as he etched out his drawings or read the latest novel.

Jay missed that.

"Stop being such a baby," he told himself, rising from the couch and kneeling in front of his chest (his treasure chest, he liked to call it in his head). "It's been over ten years."

He just wished he was better at being alone. He wished he was braver. Bolder. Like Soren. Jay's old friend had left the toxic den of vampires they'd both been raised in, and he'd had a full, exciting life before finding his mate. Soren hadn't minded being alone, had he?

But then neither had Jay, when he'd first come to Hyde Park. The novelty of it all—the humans all around, his very first job out of the house, friends to spend time with—had kept him happy and occupied. But lately a familiar melancholy had started creeping and crawling its way back in. An uninvited guest.

But oh well. Jay forced a smile—even if there was no one else there to see it, it didn't hurt to put on a happy face—and chose an activity. No crying over eternal solitude, right?

He'd draw tonight, he decided. Charcoal. He wasn't in the mood for bright colors. And he'd watch one of his favorite shows, *Gilmore Girls*. He'd seen it before, more than once, but that was okay. He liked how fast they talked and and all the references they made—he would look them up after each episode and always find something new to watch or read to pass the time.

All Jay had was time.

So much time.

Except...as he set up his supplies, as if summoned by his moment of weakness, Jay's phone dinged.

Have you tired of your experiment yet?

Jay sighed softly, scowling down at his phone. How did he always *know* like that? Jay debated ignoring it, but he didn't want to deal with the consequences.

Not yet! Four months left.

Jay left it at that and tucked his phone under the couch cushion, deciding out of sight was out of mind, and laid out his art supplies.

He already knew what he was going to draw. He couldn't help it. A familiar face, etched permanently into his mind from centuries of companionship. A beautiful older woman, with cold eyes and a stern jaw.

Veronique. Vee.

Three episodes in and Jay heard his phone buzz through the cushions. He reached for it before he could stop himself, laughing in delight when he saw the message was from Danny.

Book club Saturday. You still in?

Of course Jay was still in! He'd even gotten to choose the book this month. He'd gone for one of his old favorites: *Jane Eyre*. It was dark and broody and mysterious, so it felt appropriate for winter. And he was pretty sure no one would make fun of it the same way they would one of his Highlander romances—the ones with the big, shirtless men on the covers he liked to keep secret on his phone.

Just like that, Jay felt his melancholy lift.

He had friends here, people who wanted him around. And come Friday, he was going to open at the café for the first time. He'd learn new skills and provide humans with the caffeine they needed to start their days.

Everything was just fine.

And he had four more months of it.

Two

Alexei

Death by Coffee. What a fitting name. Maybe Alexei would find a bullet waiting for him in the small brick building. Not that he'd really expect his brother's men to be waiting to ambush him in a place like this. Still, he couldn't count it out entirely. Expecting the unexpected might be the only way to stay alive.

He hasn't found you, he scolded himself, drumming his fingers on the steering wheel, annoyed at his own thoughts. *Stop being so paranoid.*

Alexei pulled the beater he'd bought outside the Denver International Airport to a rolling stop halfway down the block from the café he'd spotted. He'd been in Hyde Park for weeks and hadn't explored any more than the seven-hundred-ish square feet of his apartment. Theoretically, that was because he was lying low—no matter how unlikely it was that he'd been tracked to the little mountain town already—but in reality he just couldn't be bothered. What was even the point of getting out of bed these days? There was nothing and nobody waiting for him. He could sleep twenty-four hours of every day and not a soul would be bothered.

That sounded pretty nice, actually.

But he'd woken up at four that morning and hadn't been able to go back to sleep this time, so after two hours of staring at the same amoeba-like water stain on his bedroom wall, he'd decided to get out of his apartment and go *somewhere*. Anywhere. And not much else was open, so why not start with coffee?

Alexei opened his car door and began the painful process of unfolding himself from the front seat. The little compact, clearly not designed for someone of his height in mind, was light-years away from the town cars he'd been used to all his life, the comfort of which he allowed himself to briefly miss before knocking the spoiled sentiment out of his head.

He debated grabbing his coat, but despite the snow on the ground, the chill was nothing compared to what he'd left behind in New York. His gray cashmere would do just fine.

Alexei's desire for a six a.m. coffee didn't seem to be a popular one that morning. The large front windows of the little café showed it to be mostly empty, its small wooden tables and cozy atmosphere shared only by an older couple reading their respective papers in the corner.

Alexei made his way inside, grimacing in annoyance at the jangling bell announcing his arrival.

"Hello!"

Alexei tapped his boots on the mat at the door, looking to the source of the greeting. There was a little guy at the counter, dressed in a truly hideous sweatshirt, and he was waving at Alexei with surprising gusto. Alexei was so distracted by the strange enthusiasm of the greeting (not to mention that eyesore of an outfit), that he was all the way to the counter before his brain processed the fact that the guy beneath the clothes could only be described as...adorable.

Distractingly so.

The barista couldn't have been any taller than five feet five, with dainty features and a mess of dark hair, the oversize, electric-blue sweatshirt with the kittens on it so large on him he'd had to roll it over about a dozen times to get it above his elbows.

Alexei had the momentary, completely bizarre thought that he wanted to steal him. To put the stranger in his pocket and take him back to his apartment, stash him there for the foreseeable future. Just...keep him.

Because apparently Alexei's recent hermitage had melted his fucking brain.

"I'm Johann," the guy chirped, oblivious to Alexei's disturbing new impulses, still waving enthusiastically even though Alexei was now directly in front of him. "But you can call me Jay. Welcome in. You've really chosen very well." His eyes—a soothing slate gray—were positively shining. "Our coffee's delicious. The best in town. Although, I wouldn't actually know. It's the only coffee I've ever had."

Alexei was staring, and not just because of the word salad he'd just been presented with. He simply couldn't look away. The guy was so...pretty. Gorgeous in a soft, unassuming way, with that little button nose, those Cupid's bow lips. And really, the bed head look he had going on was too much; it was sending Alexei's brain into dangerous territory. Like sweat-soaked sheets and a dark head bobbing between his legs and a million other dirty things he shouldn't be thinking about.

His dick was in serious danger of plumping up in his jeans just from looking at the guy.

What in the actual fuck? Alexei needed to get his head on straight. He'd seen a million and one cute twinks in the city, hosted a considerably lower number than that in his bed, and he'd never before felt like he was two steps away from leaping over a coffee shop counter and—

And what, planting a kiss on the guy? Hoisting him over his shoulder?

What was *wrong* with him?

Alexei cleared his throat, trying to find the corner of his brain that knew how to order coffee like a regular human. "I—"

"Your eyes," the barista—Jay, he'd said his name was—interrupted, leaning forward so they were nose to nose, his breath warm on Alexei's face. Alexei hadn't realized until that moment how far he himself had leaned over the counter, as if pulled by some magnetic force. The barista smelled like peppermint. "They have so many colors in them."

Alexei had nothing to say to that, but that didn't seem to bother Jay. "I can see green. Blue. Little flecks of golden brown." Jay smiled wide at him, leaning back and leaving Alexei feeling oddly bereft. "They're really very pretty."

Alexei cleared his throat for the second time, trying to find his bearings. He was taken strangely off guard by the compliment. His eyes had always been a source of discomfort for him. His older and younger brothers had gotten the ice-blue coloring of their father's, paired with his white-blond hair. Proof of their heritage, the strength of the family line. Proof Alexei had never received. Nor had he inherited his mother's eyes, neither their limpid brown color nor their warmth. His strange hazel eyes were an anomaly, one his father had always liked to prod at when he wanted Alexei to feel...other.

Alexei tried to get some words out. "Okay. Thanks. So—"

"And your hair." The barista cocked his head like a little bird. Or a curious kitten. "There's so much golden blond but also bits of brown and even some streaks of—I don't know...strawberry?"

Alexei lifted a hand to his own head, fingers touching the overly long hair he'd pulled into a loose bun that morning. He'd been meaning to cut it, maybe even dye it. He now suddenly felt quite strongly he should leave it exactly the way it was.

"And you smell really good. Like vanilla." For just a second, there was a flash of....something...in Jay's gray eyes. Almost predatory. But Alexei must have been imagining it, because the next second, it was gone, and Jay was again looking upbeat and perky, smiling brightly at him. "So what can I get for you? And what name for the order?"

Alexei's mouth moved on autopilot, his brain now seemingly permanently somewhere far away. "An Americano. Please. Alex."

Jay beamed at him. "Okay, Alex. I know how to make that."

"Good." Alexei didn't recognize his own voice, the strange husky note to it.

"It is, isn't it? Although, to be fair, I know how to make all our drinks now." Once again, Alexei had nothing to say in response. A brief stare-off ensued before Jay lifted a finger to point to the other end of the counter. "If you wait over there, it'll be out in a jiffy."

Alexei forced himself to unfreeze his muscles and move from where he stood over to where the redhead manning the espresso machine was watching him with clear amusement on her face. He didn't look back at Jay. He couldn't.

"What just happened?"

It wasn't until the redhead answered him that Alexei realized he'd asked his question out loud. She smirked at him, tamping down the espresso she'd just ground. "I'd say you got Jayed."

"Is he like that with everyone?" Alexei asked, hoping his expression was significantly more neutral than he felt. He needed to place the strange interaction he'd just had into some sort of context.

"You mean unknowingly charming the pants off everyone he meets, giving devastating and sincere compliments that leave people reeling, then flouncing away without a care in the world?"

Alexei coughed weakly, rubbing at the back of his neck. "Yeah. That."

The redhead shrugged, her smirk turning into an evil grin. "Pretty much, yep. He's like that with everyone."

Five minutes later, coffee in hand, Alexei wandered back to his car in a daze.

By the time he remembered to drink his Americano, it had gone ice-cold.

Alexei couldn't stay away after that.

There was no rhyme or reason to it. He hadn't even meant to go back to Death by Coffee the next day, not consciously. Alexei had just been driving around, and then soon he was parking in a familiar spot and then walking through that jangling door, and there Jay had been, smiling and waving.

Alexei's heart had stopped in his chest for a moment at the joyful, "You came back!" he was given on that second visit, thinking for a moment the strange attraction he felt was mutual. But he soon learned the redhead hadn't been lying: Jay was like that with everyone. Beaming smiles, sincere compliments, absurd non sequiturs.

But the frustrating thing was, no one else seemed quite so...affected by it. Not like Alexei was.

It was certainly clear—after a week of daily visits, observing every interaction more closely than was strictly sane—that Jay's regulars adored him. Alexei had watched, dumbstruck, as one older woman had actually pinched Jay's cheek, something Alexei hadn't known happened in real life.

But for the most part, as far as Alexei could tell, everyone seemed able to move on with their lives after an interaction with him. No one else stared, salivated, or masturbated furiously in the shower to thoughts of pink lips as Alexei had every night for the past week (or at least, Alexei had to assume they didn't do the last part; he wasn't exactly following anyone home to check).

The manager though. He paid Jay more attention than Alexei would have liked. He also paid Alexei more attention than Alexei would have liked, scowling at him from across the café. Not exactly prime customer service.

But the scowls were worth it for Alexei's little interactions with his strange new obsession. He could get quite a few of them, if he timed it right, coming in at a slow hour. He even found himself lengthening his orders, just to hear that sweet voice repeat them back to him.

And yes, he did realize he was acting psychotic. Possibly this was some kind of mental break after a lifetime of stress, on top of the heightened anxiety of his new life on the run. That would explain the absurdity of making himself an honest-to-God regular somewhere in his new town rather than lying low as he should have been doing.

But he told himself—in complete opposition to the paranoid reasoning he'd been living with for so long—that it was okay to let himself be seen and known in Hyde Park. That his brother was satisfied with having run Alexei off. Why track Alexei down when he finally had what he'd always wanted? Alexei out of the fucking picture. Permanently.

He also told himself, when he was feeling particularly delusional, that Jay paid him special attention.

And to be fair, the little barista did often wander over when the café was slow, asking Alexei if he wanted anything else, offering up more absurd compliments. Once he'd asked Alexei if he'd just been baking. When Alexei had told him no, Jay had cocked his head. "But you always smell so sweet. Like one of our vanilla cupcakes. Are you sure you haven't been baking?"

Alexei had never heard such a blatant fucking pickup line in his life.

Or so one would think. But that was the thing. The incredible, mind-melting frustration of it all. It *wasn't* a pickup line. Jay had said it and then just…skipped away, unbothered and completely unembarrassed by his words.

And, to be fair, Alexei had also once overheard Jay compliment his fucking cash register for opening "so smoothly and quietly." He also greeted every canine guest in the café like visiting royalty, waving and beaming and handing out dog treats like Oprah giving away a free car.

So at least Alexei factored into Jay's thinking somewhere on par with an inanimate object or someone else's pet, right?

He made himself leave each day after two hours, deciding arbitrarily that anything longer than that would be truly pathetic.

Walking home after his latest visit, feeling absurdly wrung out after what amounted to several hours sitting still in a comfortable chair, Alexei dialed the only number he knew by heart.

"If this is who I think it is, you shouldn't be calling me."

Just the sound of his younger brother's voice put Alexei at ease for the first time in six weeks. "Sascha."

Sascha's answering sigh was dramatic as hell. "Alexei. You really set off a shitstorm this time."

"I know. You're safe though?" Alexei already knew the answer. Their older brother would never hurt Sascha. The baby of the family. The only one of their trio not raised to be heartless, ruthless, and cruel.

Sascha scoffed at the question. "Of course I'm safe. *You* can't come back though. You know that, right? Ivan seems ready to shoot on sight."

More like Ivan had already hired goons to shoot on sight, and he'd be happy to have the deed done whether he was there to witness it or not, but Alexei didn't feel like splitting hairs. "I cost him a lot of money."

"You cost him his pride. That's even worse."

Alexei grunted in acknowledgment of that. Pride would always be the bigger issue with Ivan. It had to be known he was still top dog, in complete and total charge of his kingdom. Alexei purposefully fucking up a major deal, losing millions in a single act, definitely fucked with that image.

He almost had to suppress a smile at the thought, feeling somehow that Sascha would sense it on the other end of the line.

"You've found somewhere?" Sascha asked.

"I have."

"Don't tell me any details."

"I won't." And Alexei wouldn't. He loved his younger brother dearly, but Sascha had grown up spoiled, babied by both his brothers and their father. He was often careless, not out of ill intent but pure thoughtlessness.

Alexei loved him, yes, but he didn't trust him. Not with his life. With other things though...

Alexei cleared his throat. "There's a barista here, at this café I go to. He's so...strange. I think he might be an alien."

There was a moment of silence as Sascha clearly struggled to register the direction of Alexei's thoughts, and then he was barking out a sharp laugh. "You've lived in New York thirty-five years and never met someone you cared about for more than one night. Now you've been on the run six weeks and you've got yourself a *crush*?"

"It's not a crush. He's way too young for me."

"It sounds like a crush."

With anyone else, Alexei would have hung up the phone by now. He didn't take kindly to teasing. But Sascha was allowed what others weren't, and the little fucker knew it. "What would you do if you had a crush? Not that this is a crush," Alexei hurried to clarify.

"Oh my God, Alexei. Just ask him out. You're a good-looking guy. I've never seen you strike out when you're interested."

True. Incredibly true. Although, back in New York, Alexei had been operating under very different conditions. He'd never known how many of those men had been attracted to his looks—which weren't bad, he was aware enough to know—or to his perceived money and power. How many lovers had come to him because they knew his family ran the club they'd found themselves in? How many were simply attracted to the potential brush with danger? Flirting with a rumored member of the mob?

But Jay didn't seem too impressed with money or prestige, as far as Alexei could tell. He'd seen, just the other day, a suited customer trying to show off his Rolex, and Jay had countered with his own glow-in-the-dark waterproof number, of which he was apparently incredibly proud.

So what *did* get the little barista going?

Alexei hung up after a few more minutes of catch-up with Sascha, feeling foolish for having outed his little obsession, the unfamiliar emotion causing him to scowl at anyone who crossed his path on the way home.

Alexei didn't know what he wanted. He felt like a dog who wouldn't give up his bone, even as he choked on it.

He knew he didn't have space in his life for another human being, especially one as sugar sweet as the one he was currently coveting. He imagined for a moment: sweet, doll-like Jay, faced with one of his brother's men. Alexei's blood ran cold at the thought. Jay wouldn't stand a fucking chance.

No, Alexei should stay far away from him. Find a new place to haunt.

It was just that...after a lifetime of numbness, of feeling cold and distant and apathetic to everything around him, there was now this little bright spot of color. And it didn't make sense, and it probably—definitely—made Alexei a creep, but there it was. A blossoming obsession.

And that night, straining cock in hand, the shower spray beating on his back, Jay's pretty face projecting onto his closed eyelids, Alexei had to admit it. He wasn't going to leave the guy alone.

A good man would.

But Alexei had never been a good man, had he?

Three

Jay

Alex was back. *Alexei*, Jay reminded himself as the door chimed and his new favorite regular arrived. He'd told Jay the other day to call him Alexei.

Jay liked it. The little "ei" added a bit of softness to the human's name, which added a bit of softness to him as a whole. Which was kind of nice because Alexei could be a bit...intimidating.

He was big, for one. So much taller than Jay, by practically a whole foot, it seemed. And he was very, very handsome, for two. Just...quite appealing in general. His face, with its long, straight nose and rugged, masculine jawline. His build, with broad shoulders and large hands to match. Even his forearms were weirdly nice looking when he pushed his sweater sleeves back, like now. Golden hairs dotted them, the color matching the scruff on Alexei's firm jaw. Jay wanted to rub against those arms like a cat. His beastie did too.

But that would be weird, right? Humans didn't rub up against other humans they barely knew.

So no rubbing. And also, Jay had been counting something. What had he been counting?

Right, the ways in which Alexei was intimidating.

So for three, his handsome face was always kind of stern, those dark-golden brows often drawn together in a subtle frown. Not quite a scowl but also not *not* a scowl.

The nice thing was, though, those stern eyebrows always kind of relaxed around Jay. He liked watching it happen, the moment Alexei caught his eye and that frown softened to... One couldn't quite call it a smile, exactly, but it was definitely neutral at the very least. That always made Jay feel good.

Today Alexei had on a black pullover sweater and worn-looking jeans. He didn't seem to wear a coat as often as other humans. Maybe when a human was that big, they didn't get cold as easily? Jay would ask Danny about it later. His nurse friend always knew important medical facts like that.

Anyhoo, Alexei wore a lot of black and gray. Enough that Jay might normally have considered his fashion sense kind of a bummer to look at. But Jay's new favorite regular got away with it because he had those colorful eyes and the prettiest hair Jay had ever seen. And even though Alexei always wore that pretty hair up, and Jay really (like, *really*) wanted to see it down, there were always these little strands that would escape around his face, and that looked quite nice.

So really, Alexei didn't need to wear anything super bright to still be the nicest-looking thing in the room.

And oops, now he was there, at the counter. Jay had been staring again. Luckily he'd also been waving like mad, so maybe Alexei hadn't noticed.

"Jay," Alexei greeted, his voice all gruff and gravelly from the cold outside.

"Do you think I'd look good with a little bun?" Jay asked, studying Alexei's golden topknot. "My hair's not quite long enough yet, but if it were..." He reached up and tugged as many of his dark strands as he could into the semblance of a bun, even though only half of them actually made it into one, the rest falling back down around his ears. "What do you think?"

Alexei tilted his head, considering Jay's efforts carefully.

Jay liked that so, so much—the way Alexei often studied him, so intent and serious. He never brushed off Jay's questions with a laugh or an eye roll like some people did. It was why he was Jay's new favorite regular.

That and maybe also the way he smelled. So *good*. Like vanilla and sugar.

"I think you could pull it off," Alexei finally answered, that not smile, not scowl on his face.

Jay beamed at him. "Me too. What can I get you today?"

Alexei did that other thing Jay liked so much, where he leaned down low over the counter so they were both closer to eye level with each other. Jay liked it because he could see all the pretty colors in Alexei's eyes even better but also because the human smelled so, so good. It always made Jay's beastie perk up in interest (well, perk up more; his beastie was always very interested in everything Alexei).

"Are you sure you haven't been baking cupcakes?" Jay couldn't help but ask. Alexei had told him no the other day, but maybe it had just slipped his mind. He seemed like a guy who had a lot going on. Busy and important, probably. Why else would someone look so serious all the time?

Alexei huffed a not quite laugh. "No cupcakes, kotyonok."

Jay's heart warmed at the nickname Alexei had started giving him. It meant "kitten" in Russian. Jay didn't think Alexei knew *he* knew that, but Jay was afraid if he told him, Alexei might stop, so he kept his language knowledge to himself.

Alexei leaned just a hair's breadth closer. "Do you *like* cupcakes?"

"I like anything with sugar," Jay answered honestly.

"I see." Alexei's gaze traveled down to Jay's lips, just for a second. Was he imagining Jay eating a cupcake maybe? Jay felt a little hot and squirmy at the thought, which honestly happened a lot around his new regular. Something about him always had Jay's little beastie wanting to rise to the surface, as if it wanted a closer look. It had Jay half-afraid his fangs were going to pop out at any moment, which would be majorly embarrassing.

He was raised to have better control than that, after all.

Jay shook a mental finger at his beastie, pushing it back. "Your order?" he asked again. His voice sounded a bit breathless to his own ears.

"Americano. Iced, please. With a pump of...peppermint today, I think."

"Iced Americano with a pump of peppermint," Jay repeated dutifully. Alexei never ordered the exact same thing twice. "How festive!"

Alexei's brows rose slightly. "It's February, kotyonok. The holidays are long over."

Jay shrugged. "Still very festive."

"It is, isn't it." Alexei was *almost* smiling, his lips soft and relaxed, and Jay was beaming, and their faces were very close, and oh, Jay just really, really wanted a nibble. Just a little nibble of the delicious-smelling regular with the handsome face and pretty eyes and strong-looking forearms with his sleeves rolled back.

A throat cleared.

Jay peered around Alexei's broad form and was startled to see Soren standing behind him, looking beautiful as usual, his blond hair all swept back in this fancy way Jay could never even attempt, grinning his not-scary-to-Jay-but-scary-to-a-lot-of-people grin.

"Soren!" he exclaimed as Alexei handed him his card wordlessly. The almost smile had left his lips, and his eyebrows were all stern again. "You're here!"

"Surprise," Soren said dryly, stepping up to the counter in Alexei's place.

It kind of was. While Soren came into the café regularly, he usually ventured in later in the day, when Gabe went to the gym before his night shifts. Which meant maybe he'd come in earlier just to see Jay work his earlier shift. How nice of him. Jay beamed at his friend, even as his gaze strayed to Alexei, strolling to the opposite end of the counter.

Soren followed the path of his gaze. He arched a brow. "Dude looks like a mobster."

Jay's smile faltered a little. "No, he doesn't. He looks like Alexei."

Soren grinned sharply at him. "That's a mobster name."

"It isn't," Jay insisted, feeling vaguely insulted on behalf of his regular. "It's an Alexei name."

Soren waved a dismissive hand. "Just teasing, Jaybird. What would a mobster be doing in Hyde Park anyway?"

For a moment, they both stared at Alexei, who had received his Americano from Colin and was at his usual table, looking back at them with his stern expression still firmly in place. Jay waved at him. Alexei's brows furrowed deeper. How strange. Usually they relaxed when Jay waved at him. Jay tried waving with more enthusiasm. Alexei turned his face back to his drink.

Jay sighed, trying not to feel too disappointed about that. He wasn't very successful.

"He's hot. You should bang him."

Jay's cheeks heated, and he knew he must have a horrible blush on his face. Soren was always saying stuff like that.

But Alexei was a grown human man, one with nice, fancy clothes and a good smell. Jay saw the way other customers looked at him. Alexei must have quite a bit of sexual experience. What would he want with Jay in that regard? Jay wouldn't be good at any of it. He'd be…disappointing. And Jay *hated* disappointing people.

Still, his regular was pretty to look at. He made Jay's little beastie purr inside his chest. It liked having him in the café, in their sights.

Looking would have to be enough.

Jay arrived early for book club.

He'd tried not to—Soren had told him once that it was much cooler to be fashionably late for things than early—but he couldn't help it. He hadn't wanted to be in his quiet apartment for even one more minute.

And Danny never seemed to mind when Jay was early. Tonight he opened the door with his usual smile—he had such a nice, warm smile—and ushered Jay in, Ferdy wiggling like mad behind his legs. "Hi, honey."

Jay waved to Danny and the dog both. "Hi, Ferdy! Hi, Danny! You have such a nice smile. Have I told you that before?"

Danny's cheeks turned pink, which made his freckles blur to-gether and looked awfully nice with his big brown eyes all wide and happy. "Thanks, Jay. What have you got there?"

Jay presented him with his plate of hors d'oeuvres, these mini bagels that were somehow also pizzas. Human food was wild. "I brought these for our humans. Well, your human guests."

"Oh!" Danny's brow furrowed as he stared at Jay's plate. "Did you— Um, did you make these yourself?"

Jay bit back a laugh. Danny thought he had tried to cook; his worried face made sense now. Jay didn't have such a great history with that. "I bought these premade," Jay reassured him. "I only followed the directions on the box to heat them in the oven." And Jay had followed the directions *perfectly*.

The relieved smile Danny bestowed on him made Jay feel all warm and fuzzy inside. "Thanks for bringing them, honey. That was really sweet of you. Let's put them in the kitchen with the rest. I think Roman's been puttering around in there."

Jay couldn't imagine Roman "puttering around" anywhere, but he followed Danny obediently into the house, a cozy, two-story yellow abode Jay never tired of spending time in.

"*Oh.*" Jay's eyes widened in delight once they got to the kitchen.

Roman was there, looking imposing as always, even with his white button-down pushed up on his forearms and his black hair hanging loose and casual. He was surrounded by little plates, and everything smelled like garlic and butter and other delicious food scents Jay couldn't begin to identify.

It was always a treat when Roman cooked. He may have been a vampire like Jay, but he somehow still managed to make everything taste so *good*. He'd told Jay it was because he'd been French as a human.

"Roman." Danny had a lot of different ways of saying Roman's name, Jay had noticed. Sometimes he snapped it, like when Roman was rude to someone who wasn't Danny (he was never rude to Danny himself, of course); sometimes he laughed it, like when Roman said something unintentionally funny in his old-fashioned speech; and sometimes he said it like now, so full of love that even Jay, who had so little experience with the emotion, could hear it in his voice. Danny was looking at his mate with his big eyes all soft and tender. "You made so much."

Roman cleared his throat, wiping his hands on a kitchen towel and tossing it carelessly into the sink. "It is cold out, mon amour. I thought your human friends would appreciate some warm food while they discuss their book." He tore his eyes off Danny with obvious reluctance to give Jay a nod of greeting. "Yours was not a bad choice. I quite like *Jane Eyre*."

Jay rocked onto his toes, his plate of offerings still in hand, pleased beyond measure with such rare approval from the broody vamp. "It's so romantic, isn't it?"

"Mm," Roman agreed. "I have a special fondness for stories of kind, lovely humans accepting cold, damaged lovers."

"*Roman*," Danny scolded. "You aren't cold *or* damaged."

"Did I say I was? My, my, someone is projecting." There was a rare twinkle in Roman's bright-blue eyes as he swooped down to give Danny a kiss.

Jay did his best not to watch, but it was kind of too fascinating to resist....Danny just *melted* in Roman's arms the moment their lips touched. Would Jay's muscles all go soft like that, if he was kissed by a handsome man?

Jay's mind turned back to where it had been drifting quite often these days, to a very *specific* handsome man, and he squirmed, feeling himself flushing for some reason. He was speaking out loud before he knew it, interrupting Danny and Roman's kiss. "I have a new regular at the coffee shop."

Danny stepped back from Roman, his cheeks apparently permanently pink now. "Oh. That's good, right?"

"Mm-hmm. Yep." Jay held his plate up high so Ferdy, who was nosing around Jay's waist, couldn't reach it and sneak a nibble. "I always like my regulars. And this one especially. I like the way he smiles at me. Well, he doesn't *smile* at me exactly, but sometimes a corner of his mouth sort of lifts up just a little bit and it's almost like a smile? And I think if he *did* smile, it would look pretty nice. Also, he smells really good. Like vanilla and sugar. He swears he hasn't been making cupcakes, but for someone who hasn't been making cupcakes, he smells a lot like one."

Danny's face did a strange twitch as he stared first at Jay, then at Roman, then back to Jay. Apparently he didn't find what he was looking for in either of them, because in the next moment, he was calling out, "Soren!"

Jay beamed as the vampire himself appeared in the kitchen doorway in the next moment. "Soren!" he greeted happily, feeling lucky to see his friend twice in one day. "Are you joining us tonight?"

Soren leaned a shoulder against the doorjamb, looking very elegant, even in his chunky knit sweater. "Just this once. Only because Gabe is working and all my going out clothes are in the wash. And I suppose I don't mind *Jane Eyre*." He lifted a hand and studied his nails. "*Wuthering Heights* is better though."

"But it's so *sad*," Jay protested, unbelieving that his friend could prefer such a wretched story to the simple love—imprisoned wife and untimely fire notwithstanding—between Jane Eyre and Mr. Rochester.

Soren shrugged. "But everyone is so delightfully mean and unhinged. It's absolutely divine."

"Jay, sweetie," Danny interrupted gently. "Tell Soren what you just told me."

"I didn't make the bagel bites," Jay told Soren, raising his plate in demonstration. "I just heated them up from a box."

"What? No, that's—" Danny shook his head. "No, sweetheart. Tell him about the café."

"Oh! I have a new regular, and he smells really, really good."

"What do you think about that, Soren?" Danny was looking at Soren like Jay was saying something significant, his eyes all intense and his eyebrows doing some intricate things Jay couldn't comprehend.

Soren hummed, his gaze lifting from his nails to study Jay like he was some kind of puzzle. "Are you talking about the mobster, Jaybird?"

Jay's brows furrowed. "He's not a mobster. You're being prejudiced against Russians."

"He's Russian?" Danny asked, shooing Ferdy out of the kitchen when he started trying to jump up to reach Jay's plate. "Like, full Bond-villain accent?"

Soren shrugged. "No accent, but he called Jay 'kotyonok.'" He grinned at Danny and Roman, arching a brow. "It means 'kitten.'"

And now Jay was blushing even more fiercely, his face all hot for some reason. "I like when he calls me that," he defended.

Soren laughed sharply. "Yeah, I bet you do. Does your new friend know you can understand him?"

Jay sniffed. "He hasn't asked."

Danny was frowning at Soren. "You think he wouldn't like that? Like Jay's in danger?"

Soren waved a careless hand in the air. "What could a mobster possibly do to a vampire?"

This was getting frustrating. Jay resisted the urge to stomp his foot. He didn't want to be rude, but he wasn't liking at all the direction this conversation was taking. "He's not a mobster. He's my regular, and he lets me call him Alexei, and he smells like cupcakes, and I *like* him."

Danny was staring at Soren once more like Jay was saying something significant.

Soren sighed, looking Jay over again. "You think?" he asked, clearly talking to Danny even with his eyes on Jay. "The odds of it all. So unlikely..."

Jay cocked his head. "What are you two—"

"Johann." Roman cut him off, his voice softer than usual. "Why not help me set these plates up in the living room?"

Again, Jay wasn't stupid, despite what some people might think. He knew he'd said something that had set the other two off. But Roman was already ushering him out of the kitchen with one hand on his back. "Tell me more about this regular."

"Oh! Um, he's very handsome. And you already know about the cupcake smell. I guess I don't know a lot about him otherwise. But he never laughs at me. I do like that."

Roman frowned thoughtfully as he arranged his plates. Jay was about to ask why everyone was so obsessed with the regular—it wasn't like they'd seen for themselves how handsome he was, other than Soren—when the doorbell rang, signifying the other guests had arrived.

The rest of the night ended up being just as lovely as Jay had thought it would be. All six of the human book club members seemed to like the book, even the two young men from Danny's work who'd never once had a nice thing to say about romance.

Jay found himself studying those two especially while they all ate and chatted and laughed (Jay didn't always know what they were laughing about, but he liked joining in anyway).

He found himself wondering about kisses, of all things.

If either of these human men kissed him, would he go all soft and melty like Danny did with Roman?

Jay couldn't imagine it for some reason.

But then his mind turned to tan, muscled forearms and multi-colored eyes. A wide, stern mouth and the prettiest hair in Hyde Park.

And then it turned out it was quite easy to imagine after all.

Four

Alexei

Alexei nursed his third rum and coke in half as many hours, trying his best to let the alcohol shake the funk that had settled in over him.

His obsession wasn't subsiding. Not at all. If anything, it was deepening. Worsening. He couldn't seem to stay away from that fucking coffee shop. What was more, he'd walked through that goddamn jangling door that morning and Jay hadn't been at the counter, and Alexei had needed to fight the most inappropriate, gut-wrenching disappointment at that fact.

And obviously Jay wouldn't be working every single day, but he'd seemed up to that point to basically live at the damn place, and Alexei's gut—his heart—hadn't been prepared for his absence.

It had sent Alexei into a sort of…unfortunate spiral.

What the fuck was he *doing* here? Mooning over a little alien barista who waved at every living thing and had zero social awareness, especially when it came to flirting. Who was either incredibly naive or extremely diabolical with the way he had Alexei strung along by his dick without them having even so much as touched a single time.

What was Alexei hoping to accomplish even? Slow seduction via increasingly complicated coffee orders?

And then there was Jay's friend. His *friend* from the other day. Never before had Alexei been so intimidated by such a pretty face. Not by the prettiness itself. There was just a certain…menace underneath that odd grin. Alexei had spent enough time around the unhinged to recognize it. He could feel it.

And what else could he feel? Fucking jealousy, that was what. Burning in his chest. Because the way Jay had greeted the guy with such a warm, beaming smile? And okay, yes, Jay greeted *everyone* with a warm, beaming smile. But there had been familiarity there; that was for sure. And the guy—Soren—had lingered at the counter. He'd *lingered.* And he'd made Jay blush, those pale cheeks adorably pink.

What had he been saying to make Jay blush? What did Alexei have to do to have the same effect?

Alexei startled as the bartender appeared in front of him, shaking Alexei's now drained glass, rattling the remaining ice. "Another?"

Alexie grunted his assent. "Please."

It was a bad idea. He'd skipped dinner that night, and the drinks he'd consumed already had gone straight to his head. But what did it matter anyway? He was nothing more than a ghost in this town. He had no future, no connections, no purpose other than stalking the poor little barista who'd caught his eye. What did it matter if Alexei got blind drunk tonight? If he got blind drunk every single night? Who the fuck would care?

"No one," he muttered, glaring at the soggy coaster left in front of him. "Not a one."

"What was that?" The woman on the barstool next to him leaned in, her voice all husky.

Alexei kept his eye on his coaster, fighting the urge to scowl at his neighbor. She'd chosen the seat next to him, despite a plethora of open stools at the counter, and she was sitting much too close, her breast brushing his arm every now and again, and it was starting to annoy the hell out of him. He was trying to *brood*, and her perfume smelled like flowers, and it was washing away the peppermint scent that somehow still lingered in his nostrils, a full day away from any contact with Jay. "Nothing," he grumbled. "Wasn't talking to you."

He gave a nod of appreciation as the bartender placed a new drink in front of him, ignoring the annoyed harrumph from his neighbor.

This was part of why he'd never been one for bars, or at least not those outside his family's influence. With his size and his looks, he tended to get two reactions when he hit the town: women who wanted to fuck him and men who wanted to fight him. The first he had no interest in, and the second would only be appealing if it was the kind of tussle that led to the bedroom. And it never was, was it?

He hadn't ever gotten to explore the gay scene as much as he'd like; not when his father had been such an unrepentant, bigoted asshole. And not when, even after his father's death, Alexei's nights had so often been spent monitoring their family's more popular assets: the clubs and the underground gambling dens. Ivan liked having Alexei out and about in those places, liked flaunting Alexei's size and admittedly intimidating presence.

In truth, it had always irked Ivan that he couldn't use Alexei's size to his own advantage even more. How he would have loved to have Alexei as his personal bodyguard, his loyal fucking dog. But they both knew Alexei would never sacrifice his life for his brother's, would never willingly take a bullet or any other bit of violence meant for him.

How long had Ivan wanted Alexei out of the picture? Since they'd both been in diapers? Since their mother had left them behind?

Probably for as long as Alexei had wanted to be out himself. Since the first time their father had taken them to see some broken-bone retribution, deciding that Ivan being old enough to be inaugurated into the family business meant Alexei had to suck it up and face it too.

Ten years old, practically a man, right, Alyosha?

And now he *was* out. He was hidden, he was hundreds of miles away, and he wasn't sure if he was any better off. He might not be actively committing any crimes, but was he really any more of a good person than he'd been before? The world was just as dull and gray as it had ever been, just without the bright splashes of blood to color it in violence.

Instead, he had his bright splash of Jay.

Except today he *didn't.*

Alexei cut himself off after draining the fourth drink faster than he should have. Any more than that and he'd be reminiscing past the point where it was healthy or sane. He summoned the bartender with a raised finger, paid his bill, and stumbled out of the bar, maybe not as steady on his feet as he should have been, but that was the natural consequence of deciding to drink his dinner.

And yes, maybe the bar he'd chosen had been the one conveniently closest to a certain coffee shop. The one he was now walking past at a much slower pace than necessary, even though Jay would have left hours ago, had he even been there that day. Alexei couldn't resist the compulsion to stay close, and he didn't know why.

Except for the alluring thought that maybe he'd get to smell peppermint again.

Actually...

Alexei didn't smell anything, but there *was* a strange sound coming from the alley next to the café. A whimper, maybe?

He knew better than to check, to stick his nose where it didn't belong. But his brain was a little mushy from booze, and in general he'd been living for weeks in a state of mind light-years away from any sort of common sense, so what the hell.

He strode into the alleyway, straightening his posture and righting his stumbling steps, a lifetime spent masking any weakness aiding him in hiding his semidrunken state.

He realized about ten seconds too late that he was interrupting an apparently intimate moment between two shadowed people, all pressed up against each other and probably doing things they had no need of Alexei as witness of. Because what the fuck else had Alexei been expecting?

"Fuck. Sorry, I'll—" Alexei's mouth snapped shut, his brain freezing completely, the apology left hanging half-finished in the night air.

Because his entrance had the automatic light above the back door of Death by Coffee turning on, and it was illuminating exactly who those two figures were.

The tall, gangly guy pressed back against the wall, looking flushed and harried, was clearly the manager, Colin, and in his arms, half a foot shorter, with a head of thick dark hair...

Alexei's first coherent thought after his brain came stuttering back online was that it was a shame the manager had to die.

Really, he seemed like an okay kind of guy, beyond his daily glaring at Alexei in the café. But he had his hands on Jay's shoulders, and even with the shadows in the alley, it was clear Jay was...kissing his neck?

Because that little figure was definitely Jay. Even from behind, Alexei couldn't mistake him for anyone else. And not just because of that hideous fucking sweater.

And why wasn't Jay wearing a fucking *coat*? It was freezing outside.

"What the fuck!" Colin's hazy gaze focused, and he glared at Alexei with more intensity than usual, clutching at Jay's shoulders as if to shake him off.

Colin's yell had Jay turning around, and Alexei braced himself for those big, beautiful gray eyes—for the aborted lust he might find in them—but when Jay turned fully, he only looked...odd. Different.

Very, oddly different.

Because Jay's eyes didn't look gray at all. They were completely black, no whites showing. And his cute little lips were covered in—

Was that *blood*?

"What sort of kinky fucking..." Alexei trailed off, staring fixedly at his obsession, his fucking barista crush.

Because there was something strange about Jay's teeth too. Like he had on a pair of those Halloween-store vampire fangs or something.

Jay's eyes—his weirdly black fucking eyes—widened as he took Alexei in. "Oh no," he breathed, licking…whatever that was…off his lips, looking positively mournful as he stared at Alexei, Colin glaring over his head. "Well…this is very bad."

Five

Jay

T his was all very bad indeed.

Jay knew that. He knew he needed to take action, to be decisive.

But he also knew he was having an extremely hard time focusing.

He was a little revved up from feeding—especially since he hadn't gotten to finish—and Alexei smelled so very *good*. Jay's little beastie really wanted a taste. Just one itty-bitty taste.

But that would be bad, right?

Jay licked the blood off his lips, very conscious of Colin standing directly behind him. *Right.* No tasting his regular.

But oof. His beastie did *not* agree with that statement.

Alexei was staring, his wide mouth a bit slack, and with Jay's vampire face out, he could see every bit of color in those extremely pretty eyes of his. Hazel, that was what they were technically called. He'd had to look it up to be sure; it didn't seem like a big enough word to capture just how compelling he found them.

"What— Your teeth...," Alexei rasped.

Oh. Right. Jay's teeth. His *fangs*.

Jay took a few deep breaths, pushing his beastie back within himself, the task requiring a little extra effort than normal. He wiped his mouth with the back of his sweater sleeve, hoping he was managing to get all the drops of blood.

He could get a little...messy, when he was hungry.

The worst part was he had barely been getting started when Alexei had stumbled into their feeding. He still *was* quite hungry.

But he'd have to deal with that later. Right now he had a shocked human to somehow placate.

Human face firmly in place, Jay started with a friendly wave. "Hello, Alexei. Fancy seeing you here."

At closer inspection, Alexei, although handsome as ever, was looking quite mussed: those pretty eyes were glazed over, his lovely hair was loose from his bun, and there was a slight boozy smell layered over his usual delicious scent.

The man was definitely drunk. Or at least, probably drunk. Jay didn't actually have all that much experience with drunk humans; Vee had always wanted sober prey so as not to get sloppy from drinking their alcohol-laden blood.

Alexei was also apparently speechless now that Jay's face had changed right in front of his eyes. He hadn't answered Jay's greeting at all. Jay supposed the transformation must be a little startling, if one wasn't used to it.

Jay glanced over his shoulder, back at Colin. "Maybe you should head out. I can get Alexei where he needs to go."

Colin's brow was furrowed, his pink cheeks contrasting with his blue hair. "But—but he saw..."

"It's okay," Jay soothed. "I'll explain it to him."

Colin frowned down at Jay, a stubborn set to his jaw, which Jay supposed he should have expected. His manager was very protective of Jay, ever since Jay had told him the truth of what he was. "I'll be okay, Colin," Jay reassured. "Be sure to drink plenty of water when you get home. I only took a little, but...still."

He turned back to Alexei, who was pointing an unsteady finger at the pair of them, a new, hard glint to his eyes. "The two of you...together?"

Did he mean romantically? "No," Jay told him, biting back a giggle at the thought.

"Yes," said Colin at the same time.

"Colin," Jay reprimanded, frowning back at the lanky human.

Colin stepped a bit closer, leaning down to whisper in Jay's ear. "That would be the simplest explanation to what he's just seen. The kind of thing someone might expect: two people hooking up in an alley."

Jay supposed that could be true, even though hooking up with someone in an alley didn't sound all that great to him, personally. But it would also be a lie. And Jay did *not* like lies.

He stepped forward, away from Colin and toward Alexei. "We're not boyfriends. I'm just a vampire."

Now it was Colin's turn to say his name like a reprimand. "*Jay*. You can't go around telling everybody you're a vampire."

"I'm not telling *everybody*," Jay said, his voice rising a bit in his defensiveness. "This makes two people I've told. You and now Alexei." Colin still looked disapproving, so Jay tried to find a positive spin. "Now the two of you have something in common!"

"A vampire." Alexei gave a strange, coughing laugh, crossing his arms over his chest. "You two are into some kinky shit."

Jay's brow furrowed. "It's not a sex thing. Here, look." He let out his little beastie again, careful to remind it that they would *not* be biting the nice-smelling human, and stepped closer so Alexei could get a better look. "See?" Jay smiled wide, pointing to his teeth. "Fangs."

Unfortunately, Alexei didn't seem to find Jay's fangs all that reassuring. Jay watched as the blood drained from Alexei's face, leaving him looking decidedly pale. He really hoped the human wasn't going to faint on him. Jay was strong enough to carry him, sure, but he had no idea where Alexei lived.

"Holy fucking fuck." Alexei stared at Jay's mouth for another moment, rubbed at his brow with two fingers, and then waved a hand at Colin. "So you weren't kissing his neck."

"I told you, it's not sexual." Jay shot a glance over his shoulder at Colin, who still had a pretty blush on his cheeks. "Well, not *totally* sexual. Feeding can be very pleasurable to huma—"

"Jay," Colin pleaded.

Uh-oh. Was that not polite to share? Jay cocked his head. "You don't want him to know that part?"

Colin ran a hand through his blue hair, sighing. "Just...not while I'm around. I don't want to have to look him in the eyes."

Jay nodded in understanding, even if he didn't actually fully understand. He didn't think there was anything wrong with his arrangement with Colin. Jay needed to eat; Colin had been curious about some of the physical responses to feeding. It worked well for both of them.

Jay hadn't known all that when he'd first approached Colin about feeding though. All he'd known was that his manager was kind, already sort of protective, and seemed to have a steady enough head on his shoulders that he maybe wouldn't freak out about the existence of vampires.

And Jay had really, really needed to eat.

Alexei, meanwhile, had moved even closer, his broad frame positively looming over Jay's, and Jay had to force himself to take regular, even breaths—rather than inhale greedily—because even with that layer of booze, the human still smelled so very good.

He was so focused on his breathing he didn't notice Alexei move, but before Jay knew it, Alexei had gripped him by the upper arms—he was quite strong, for a human—and was peering down at Jay's eyes. "Whoa."

"Pretty neat, huh?" Jay liked his vampire face. He thought it gave him a bit of toughness he normally lacked.

Alexei looked over Jay's shoulder to Colin again. "You were drinking his blood?"

Jay bounced onto his toes, pleased they were finally getting through to the probably drunk human. "Yes."

Alexei went back to studying Jay's face again, and Jay tried not to squirm under the scrutiny. All the attention made him want to do something weird, like lick Alexei's strong, straight nose.

"Do you want to drink *my* blood?" Alexie asked.

Jay's lips parted as his beastie took sharp notice. "Um...are you offering?" he asked, even knowing that wouldn't be a good idea. Mostly because Alexei was maybe drunk and possibly didn't really understand what he was consenting to. And also because if Jay drank from him, they would both be drunk, and that probably wouldn't help the situation at all.

Alexei had released one of Jay's arms, and his finger was now a hairbreadth from Jay's mouth. "I just— Well, do you?"

Jay still couldn't tell if Alexei was legitimately offering or just curious. "You smell very good," he admitted, tongue darting out to wet his lips. "But not right now, thank you."

He pushed his human face forward again, and then for some reason, Alexei was running a finger over Jay's lips, and ohh, that felt very, very nice.

Jay closed his eyes, leaning in a bit to the sensation. It was pleasant to be touched so nicely, even a little bit.

A throat cleared from behind them, and Jay was brought back to his senses with a start. "Oh. Right." He took a step back, surprised when Alexei readily released him. "Alexei, where do you live? We'll get you home."

But Alexei was already shaking his head with uncharacteristic aggression, his free tendrils of hair whipping around his head. "No, no, no. You can't tell me vampires exist, that you *are* one, and then just send me on my way."

Jay frowned. "Well, you can't stay here. It's freezing. You're starting to shiver." Alexei's finger had been quite cold against Jay's lips. Nice but cold.

Alexei continued to shake his head, and then Jay had a wonderful, splendid, terrible idea. "Alexei, do you want to come home with me?"

Jay was pleased that Alexei handled the walk home just fine.

Well, he did keep leaning on Jay, putting a good portion of his weight onto Jay's shoulders. That part was fine; Jay was super strong. But the issue was the human smelled so good, and Jay was so hungry, and his fangs kept wanting to pop out.

His little beastie even started speaking to him, which it rarely ever did. *Just a little taste*, it pleaded.

No, beastie. No biting without permission.

Jay would have to make new arrangements with Colin in the morning. But for now—after convincing Colin that yes, the two of them would be just fine alone and no, he didn't need to compel Alexei to forgetfulness right then and there—they were at Jay's little duplex in no time at all.

Jay was surprisingly nervous approaching his apartment, his stomach a funny little ball of knots. He didn't have guests often. He wished he did, but Soren and Danny both had proper houses, so he often just went over to theirs when they spent time together.

He tried to make some conversation to cover his nerves as he unlocked the door for them. "So, Alexei. Do you get drunk often?"

Alexei was close on his heels, enough so that Jay could feel how cold the human was from the frozen night air. He seemed to stiffen even further at Jay's question. "What? No. I just—I forgot to eat dinner."

"You need to eat?" Jay turned to ask the question, and whoa, Alexei's face was very close to his. The human's nose was a little red at the tip from the chill. Jay hummed in thought. "You need to eat, and you're cold."

Jay's absent humming turned into a full tune as he thought it over. He could definitely work with that. He didn't need to be nervous at all. He was very good at making people comfortable—it had, after all, been his sole purpose for over two centuries. Well, not to make humans comfortable, exactly, but it couldn't be that different with vampires, could it?

He grabbed hold of Alexei's hand, taking a second to enjoy the way the human's large palm swallowed his so easily. He was so much larger than Jay, and Jay had to admit he liked that about his regular. He could easily imagine being held, possibly hugged, maybe even pressed down onto a mattress...

But no. This wasn't the time. The human needed food and warmth, not Jay's lustful thoughts. Jay shook them right out of his head.

He pulled Alexei to the couch in the living room before rising to his tiptoes to press down on the big human's shoulders, gently guiding him into a seated position. Alexei folded himself down easily, his wide, dazed eyes focused on Jay all the while.

Jay patted Alexei's chest (so nice and firm) and went off to collect all the blankets from around the room—good thing he'd bought so many in his time here. He started layering them onto Alexei, unsure how many the human needed to warm himself. But after the fifth blanket, Alexei halted his movement by placing his large hand—he really had such nice hands, tan and slightly calloused—onto Jay's arm.

"Show me again," Alexei requested. "In the light."

Jay let out a little sigh. He had things to attend to just now, but he supposed it was the polite thing to do, to cede to a guest's request. "One more time," he said, making his voice as stern as he could, which probably wasn't very stern at all. "Then we need to feed you."

Jay pushed his beastie forward again. It came easily at his call, preening a little at the attention Alexei showered it with, those pretty eyes tracking Jay's newly black pair.

Alexei released Jay's arm and lifted his hand, pressing against the front of Jay's fang with one finger. Jay shivered, a tingle going down his spine. No one had ever touched his fangs like that before. Were fangs an erogenous zone? Or was it just that it was Alexei touching him?

He'd have to ask Soren later. That sounded like something he would know.

When Alexei moved to press his finger against the pointed tip, Jay stopped him with a hand to his wrist. "I don't think that's such a good idea. If I cut you— Well, um, it's just you smell really, really good," he tried to explain, not sure if he was getting through to the dazed human or not.

Alexei only stared.

Jay pushed his beastie back, ignoring its grumbling protests. Time to get back to business. "I'm going to make you some miniature pizza bagels," he said, stepping back from the couch. "But don't worry, they come from a box."

"Why would I be worried?" Alexei twisted his torso, tracking Jay's entry into the kitchen.

The duplex had an open floor plan, without a wall between the two rooms, so really, he could watch as much as he wanted while Jay prepared his food. Jay was fine with an audience because he was going to follow the directions *perfectly*. Maybe Alexei would even be impressed.

"I can't cook because everything I make comes out terrible and inedible, and also, I started a small fire once, and that upset my friends," Jay explained, pushing the buttons to preheat the oven.

Alexei took a moment with that information. "Has anyone ever tried to teach you?" he asked eventually.

"Well, no, but I've followed recipes from the internet."

"It's different having someone to show you in person. Cooking is an art. It's hard to learn just from reading. It helps to have someone to direct you."

Jay turned from the oven, smiling at the thought. "Oh! I'm *very* good at following directions."

"I bet you are, kotyonok." Alexei's voice came out kind of throaty and husky and weirdly sexy. Maybe from being in the cold too long? Jay had to turn back around to hide his blush.

He hummed to cover his embarrassment, pulling the little box out of the freezer. "It doesn't seem quite fair though. Roman's such a good cook, and *he's* a vampire, so it's not like we *can't* have a knack for cooking. It's not a species thing, I don't think."

There was a weighty silence from behind him.

Oh, shoot. Shoot, shoot, shoot. Jay hadn't meant to mention anything about the others. He'd been so *good* until now. He'd never even once told Colin there were more of his kind in town.

But there was something about the careful, close way Alexei always watched him that had Jay just wanting to talk all day long. People rarely paid attention to him, not like this. Sure, they'd be amused when he said something unintentionally funny, maybe even momentarily charmed by his admittedly weird ways. But then they would just pat his head—metaphorically or sometimes literally—and move on.

But Alexei... He watched. Stared, even.

And Jay liked it.

"There are more of you here?" Alexei finally asked. "Vampires?"

"Um..." Jay dithered over answering, filling a water glass and bringing it over to the couch while he thought it over. (Ferdy always needed water after a run, and Alexei had just had a walk, so that was probably a good idea for him too.)

He was pleased when Alexei gulped it down easily. He also felt a surprisingly warm tingling in his belly, watching Alexei's Adam's apple bob.

Alexei looked good doing anything and everything, it seemed.

"There are others," Jay admitted quietly, watching the human drink.

Alexei set the glass down, wiping his mouth with the back of his hand. Very uncivilized of him. Jay liked it. "I'm not much of a cook, but I can teach you to make syrniki. They're like Russian pancakes." He stared down at his glass. "My grandmother taught me."

"Oh," Jay breathed. What an incredibly nice offer from a new friend. Because that was what they were becoming, right? That was what happened when one person came to another person's home and shared food and secrets? "Oh yes, I'd like that very much."

Twenty minutes later and Alexei had wolfed down an entire box of the little pizza bagels. He'd assured Jay one box would be enough. "Just needed to soak up some of the rum."

The human *did* look a little more alert now. His eyes were sharper, that glazed look gone. He was fiddling with his empty plate, turning it round and round on the coffee table. He'd been more or less silent, eating his food, but now he seemed ready to ask some questions. "How long have you been...feeding...on Colin? And what did you mean that bites are pleasurable?"

Jay, seated next to him on the couch now, folded his hands on his lap, considering how to answer. Technically, Colin had given him permission to share, as long as he wasn't present to be embarrassed by it all. So Jay did his best to lay it all out carefully and concisely.

"I've been feeding on Colin since shortly after he hired me. Once every two weeks." Which honestly left Jay pretty hungry a lot of the time, but he didn't want to overfeed on his singular food source. "Vampire bites can be very...arousing, for the human involved. And Colin... Well, um, as he put it to me: he likes the idea of sex in theory but doesn't always feel...into it...in real life. He was intrigued by the bite's arousal effects. We made an arrangement, with full knowledge and full consent from both parties." Jay liked adding that last part. He was proud of how he'd handled the task of feeding in Hyde Park.

"So why aren't you two fucking?" Alexei asked, shocking Jay a little with his bluntness. "Are bites not arousing for vampires as well?"

Jay shifted on the couch. He was honestly a little surprised Alexei was so much more interested in the sex part than the drinking-blood-from-a-coworker part. But maybe that was just how human brains worked. It had been so long since Jay had been one himself; perhaps he was out of touch. "Well...yes, they are. But Colin doesn't actually want sex from me—we're really not each other's type—and also I-I'm sort of lacking in experience anyway. I wouldn't be a good guide for all that."

Alexei's eyes on him were very intense, his pupils looking larger than before. "How lacking?" he asked, his voice husky again. Maybe it wasn't from the cold after all.

"I'm a virgin," Jay admitted, making sure he kept his chin held high as he said it. He refused to be embarrassed by his inexperience. Well, he refused to *show* his embarrassment, at least.

He watched in fascination as Alexei's pupils dilated even further. Alexei swayed a little toward Jay—maybe he hadn't sobered up as much as they'd thought—then seemed to catch himself, clearing his throat and rubbing at the back of his neck. "You don't have any interest in sex?"

"Oh!" Jay almost giggled at the thought. "No, I do. Very much. But I had some strange circumstances for my first two centuries, and then, well...it's hard to know where to start when you've been...sheltered, like I have."

Alexei took his time processing that information. Jay liked the way he did that, always considering the things Jay said very carefully. When he eventually spoke, he switched directions once again. "Are you still hungry? I interrupted you."

Oh God. There went Jay's fangs.

Alexei's lips twitched. "Do you want to bite me, kotyonok?"

Jay covered his mouth with one hand, embarrassed. It was just...the human kept offering himself up. What was Jay supposed to do? Or maybe Alexei was only curious? Jay studied his face for a moment, trying to gauge how genuine the offer was. He really *was* hungry.

But then Alexei cheated. He tilted his head, displaying that strong, tanned neck. God, why did he have to look so good? And *smell* so good? Alexei's pretty eyes were half-lidded, almost taunting. Like he knew exactly how much he was tempting Jay.

How did one know when a human was too tipsy for a feeding?

"What day is it today?" Jay asked through the hand covering his mouth. He'd pushed his fangs back again, but he wasn't taking any chances.

"February 4," Alexei answered promptly.

"And where are we right now?"

"Your house. In Hyde Park." Alexei's eyes lit up, and he huffed a short laugh as he seemed to realize what Jay was doing. "You know I had a few rum and cokes, not a concussion, right?"

Jay flapped his free hand in the air, strangely embarrassed. "Well, I don't know!"

Alexei shifted closer on the couch. "I know what I'm offering."

Jay cocked his head, too tempted for words. Still. "But what *are* you offering?"

"Feed from me. I like the idea of giving you something you need, kotyonok. Let me be of use to you. Please."

Well, wasn't Alexei turning out to be the nicest human ever? Jay didn't know what to do with the warmth filling his chest. It was so rare anyone asked how they could be of use to Jay without wanting something in return. He couldn't resist it. He let the beastie out again, fangs popping down. "I'm going to come closer," he warned, finally lowering his hand from his mouth.

But Alexei didn't seem even the least bit frightened. "Yes," he purred.

It was almost like *he* was the hunter here, not Jay. But that was a silly thought.

Jay climbed up into Alexei's lap. He supposed he could have shuffled closer to him on the couch instead—maybe that would have been more polite?—but he couldn't resist this golden opportunity for further physical connection.

And maybe Jay just really wanted to be held. The human looked so strong and smelled so good. Was it so horrible that Jay wanted to be as close as possible?

Alexei tilted his head to the side, baring his neck again.

Jay bit in.

Six

Alexei

A lexei felt a sharp pinch, a brief burn, and then...oh *fuck*.

He sucked in a sharp breath, shocked in spite of himself at the lust flooding his body, the tendrils of arousal that started at his neck and raced through his veins, the strange sensation plumping his cock in an instant.

He knew—he'd been warned—the bite would be pleasurable, but he'd expected it to be something like when a doctor said a shot wasn't going to hurt. A little fib. A white lie. A necessary obfuscation to achieve the desired result.

But Jay had been truthful. It felt good.

It felt so. Fucking. *Good*.

Alexei grabbed more firmly onto the little vampire's hips, pleased beyond measure at the intimacy of the feeding position Jay had chosen: on Alexei's lap, that pert bottom pressed up against Alexei's hardening cock.

He breathed Jay in, that wonderful peppermint scent.

He should always be here, Alexei thought dreamily, listening to the strangely erotic sounds of Jay's greedy gulping. *In my arms*.

He found himself leaning further back against the couch and pressing a hand to the back of Jay's dark head, urging him closer. "Take as much as you need, kotyonok. Drink your fill."

Alexei knew—in that back corner of his mind, the tiny place unclouded by this obsessive want—that he should theoretically be more freaked out at the moment. He'd found out barely an hour ago that vampires existed (and that sweet, adorable, waves-at-dogs Jay was one), and now here he was letting Jay feast on his neck?

Alexei should probably be considering the very real possibility that at some point that night, he'd truly snapped, and this was all some sort of elaborate illusion taking place after his losing his fucking mind.

But the sensations were too clear, too real. Jay's hungry little noises, the warmth of his small body, the ache of Alexei's erection straining against his zipper. He felt gratified that the vampire was hard as well, grinding himself against Alexei's bulge, seemingly unconsciously.

Alexei felt a hot surge of jealousy, thinking of Jay doing this with Colin, but the emotion passed quickly. Because really, what Alexei had encountered in the alleyway hadn't looked anywhere near this intimate.

There was a difference between how Jay felt about the two of them; Alexei was becoming sure of it.

And that was the crux of it all, wasn't it? Why Alexei was allowing this (not just allowing but practically begging for it). Because here he'd been wanting to get closer to Jay, to be special to him in some way, and this wonderful, bloody door had opened for them both.

Alexei could give Jay something vital. Something necessary to his very existence. Something horrifically intimate that could potentially open even more doors to even more intimacies.

Alexei sank into the couch cushions, feeling both wound up beyond belief and also unbearably loose and relaxed. A little dizzy too, but that was a small price to pay.

The feeding had been going on for long enough Alexei had serious concerns he was going to come in his pants like a teenager with his first grope when Jay finally pulled back, his fangs sliding out of Alexei's skin. But it didn't do much to lessen the arousal when Jay started licking gently at Alexei's neck.

He really was a kitten.

"Trying to get every last drop?" Alexei teased softly, his muscles lax against the couch cushions.

Jay gave one last lick before sitting back, his lovely face flushed and brown hair mussed well beyond its usual bed head status. The black had already receded from his eyes, and there were dark-red drops of Alexei's blood on his chin. Alexei was incredibly gratified to note Jay made no move to crawl off his lap. "My saliva has healing properties," Jay said softly. "I was closing the bite."

Alexei squeezed gently at his hips. "Well, look at you. What other special abilities are you hiding, kotyonok?"

Jay worried at his blood-specked lip with blunt teeth a moment before answering in a very serious tone, "I'm fast. Quite strong. I don't need much sleep. I don't age, at least not physically. And I'm next to impossible to kill."

Next to impossible to kill.

A certain tightness unfurled in Alexei's chest at Jay's words. Here he'd been thinking the barista he'd been lusting after was too fragile, too gentle, too—

"How old are you?" he asked the vampire abruptly.

Jay cocked his head. "Somewhere around two hundred and fifty, I think?"

Alexei couldn't help it. He threw his head back and laughed, low and loose and so relaxed he thought he might sink all the way through the couch and end up somehow on the floor. He'd been thinking he was a potential cradle robber, lusting after some college-aged kid. But Jay was older than him by *multiple fucking centuries.*

It was the funniest thing he'd heard in years. Maybe ever.

When he was finished, forced to release his hold on Jay's hips to wipe tears from his eyes, he found the vampire staring at him, gray eyes wide and seemingly delighted. "You have the nicest laugh," Jay breathed.

"Thank you. It doesn't come out often, I suppose."

Jay beamed at him. "I've never seen you smile before tonight. And now you *laughed*." He hummed happily before cocking his head, his smile fading into a strange almost pout. "You're really not afraid of me?"

Alexei placed his hands back on Jay's hips, the fleece material of his pants soft against Alexei's skin. "Should I be?"

Jay shook his head somberly. "No. I would *never* hurt you. I love humans. I try to be very respectful. I'll never bite without permission."

"You have my blanket permission, kotyonok."

"Oh." Jay bit at his lip again. "But why?"

Alexei cleared his throat, trying to figure out how to say what he felt without sounding like an obsessive psycho. "I meant what I said earlier. About giving you something you need. I've become very....fond of you. But also because I enjoyed that very much. Did you?"

Jay nodded enthusiastically. "Yes. You're very delicious, you know."

Alexei groaned. Fuck, Jay couldn't go around saying stuff like that, not when Alexei was so keyed up from that fucking bite.

He could feel Jay tense under his hands, the vampire seemingly alarmed by the sound. "What's wrong?" Jay asked. "Do you need more food? Water? Am I too heavy on your lap?"

Alexei's arms moved without permission, banding around Jay's waist so the vampire couldn't escape. "No. I'm just—" He paused a moment to think. With anyone else, he might have considered teasing a bit, but he had a feeling with Jay, he needed to be quite literal to get this ship sailing. "I'm very attracted to you, Jay."

"*Oh.*" Alexei watched in fascination as Jay went pink all the way to the tips of his ears.

That was promising, right?

He tried to keep his voice soft, gentle, nonthreatening. "Do you find me attractive, kitten?"

Jay's small hand clenched against Alexei's arm. "Oh yes. I think you have the prettiest eyes and prettiest hair, and you're the most handsome man in the coffee shop."

Alexei could work with that. He could *definitely* work with that. "You said you have no experience. Sexually. Would you like to remedy that?"

Jay's tongue darted out, wetting his lips. "You want to, um, show me sex stuff?"

Alexei let out a long, slow breath. "Yes. I would very much like to show you sex stuff, if you like."

Jay's eyes flashed, and his hands moved up to clutch at the collar of Alexei's shirt. "And let me bite you?"

"Yes."

"And teach me how to make syrniki?"

Alexei blinked. He'd forgotten he'd said that, honestly. But he would take literally any excuse to get closer to this creature, even if it was in the kitchen. "Yes."

"It's like Christmas," Jay whispered, toying with Alexei's collar. Then he shot him what Alexei had to assume was supposed to be a stern look. "But not tonight. I got light-headed just from drinking you. You're tipsy," he accused, his brow furrowing even further.

Alexei hadn't realized how much his muscles had tensed from waiting on Jay's answer until he felt himself relax back once more against the cushions. He had the strangest urge to start laughing again. "Perhaps I am. But the offer will stand in the morning, I promise you that."

Jay ducked his head, but Alexei didn't miss the shy smile gracing his lips.

So fucking adorable.

After that, Alexei was subjected to more of Jay's caretaking. He was given another glass of water and was forced to refuse more pizza bagels three separate times before Jay was willing to believe Alexei was actually full.

When Jay told Alexei he wouldn't be sleeping himself for many more hours, Alexei insisted on remaining on the couch to be near him, assuring Jay multiple times that not sleeping on the bed wasn't going to cause permanent damage to his fragile mortal body (how bizarre, to find out *he* was the delicate one in this dynamic).

His eyelids started dropping as he watched Jay draw what was looking to become an exquisite portrait of a woman's face in pencil.

Alexei drifted off wondering who she might be.

Alexei woke up to the smell of peppermint invading his nostrils. He breathed in deep, tightening his hold on the warm bundle in his arms. The peppermint was nice, cutting through the little bit of hangover fog he had going on.

And cutting through the fog was good. Very good. Because Alexei had a lot to process, didn't he? Jay and Colin in the alleyway. The existence of vampires (which begged the question, the existence of what else?). Jay biting him on the couch.

And the bite. That fucking bite. Nothing could have prepared Alexei for how good getting the blood sucked out of his goddamn body was going to feel.

His morning wood gave a little jerk at the thought of it.

"You're awake?" Jay's soft voice had Alexei opening his eyes with a start, at the same moment he realized the bundle in his arms wasn't one of the couch pillows after all.

"You weren't up here with me when I fell asleep," Alexei pointed out mildly, his voice husky with sleep, as he tightened his arms almost against his will. Jay had definitely still been sitting on the floor in front of the couch when Alexei's eyes had drifted shut.

Jay giggled, an absurdly adorable sound. "Well, you sort of pulled me up on the couch with you in the middle of the night."

"I pulled you up in my sleep?" Alexei asked, incredulous.

Except that actually sounded just about right. His obsession with the barista—the *vampire* barista—was so deeply ingrained at this point he wasn't at all surprised it had seeped even into his subconscious.

"I think so?" Jay answered with a shrug, his shoulder bumping up against Alexei's chest. Jay's back was to Alexei's front, with Alexei's erection nestled right up against that surprisingly pert little butt. It took all Alexei's willpower to resist thrusting into it. "You were all grumbly and mumbly, and your eyes were only half-open. I don't mind though." Jay said the last part tentatively, the tips of his ears going pink in front of Alexei's eyes. "The cuddling is nice."

Alexei snorted with amusement, unable to keep himself from bending forward to nose the back of Jay's neck. "You're just a literal cupcake, aren't you?"

"Well, not a *literal* cupcake," Jay giggled.

Right. Because Jay was a literal *vampire.* An ancient creature who drank people's blood and was somehow still a virgin after multiple centuries of living. And while Alexei knew his brain should be more focused on the former, he was really having a hard time pulling his dirty fucking mind away from the latter.

He still couldn't believe he'd been worried Jay was too *young* for him.

"We'll consider the cuddling part of your...education."

"Is cuddling a big part of sex?" Jay wiggled against him as he asked the question, and Alexei couldn't for the life of him tell if he was doing it on purpose.

"Yes," Alexei lied.

It wasn't, not to him. He'd never opened himself up to the potential vulnerability of holding his former partners, had never stayed the night with them. But he liked having Jay in his arms. For such a slender little thing, he was surprisingly soft, and he smelled unbearably good, and when he was nervous, he apparently did this odd wiggling thing like a little puppy, and that felt awfully nice pressed against Alexei's dick right about now.

Except...

Alexei sighed, reluctantly loosening his hold. "I'm afraid I need to get up."

Jay twisted his upper body until he was peering back at Alexei, his brows furrowed. "Oh," he said sadly. "Did you, um, change your mind? About the sex stuff?"

"Fuck no," Alexei said, a bit more harshly than he had intended, his arms tightening once more. He made an effort to soften his voice. "Not at all. I just need to use the restroom, kitten."

Honestly, with all the water Jay had had him chugging the night before, it was a miracle Alexei had slept the entire night without having to get up to pee.

He sat up carefully, finally releasing his captive vampire, mindful of each movement of his potential hangover. He wasn't in his twenties anymore. But really, Alexei's head didn't feel too bad, all things considered.

It probably had something to do with all the pizza bagels Jay had fed him.

Jay led him to the bathroom, although the guidance probably wasn't necessary, considering there were only two possible doors to choose from. Alexei paused in the doorway, rubbing at the back of his neck. His hair had come loose sometime in the night. "Do vampires happen to use toothpaste?"

For some reason, the question seemed to delight Jay, who bounced up on his toes in his excitement. "Oh! Yes to toothpaste. And I even have a toothbrush, never used." He hustled into the bathroom and dug around in the cabinet, triumphantly brandishing a still-packaged toothbrush. "I keep them for guests, but then I never have guests, so it's just...here."

Alexei took the toothbrush from him, lips twitching a little at Jay's enthusiasm, and then they both just stood there, staring at each other. Eventually Alexei cleared his throat. "Still have to pee, kitten."

"Oh!" Jay flushed. As of the past twenty-four hours, he seemed to do that quite a lot around Alexei. It was incredibly endearing. "I'll get out of your way."

Alexei did his business quickly, and by the time he came out of the bathroom, Jay had already arranged a tall glass of water and a plate of what looked like Pop-Tarts on the coffee table, standing off to the side like the maître d' of some fancy restaurant.

"For me?" Alexei asked, making his way over to the couch.

Jay nodded shyly, remaining standing even as Alexei sat, and Alexei gulped his water dutifully under the vampire's watchful eye. He left the Pop-Tarts alone for the moment; he wasn't interested in the food just yet.

"Come here, please," he requested, patting the couch next to him.

But Jay, moving *alarmingly* fast, took his request in a much more interesting direction, and he was perched and straddling Alexei's lap before he could even blink.

"Vamp speed?" Alexei asked, careful to keep his voice light. He didn't want the little guy to think he was scared of him or anything.

"Uh-huh," Jay answered absently, his gaze on Alexei's mouth.

Alexei bit back a smile. Jay was wearing worn sweatpants, incredibly soft-looking, and a T-shirt that had to be about three sizes too big. It was easy enough for Alexei to slip his hands up under all that fabric, rubbing his thumbs against the soft skin of Jay's stomach. "Would you like to start with a kiss, kitten?"

Gray eyes met his, a fervid hunger in their depths. "Can we?"

Alexei barely managed a nod before Jay was leaning forward eagerly, pressing those sweet pink lips against Alexei's own. He took a long moment like that, just a light, steady brush of their lips. Alexei let him go at his own pace, keeping the kiss soft and easy, the scent of peppermint washing over him. And then Jay was slipping his tongue in Alexei's mouth, and Alexei couldn't help himself.

He groaned, a husky, desperate sound, wrapping his arms around Jay and pulling him closer, deepening the kiss.

Jay gave a soft, breathy moan of his own, melting into Alexei's body, one hand gripping Alexei's shirt as if to keep himself upright that way. Alexei palmed the back of Jay's head, doing his part to keep the vampire in place, plundering Jay's mouth with days and days of pent-up lust and longing. Jay met his pace, the eager thing, the greedy little noises coming out of his mouth an echo of the sounds he'd made feeding from Alexei the night before.

It was Alexei who broke the kiss first, out of a need for oxygen more than anything else. He stared, panting, at the little vampire on his lap. Never in his life had Alexei been so torn apart by a single kiss.

Jay was beaming at him, panting in turn. "I melted."

"I'm sorry?"

"My first kiss with tongue," Jay mused rather than explaining.

"That was your first *kiss*?" In his lust-fogged state, Alexei didn't quite manage to keep the shock out of his voice.

Jay stiffened in his arms, and Alexei regretted his words immediately. "My first kiss with *tongue*," Jay repeated, his sweet voice laced with defensiveness.

Alexei had so many fucking questions about Jay's past he didn't ever know where to start. "Can I ask why..." He trailed off, unsure how best to phrase the question, Why haven't you had sex in over two hundred years? without sounding like a complete asshole.

Jay seemed to catch his meaning anyway. "You can, but I don't feel like explaining this morning. This is a *good* morning."

On that they could agree.

Alexei felt like he should offer truth for truth. He kept stealing Jay's secrets and giving nothing in return. "I'm in hiding. From my brother. Our family business has some...criminal elements to it. I pissed him off before I left." He cleared his throat, unsure of how much detail to go into. "I don't know if he's even looking for me anymore, but if he found me...it could get dangerous."

Jay's gray eyes were serious, his nod solemn. "I'll protect you, Alexei."

Alexei couldn't help it. He kissed him again, hungry and obsessive and wanting the vampire in his arms so much it physically *hurt*.

He broke it off first again, Jay giving the impression he could kiss for hours and never tire of it. "There's so much I want to do to you. Jesus fucking Christ. I don't want to go too fast."

Jay licked his lips, as if chasing Alexei's taste. "I've waited over two hundred years. There's no such thing as too fast."

"Well, exactly. But—"

Jay's brow furrowed, and the hand in Alexei's shirt tugged sharply. "I'm not a baby. I'm not naive. I'm not some ingenue. I'm just...inexperienced."

"No, you're not a baby." Alexei pressed a kiss to Jay's neck, then whispered in his ear. "You're a kitten."

Jay leaned back, a smile on his face, his defensiveness instantly forgotten. "You made a little joke." He started stroking Alexei's hair, lifting a strand between two fingers. "This is nice. I like it all down like this."

Alexei allowed himself to close his eyes, reveling in the soft touch. How long had it been since he'd been petted, stroked, cared for?

He could feel Jay watching him closely. Alexei tried to gauge where best to start. He'd never...deflowered anyone before.

Might as well start with the basics. "So you've touched yourself, then?" he asked.

"Yes, I like to." Jay continued his soft petting of Alexei's hair. "Sometimes I do it a lot. I read my books and get turned on, or sometimes I watch porn, and then I stroke myself under the covers."

Holy fuck. That had Alexei's eyes opening, his cock suddenly straining against his zipper hard enough to hurt. "Well, fuck. That—that's great, kitten." Jay was smiling almost mischievously at him, and Alexei had to wonder once again how much of the maddening little things the vampire was doing were on purpose. He swallowed, mouth dry. "You want to show me how you do it?"

He figured Jay would maybe be more comfortable starting with what he knew, but Jay was already shaking his head, biting at that fucking lip again. "I'd like to—I want—" He heaved a breath, finding his words. "I've never touched someone *else* that way."

Alexei let out his own slow exhale. "You want to touch me, kitten?"

Jay nodded eagerly, his hands clenching into Alexei's hair, Alexei's scalp stinging at the pull. "Yes. That."

Seven

Jay

Jay was nodding so furiously it was making him a little dizzy. "Yes. Touching. Me touching you. That's what I want."

He couldn't even feel embarrassed by his eagerness, not when Alexei was actually smiling at him again (and not one of his not smiles, but a real, honest-to-goodness *smile*), looking so handsome with his pretty hair and pretty eyes and his wide mouth looking so soft and happy, just for Jay.

Was Jay maybe dreaming? This all sort of felt like it. Except he'd never had a dream this good, sitting on this big human's lap, being told he could have everything he'd ever wanted. (And okay, maybe touching Alexei's cock wasn't *everything* Jay had ever wanted, but really, it was way, way up there.)

Jay reluctantly released his grip on that pretty blond hair, scooting back a little to give Alexei room to maneuver. The scent of vanilla was everywhere around him, and his beastie kept wanting to come out to play again.

No way, Jay reprimanded. *This is for me. You had your bite last night.*

His beastie preened at the reminder, even while annoyance buzzed at Jay's chastising. They both agreed the human had tasted so very delicious. And with Alexei's bigger size (what was he, six feet four?), Jay had been able to take more blood than he had when feeding from Colin. There was an art to it, taking just enough, recognizing the rise in heart rate, the signs of impending hypovolemia (Danny had taught Jay that word; it was such a useful one). But Jay finally felt *full* for the first time in a long while.

And all that was suddenly very beside the point because Alexei was unbuttoning his jeans (and oh God, had Jay really made the poor human sleep in stiff denim?) and pulling them down his hips, taking whatever underwear he'd had on with them. Jay raised his own butt to get himself out of the way, but his gaze remained firmly on his prize.

Goodness gracious.

Jay had seen other men's cocks before, of course—the den he'd been raised in wasn't exactly puritanical with its nudity standards—but never one that was his to touch. His to *play* with.

"You're bigger than I am," he found himself saying, nibbling at his lower lip.

Alexei graced him with a soft chuckle. "Well, that makes sense, kitten. I'm a bigger guy."

Jay hummed his agreement, even knowing it didn't always work that way. He liked the size of Alexei's body very much. Jay felt so secure in the big human's lap, settled on his strong, broad thighs.

Alexei's cock was standing at attention, and Jay felt a fierce, burning satisfaction, knowing the human was attracted to him enough to be hard without Jay having even touched him yet. He was uncut, like Jay, but the red head of his cock was peeking out from the hood of his foreskin.

Jay wanted to lick it. He really did. He wanted his mouth all over that thing.

But he was also very keyed up and turned on, and he didn't trust his fangs not to come out accidentally, so maybe it was best if he kept his mouth to himself for now.

Jay looked up from the source of his fascination to see amusement shining in Alexei's colorful eyes. It wasn't mocking or cruel though. Jay knew the difference. "You're looking at my cock like it's a slice of birthday cake," Alexei said.

"Oh, much better than cake," Jay breathed, twisting his hands together to keep himself from grabbing too soon.

Alexei noticed the movement because of course he did. "You can touch," he told Jay.

Jay reached out with one finger, petting at the silky head, spreading the drops of precum around. When his finger dipped under Alexei's foreskin, the human hissed softly.

Jay halted his movements. "Does that feel good?" he asked tentatively.

"Everything about you feels good, kitten."

Warmth hummed in Jay's chest. He felt exactly the same way. Still. "I don't know what I'm doing," he reminded Alexei.

"I know enough for the both of us."

"Have you been with many people?" Jay asked, pushing the excess skin back from Alexei's cock head and tracing at a vein with his finger.

"Not too many." Alexei was sounding a little strained. "Enough."

Jay's beastie gave a restless shake at that. It was feeling awfully possessive, really. But Jay was glad at least one of them knew what he was doing. He tore his gaze off his own hand and met Alexei's eyes again. "Show me what to do, please."

Alexei immediately wrapped his broad hand around Jay's and started moving them both, working his cock in the rhythm Jay had to assume he preferred. It was surprisingly slow, and when Jay cocked his head, considering that, Alexei seemed to read his mind, answering the unspoken question. "I don't want this to end too quickly."

Jay couldn't help preening a little at that. He loved that this human was attracted to him. That he was worried Jay would give him too *much* pleasure rather than too little.

They stroked together for who could say how long, and then Alexei removed his hand and let Jay take over. Jay was fascinated with all the little grunts and groans he was able to draw out of Alexei's once taciturn mouth, the little "perfect" he would occasionally throw out.

But soon it wasn't enough. Jay squirmed on Alexei's thighs, strangely restless. "I want to be kissing you," he grumbled.

Maybe that was rude to say? Would Alexei think he was getting greedy?

But Alexei's eyes, half-lidded and drowsy-looking, flashed with heat. "Fucking hell, kitten. Anytime you want."

Jay scooted forward, eager. He licked into the human's mouth, humming with happiness at the taste. It took him a minute to realize his hand had stopped moving. Alexei hadn't made any protest, had just taken Jay's kissing in glorious stride. Jay broke the kiss, frustrated with himself. "It's hard to focus," he complained. "You smell so good."

He wasn't sure if Alexei would understand what he meant by that. Jay wanted to...burrow, almost. To bury himself in the sensation of being kissed, in the wonderful feeling of Alexei holding him, surrounding him. But it was hard to do that and also do a good job with his hand on Alexei's cock.

How did everyone else manage multitasking like this?

Alexei didn't look frustrated with him though. He smiled lazily—so pretty, when he smiled like that—and traced a finger around the waistline of Jay's sweatpants. "Can I touch you instead, kitten? Show you how good it feels?"

How was Jay supposed to say no? He nodded, not trusting his own voice, leaning back so Alexei could delve into Jay's pants, fishing out Jay's leaking, aching cock. Jay moaned at the contact.

"Gorgeous," Alexei murmured, licking his lips like Jay was some sort of delicious dessert he was about to cut into.

Jay's face felt hot. "I'm not gorgeous," he protested.

He wasn't. Cute, maybe. Adorable, sometimes. Weird, often. But nobody ever called him gorgeous.

He squeaked when Alexei gave his cock a little tug. "You are. So gorgeous."

Jay couldn't find it in himself to correct him again. There was a hand. On his cock. Not Jay's hand. Someone *else's* hand.

Jay had thought they'd be working together; Alexei working his cock and him working Alexei's, but instead, the human gently knocked Jay's hand away, wrapping both their members in his big grip.

Jay whimpered. Ohh, that was nice. So very nice. He liked that quite a bit. The way it felt. The way it *looked*: the two of them pressed together, the difference in their sizes so apparent and so weirdly...hot.

Like, super-duper hot.

Alexei used his free hand to cup the back of Jay's head, pulling him in for another kiss. Jay whimpered again into his mouth as Alexei set an easy rhythm. "Is that good, kitten?"

"Uh-huh. Yeah. Yes. But I should— For you. I should be making *you* feel good."

Alexei's laugh was low and throaty. "Do you know how long I've wanted you on my lap like this? You *are* making me feel good, kitten. The way you smell. The way you look right now, flushed and fucked out and desperate. Move your hips. Just like that. Fuck into my fist. We're not stopping until your cum is coating us both."

Well, holy hell. Jay hadn't known people talked like that outside of dirty books and porn. But he liked it. He liked it *so much*. Alexei's hand felt way better than his own ever had, especially with the soft, sticky slide of their cocks pressed together. Even more so with Alexei's mouth pressed to his, their tongues brushing up against each other.

Jay didn't realize he'd changed until the coppery sweet taste of blood filled his mouth. Alexei must have cut his tongue on Jay's fang. His body jerked underneath Jay's, and the human groaned loudly.

And then Jay could feel it. A new warmth on his cock. It was cum. Alexei's *cum*. Jay whined, so turned on he couldn't communicate properly, could only suck Alexei's tongue into his mouth even harder as he and his beastie both reveled in the taste.

Alexei didn't stop. He was so much more responsible than Jay that way, because his hand kept moving, bringing Jay up, up to the edge, until all that heat and electricity that had been building steadily in his stomach, in his spine, just...exploded.

Jay tore his mouth away and tucked his head against Alexei's neck as his body shuddered with the force of it.

He nuzzled there, even after the trembling stopped. Not to bite, just because it felt so dang good all curled up against him, feeling the steady movement of Alexei's chest as he panted.

Jay had done that. He'd made Alexei come.

Well, *he* hadn't done that, exactly. Alexei had. But it was Jay's presence that had had him so turned on. That was what Alexei had said, when he'd been saying all those nice, dirty words.

After a long moment, Jay felt Alexei's hand on his cheek, urging him up. Before Jay could even think to push the beastie back fully, Alexei was grabbing onto his face with both hands, staring so intensely. So...intimately.

He smiled at Jay, and Jay felt positively spoiled with the number of those smiles he was getting from his stern regular. "Like I said," Alexei murmured. "Gorgeous."

Jay felt too good to protest this time. So relaxed. So content. So full.

He smiled back at Alexei, probably a little goofily. "I think you're the nicest human I've ever met."

Alexei laughed then. A full laugh, easy and smooth. "I'm really, really not. But I like being nice to you."

Jay liked it too.

Jay loved when family dinner fell on a Monday.

It made up for him not having any work to do, no café to go to, even to pop in and check in on his coworkers. He did that sometimes, and Alicia always made sure to give him a free coffee drink, winking and warning him not to tell Colin, and then Colin would always make sure to give him a free pastry, frowning and warning him not to tell Alicia.

He wasn't allowed to bring any food to family dinner, of course, but he was allowed to bring the wine. Roman had admitted, after extensive taste tests, that Jay knew how to choose a wine.

Because I taught you so well, Johann.

Vee's voice in his head caught Jay by surprise. He hadn't heard it in...well, not since he'd seen Alexei in the alleyway. How funny, that he didn't really hear her in his head when Alexei was around. Too many other things to focus on, he supposed.

Alexei's scrumptious smell. The way it felt touching him. The way it felt being touched by him. Jay did a little happy shimmy at the memory, pressing Danny's doorbell even though he knew he was welcome to come in without doing so, just because he liked hearing the little chime.

Maybe by next week, he'd even be able to bring something he'd made himself! Syrniki. Wouldn't that be nice.

He was ushered in by Danny, who let Jay open the wine and fill up glasses while he and Roman put the finishing touches on dinner—some creamy French chicken dish that smelled like yummy garlic.

Jay liked that Danny insisted on a weekly family dinner with human food, even though none of them technically needed it. He liked even more that Danny included *Jay* in it, even though he wasn't technically family, neither a Kingman brother nor significant other.

Soren and Gabe arrived not too long after Jay, holding hands like they always did anytime they were in the same room. Danny liked to tease that they were Velcroed together, but Jay could tell it made him happy to see it. Danny always got this glowing, pleased look, seeing his older brother so content.

Gabe and Danny hugged while Soren—who was the most dressed up of all of them, wearing some elegant silk blouse and tapered black pants—shot Jay a smirk. "Jaybird, what have I told you about arriving fashionably late?"

"That I'm terrible at it because I'm too eager for everything all the time."

"Exactly," Soren said, but he gave Jay a kiss on the cheek anyway, which was unexpected and extra nice.

Gabe gave Jay a little shoulder squeeze in greeting, looking like he'd let Soren dress him again; his shirt was much too tight for it to have been his own choice in clothing.

Jay beamed up at him. He liked Soren's mate. He was very nice to Jay and also quite handsome. He might even have been Jay's type—tall and strong with nicely large hands—if he weren't so perfect for Soren already. Gabe's presence in Soren's life had made Jay's old friend kind of...soft, in a way he'd never been before. Jay approved. Soren deserved nice things. He'd had too much bad in his life before, and it wasn't really fair at all, because underneath all the snark and the sass, he had a big, giant heart.

That was a little secret, though, just among the family. And Jay.

They all sat down to eat, catching up on hospital gossip (in the case of Danny and Gabe), and Ferdy updates (in the case of Danny and Soren). Roman mostly watched his mate, his every reaction to the conversation in tune with what made Danny smile, or frown, or wave his fork around in excitement.

And Jay watched *everyone*, happy to be surrounded by such nice vampires. He didn't know what he'd done to deserve it—or rather, he *did* know he hadn't done a single thing—but he felt very lucky anyway.

He waited until dessert—a flourless chocolate cake Danny had baked—to make his announcement, setting his fork down next to his plate and folding his hands in the way he'd seen serious businesspeople do in movies. "So. I'm seeing someone."

The surrounding conversation halted immediately, and three pairs of eyes blinked in astonishment—practically in unison, which kind of made Jay want to giggle. But he was busy making a serious announcement, so he took a sip of wine instead.

"You're *dating* someone?" Danny finally asked, reaching a hand out to grab Roman's arm for some reason.

Jay cocked his head, considering. "Well, I'm not sure if it's dating, exactly. I'm biting him, and he's teaching me about sex and also some cooking. Or maybe baking?" Jay wasn't sure, actually, if pancakes counted as cooking or baking.

Danny gave a strangled cough. "He— I'm sorry, what? I could have taught you that, if you wanted."

At Roman's, "Not fucking likely," Danny clarified, "The baking. I could teach you the *baking*. I've gotten pretty good at it."

"Oh God, this is that mobster, isn't it?" Soren asked, shooting a weird look at Danny, whose eyes widened.

"The one you like the smell of? *Oh*." Danny shot his own meaningful look back at Soren.

"Stop *doing* that," Jay snapped, then slapped his hand over his mouth in horror. Oh no. Oh no, no, no. He did *not* snap at his friends. That wasn't acceptable behavior. Not one bit.

Rude boy. Not fit for company. Vee's voice in his head sounded almost gleeful chastising him. Of course it did. She'd always loved finding fault. And there was so much fault to find.

Jay's chest felt tight, his stomach a strange, solid rock. "I'm sorry, everyone. I'll go." He pushed his chair back from the table.

"What? Why would you go?" Danny's brow furrowed, and he looked around the table, seeming to search his dinner companions' faces for answers.

"I was rude," Jay admitted, biting his lips hard enough to sting. "I should leave. Rude people shouldn't be around company."

"Fucking Veronique," Soren muttered, taking a gulp of his wine.

"It's not— She just—" Jay knew how Soren felt about his old companion. That she had a cruelty to her, that she hadn't treated Jay as well as she should have. All of which may have been true, but also...she'd taken care of him. She'd kept Jay at her side for centuries, his only consistent company for so long. "Don't start on her, please," he begged.

Soren's pale eyes—harsh and cold in his old anger toward Vee—softened at Jay's plea, and he let out a long sigh. "Okay, Jaybird. Just stay, please. You're allowed to be rude sometimes. Christ, I'm rude ninety-nine percent of the time."

Some of that tight pressure in Jay's chest released at Soren's words, and he found himself letting out a weak giggle, pulling his chair back into the table and straightening his fork. "I just don't like when you talk *around* me instead of *to* me. Even when you do it with your eyes."

"Who, us?" Soren gave Jay his most innocent look, which wasn't very innocent at all.

Danny waved his napkin at Soren in admonishment, turning to Jay with his big brown eyes all sympathetic and apologetic. "I'm sorry, sweetie. It's just...we worry a little."

Gabe cleared his throat. "Like, should you really be dating a human? Isn't that dangerous, if they're not even your ma— Ow!" Gabe glared accusingly at Soren. "What are you doing?"

Soren lifted his head from where he'd been peering beneath the tablecloth, arching a golden brow at his mate. "Just looking to see how you could possibly manage to fit such big feet into your mouth at every opportunity."

Gabe smirked at him. "You know what they say, baby brat. Big feet, big—"

"Please, for the love of God, don't finish that sentence," Danny begged.

Gabe only laughed, his anger apparently instantly forgotten, and stole a kiss from Soren, who pretended to be annoyed but whose fingers, Jay noticed, twined around Gabe's, holding hands even as he fussed.

Then all the attention in the room was once again on Jay.

Danny cleared his throat. "Sweetie, we just worry. You know, if you don't, um, have a lot of experience, and you get worked up..."

Jay nodded, immediately understanding the direction of Danny's concern. "Don't worry," he reassured his friends. "He already knows I'm a vampire. He saw me feeding on Colin."

Soren gave a sharp bark of laughter. "Your *manager*? Please tell me you were able to compel him to forget."

Jay cocked his head. "But I never compel people. That's why I've been feeding on Colin."

"*Been* feeding on Colin?" Danny asked. "Colin...knows? About us?"

"Just about me," Jay reassured him. "I wouldn't tell him about you all." He bit at his lip, considering. "But I kind of slipped with Alexei in that regard." Technically he'd only told the human about Roman, but Jay had a feeling it wouldn't be his only slipup. He'd rather just have it all out in the open now and not worry about it later.

Roman, silent up to this point, sighed heavily, folding his napkin carefully on the table, then looked to Soren. "We'll need you to do some cleanup. At the very least compel the manager."

Soren was nodding along in agreement.

"No." Jay didn't snap this time, but he did make sure his voice carried. "No compelling. Colin and I have an agreement."

Soren looked at Jay like his words from earlier were finally sinking in. "You *never* compel humans? But— How have you been feeding all this time, Jaybird?"

Jay fidgeted with his fork. "Vee always got me my blood, before. And after she died, I had a...friend. I don't judge you all for it, but I don't like doing it. It's a lie."

"You think I'm a liar?" Soren's voice held a dangerous note Jay knew all too well—one he didn't use very often with Jay—but for once, Jay refused to back down.

He held Soren's gaze. "I think you don't mind using deception in order to get what you need. That's fine. I just don't work that way."

"Fucking Veronique," Soren muttered for the second time.

Jay resisted the urge to raise his voice. "You can't blame her for everything."

"Can you honestly tell me it has nothing to do with her?"

Jay couldn't, and it made him almost *angry* that he couldn't. So much of his personality could be attributed to one person. One person who hadn't even loved him. Not really. He knew that, somewhere underneath the loyalty and the long-standing habit of his devotion.

Jay wanted to be his own person. To be independent. He really did. But it was hard, and it was lonely, and he just didn't want to mess with poor humans' brains to do so.

"Okay. Let's take stock." Danny was using what he called his stern nurse voice. "The manager of the café where Jay works knows he's a vampire and has for some time. Is that right, Jay?"

"Right." Jay nodded, glad they were all finally getting on the same page.

"And now your new...regular...also knows, and maybe also about some of us too, and he's seducing you with his body and his blood and maybe also his baking prowess. Is *that* right, Jay?"

"Right," Jay agreed, although with a little less certainty this time. He wasn't so sure it was a seduction going on, not when Jay had agreed so readily. "Just hand stuff so far, but I'm hoping to get to mouth stuff very soon."

"How is this my goddamn life?" Roman muttered, downing the rest of his wine in one swallow.

"And we're just going to support the revealing of all our secrets so Jay can get some action?" Gabe asked, sounding pretty cranky about the whole idea.

Soren and Danny looked at each other, once again communicating something without words. Jay didn't protest because it seemed like this time they were talking around everybody, not just him.

Also, it was kind of funny to see Gabe and Roman so put out about it.

Finally Danny nodded, and Soren cleared his throat. "Yes, Highness. Yes, we are."

Jay beamed at each person seated at the table in turn.

All in all, that had gone better than expected.

Eight

Jay

It wasn't until Jay got home and started drawing, sitting cross-legged on the floor of his living room, his pencil sketching an all-too-familiar female face, that the bad thoughts and feelings surfaced again.

He considered Soren's anger toward Jay's maker, his clear irritation with Jay for his inability to renounce her.

Jay couldn't help feeling like it was just a bit unfair though. Jay and Soren were different in that way; they always had been. They may have been raised in the same toxic den, taught the same lessons: obey your maker, humans are cattle, no vampire makes it alone in the outside world. But Soren had been brave—he'd *always* been so brave—and he'd escaped anyway.

True, Soren's maker had definitely been the kind of vampire to run from; Hendrick had been much crueler, more physically violent, and more aggressive than Vee. And he'd wanted certain things from Soren Vee had never wanted from Jay. Vee had wanted a...servant, Jay supposed it came down to. And not of the sexual kind. Someone to keep things neat and tidy and put on a good face for visitors. Someone to keep her company—reading quietly or playing the piano concertos she'd taught him—during the long, cold nights. Someone to never talk back and never contradict her and never look dirty or unkempt or wild. And as long as he'd done all those things perfectly, she'd been...kind. She hadn't yelled or hit. Sometimes she'd even hugged him, or praised him when he'd done a particularly good job. Those were the very best moments,

And if he hadn't done all those things absolutely perfectly, then Jay had been simply...left alone.

Which wasn't so bad, right? Not compared to what Soren had been through, that was for sure.

Locked in a room by himself for hours or days, nothing to look at or play with or read. It could have been worse. Jay had learned to pass the time in his head. He sometimes still did, even without meaning to. He sometimes lost hours that way.

It didn't happen when he was around people though.

Jay's pencil paused. His throat felt thick, like it was hard to swallow. He wished he weren't alone now. He wished...

He wanted to call Alexei, to ask the human to distract him with his good smell and his nice hands. But calling someone in the middle of the night, just because he was lonely...that was for boyfriends, wasn't it? Alexei wasn't Jay's boyfriend.

Jay was never going to get to have a boyfriend, was he?

Jay stabbed his pencil back into his paper, running back over the familiar lines, an angry, roiling heat filling his gut. He shouldn't mind being alone. He should be able to be brave. He should be able to raise his voice at the dinner table without feeling like he needed to be punished.

Jay tried it, tried tasting the words out loud. "Fucking Veronique." He tried again, putting as much spite and malice as he could into the words. "*Fucking Veronique.*"

It wasn't enough.

He scribbled over his drawing, crossing out the eyes with heavy, repeated strokes. He turned the whole page into a mass of gray-black sludge, then crumpled it into a little ball and threw it at the wall. *Fucking Veronique.*

He started on a new paper, a new face. A long, straight nose. Pretty eyes with so many different colors, none of which Jay could capture with just a pencil, but the kindness in them he could. The way that stern brow turned soft just for Jay. The little crinkles at the corners of those eyes when they were smiling at him, telling him he was good and perfect and gorgeous.

Jay let the motions of his pencil soothe him.

He was growing. He was changing. He *was*.

He could be more than what his maker had made of him.

Seconds or minutes or hours later—he couldn't be sure, really, only knew that his drawing was finished and he'd since been staring at the wall—Jay's phone dinged with a text.

They grow impatient.

Jay considered throwing his phone against the wall like he had with Vee's ruined portrait, how satisfying the crunch of it would be. But then how would Alexei get a hold of him? They were going to make syrniki tomorrow. Jay needed to be available.

So he kept his phone intact, sending a reply instead.

I'm learning how to make pancakes.

Then he let himself drift off, back into his own head. Maybe when he came to, it would be morning, and he'd be that much closer to his cooking lesson.

Johann closed his eyes and let the sun beat down on his face, his feet resting up on the fence, his back firmly planted in the grass. Most likely any minute now, his uncle would call him in to help with the horses, but for now he could take a minute to enjoy the warmth of the spring day.

"My, my. Don't you look comfortable."

Johann peeled one eye open, startling when he realized there was a woman looking down at him, her face mostly hidden by a large sun hat.

"Oh!" Johann scrambled up, brushing his breeches and doing his best not to stumble as the blood rushed back down from his head. "Can I help you, Madam?"

"I'm not quite sure yet."

Johann couldn't see her eyes, but he could tell the woman was looking him over slowly by the way her hatted head tilted. She had three inches on him at least, and she was really very elegant. Much too elegant for the countryside, and her German had a slight accent to it Johann couldn't quite place. Perhaps she wasn't native to Austria.

"You're very young, I think" was the woman's final verdict after her perusal. "How old exactly?"

Johann cleared his throat. "I've just turned nineteen."

She gave a thoughtful hum. "And you still reside with your parents?"

"My aunt and uncle. My parents have passed."

"No wife of your own yet?"

Johann shook his head, unable to find words, too embarrassed that she'd even asked.

She laughed softly then. And it wasn't necessarily a mean sound, but it wasn't necessarily a nice one either. "What do you do all day, then, other than sitting upside down in the dirt?"

Johann resisted the urge to scratch at his neck, running a hand along the fence instead. "I help around the farm. My aunt and uncle don't have children of their own."

The woman's head tilted. "You're good at following instruction?"

"Yes, Madam."

She was silent then, studying him some more. It was starting to make Johann uneasy, the way she looked at him. The way he couldn't quite see her face. "You have a very fine bone structure, under all that dirt," she mused. "Not displeasing at all."

"Thank you, Madam." Johann very much wanted to go home now. He wanted the firm comfort of his uncle's hand on his shoulder, the warm reassurance of his aunt's smile at the supper table.

"And you're very polite."

His response was automatic. "Thank you, Madam."

She seemed to come to some conclusion then, nodding sharply. "You'll do. Come with me."

That...wasn't right. Johann shook his head. This woman may have been above his station, but that was taking things too far. He didn't want to go anywhere with her, this person who studied him like an insect. Or a meal. "Oh no. I'm sorry, but I have to get back."

"You will come with me now."

The sharp edge in her voice had Johann's heart rate speeding. He tried to step back, but the fence was directly behind him, and he only ended up feeling all the more trapped. "I beg your pardon"—she'd liked that he was polite, right? Maybe if he was polite, she'd leave him alone—"but I won't."

The woman pushed up her hat then, and Johann caught only a flash of brown eyes before they...changed. It was like her pupils expanded rapidly, the black taking over. And then she smiled, and her teeth were sharp. Like a demon's.

Like a beast's.

Jay opened his mouth to scream, but she spoke before he could, those black eyes on his, her voice much rougher than before. "You're not afraid, little lad. You aren't frightened of me."

The tension seeped out of Johann's muscles in an instant with her words, his mouth snapping shut of its own accord. Of course Johann wasn't afraid. Why would he be?

"What's your name, little one?"

"Johann. Johann Barre."

"You'll come with me," she ordered, not offering up her own name. "You won't complain."

"I won't complain." Of course Johann wouldn't complain. Why would he?

Her lips twitched into a satisfied smile. "We'll try you out. If you please me, I'll grant you a gift. Eternal life. Eternal youth. Would you like that?"

"No, Madam," Johann answered honestly. He knew how the natural world worked, the ordinary cycles of men and beasts. To live forever would be...wrong. Out of order.

But she corrected him instantly, the smile dropping from her face. "You would like that. Tell me so."

"I would like that." And suddenly, just like that, the idea of eternal life sounded completely fine. Not unnatural at all.

She turned from him then, gesturing imperiously with one hand. "Come along."

So Johann followed the finely dressed woman off his uncle's property, to the carriage waiting for them on the dirt road. With every step, he felt...wrong...in his own mind. Like there was a tiny, dark corner that knew he was afraid. Very afraid. But he couldn't quite access it and found it difficult to even want to try.

It was months of that, as Jay learned how to be a proper gentleman under Veronique's compulsion. Months of hidden, inaccessible fear. A knowledge that he wasn't where he was supposed to be but that he couldn't quite find it in himself to care about the way he should.

It turned out Veronique had a very special talent, even for those of her kind. It wasn't every vampire who could control a human's mind for such an extended period, with such little effort.

When she finally turned Johann—granting him her unwanted gift—the compulsion no longer worked on him, but by that time, he was in a foreign country, surrounded by bloodthirsty strangers, suddenly quite literally bloodthirsty himself. He simply had to adapt, in order to survive.

As he saw other vampires in the den turn their humans, as he saw the way some of those matches turned out—those newly turned vampires who were too hostile to their makers put down like dogs—Johann realized it could have been much worse.

Really it could have all been so much worse.

Nine

Alexei

Foolish, ridiculous, obsessive Alexei.

Even knowing Jay wouldn't be working that morning—that he had the day off and would in fact be at Alexei's apartment later that day—couldn't seem to stop Alexei's new habit of stalking the coffee shop. He associated it with his little vampire barista, and that seemed like enough to keep him in its thrall.

On top of that, not seeing Jay the day before had been torture.

Alexei had already been obsessed; he knew that. But now that he'd heard the desperate, eager sounds Jay made when touched? The lost, blissed-out look, the frantic movement of his hips when chasing his release?

Alexei was a fucking goner.

And it wasn't just the revelation of sex with Jay that had him spiraling. It was the mind-blowing realization that Jay was so much more than he had seemed (and what he'd seemed to be had already been captivating enough).

Jay may have looked like a literal doll, but he wasn't delicate; he was strong—vastly stronger than Alexei. Jay may have looked more than a decade younger than Alexei, but he had multiple centuries of life experience. And Jay may have been good and kind and the type of person who made everyone around him smile, but he also had a quite literal thirst for blood.

The contradictions only made him that much more alluring. Alexei couldn't think of anything else.

A smirking Alicia greeted Alexei at the counter. "You know he isn't here," she immediately felt the need to point out, flicking the ends of her ponytail over her shoulder.

"Pardon?" Alexei feigned ignorance, scanning the café menu like he hadn't been coming there daily for almost two weeks.

The redhead didn't cut him any slack. "Our young Jay," she drawled. "The one you watch oh so carefully every single day. He's not here today."

How fucking marvelous to realize Alexei had been about as subtle as a hand grenade in his obsession. His father would have murdered him for his carelessness. *Never let them know your thoughts or emotions. Best not to have the latter at all.*

And Alexei's father never had. Let him know, that was—Alexei had no idea to this day if his father had ever even loved him. He'd never said, and he had most certainly never shown.

Alexei pulled his wallet out of his pocket to give himself something to do, keeping his face carefully blank. "I already know he's not."

Alicia's smirk deepened, a dimple appearing on her left cheek. "Oh, you *know*, do you?"

He tapped his card on the counter. "Americano. Please."

Alicia blew out a breath, clearly frustrated with his reticence, but rang him up anyway. "Be careful with him," she warned, the smirk dropping from her face as she handed him back his card.

"Hm?" Alexei didn't usually enjoy playing coy, but he also wasn't in the habit of discussing his love life with local baristas.

Only local *Jay* baristas.

"He watches you just as much" was all Alicia said, winking as she set off to make his drink.

An uncomfortable amount of warmth bloomed in Alexei's chest at her words. Fucking hell. How pathetic he was, to be that desperate for any sign he was special to Jay.

He waited for his coffee before settling in at his usual table. He wouldn't stay at the café for hours this time—he had a date to set up, after all—but he could linger for a minute.

He wasn't really all that surprised when a black cloud of scowling café manager sat down at Alexei's table.

He sipped his espresso calmly while Colin tried to murder him with his eyes alone. Alexei had been in the presence of mobsters since he'd been toddling age; he wasn't going to be intimidated by six feet something of malnourished Colorado punk.

Intimidation tactic clearly failing, Colin leaned back in his chair, crossing his arms over his chest. "You know his secret."

It sounded like an accusation. Alexei inclined his head. "I do."

"You can't tell anyone," Colin warned, his fingers tapping against his bicep.

"I would never."

Colin nodded sharply before giving Alexei a sidelong look. "Did he bite you?"

Alexei cocked a brow. "Is that any of your business?"

"I'll take that as a yes," Colin muttered. "Feels good, huh?"

Alexei just raised his brow again, not giving an inch.

With a sigh, Colin slouched down in his seat. "I just worry about him is all. It takes a lot of control, to be bitten and not...you know. And that's with him not even being my type."

To be drunk from and not fuck Jay into total oblivion was what Alexei assumed Colin was getting at. "And why wouldn't I...*you know*?" Alexei taunted.

Maybe if he pissed Colin off enough, the guy would leave the table and let him drink his coffee in peace.

He was given a new, deepened glare in return, but Colin made no move to shove off. Unfortunate.

Alexei sighed, pushing his coffee to the side and crossing his own arms, giving Colin a level stare. Apparently this conversation was happening whether he wanted it to or not. "Why is everyone acting like he's a babe in the woods and I'm the big, bad wolf? He's my elder by *hundreds* of years."

Alexei hissed as he received a sharp kick to his shin, Colin looking around the room as if KGB spies were clocking their conversation. "Lower your voice, dude. It's because he's—"

"Inexperienced. Yes, I know. So were we all at some point."

Colin shot him a withering look. The guy certainly knew a hundred different ways to glower. "No. It's because he's sweet and kind and lovely and *himself* in a way very few people are."

Alexei shifted in his seat. That was actually a point he couldn't argue. So he folded instead. "I know all that. Why do you think I'm so obsessed with him?"

Colin gave a mirthless laugh. "You are, aren't you? Here every day..." But Alexei's declaration seemed to ease something in him, the tension slowly leaving his lanky frame. "Are you going to let him keep biting me?" he asked, voice deceptively light.

Not on your fucking life. But rather than start another fight, Alexei shrugged. "It's not up to me. But I'm not going to lie. I'd be...discouraging, if he asked."

Colin nodded glumly, pinching at his lip. "Need to find myself another vampire," he muttered, more to himself than to Alexei.

"Jay told me you're...asexual. Is that right?" Alexei wasn't sure why he pried, other than a desire to know more about the relationship between Colin and Jay. To assess the potential threat to his own budding connection.

Colin's brows rose. "And why would you think that's an okay question to ask someone you barely know?"

Because I'm entranced and obsessive and I need to know the exact nature of your relationship or I'll simply pass the fuck away. "Because I want to understand."

For such a moody fuck, Colin seemed to take that at face value. "Jay actually used that term?"

"Not quite."

"I'm not, exactly. Or maybe...somewhere on the spectrum. I just have trouble getting out of my own head, in the moment. And I don't like most people. You included, by the way. It wasn't about sex with him. It's just..." He lowered his voice to a whisper. "Monsters are *real*. How could I not want to experiment a bit, knowing that?" He shrugged. "Plus, Jay needed a friend."

I'll be his friend, Alexei thought, the possessive yearning hot and liquid in his chest. Maybe Colin was right to be concerned. "Jay said he has people of a kind. Here in town."

Colin nodded. "Yeah, he has a few friends he's close to, I guess. But you'd have to be blind not to see he's lonely as hell, even so. The more people around him, the better, I think."

There was a long moment of silence as they both processed that thought. Eventually, Alexei cleared his throat, offering his own version of a cease-fire. "I won't hurt him, you know. Just because I'm attracted to him doesn't mean I'm some dastardly villain."

"And when he falls in love with you because he's affection-deprived, touch-starved, and you're his fucking first?"

That answered the question of whether Colin knew Jay was a virgin. It also sounded like the perfect fucking outcome to Alexei. But to say so would be giving away more cards than he was willing. So he only shrugged, aware Colin still probably thought he was a complete asshole. "We'll cross that bridge if we ever come to it."

Colin still didn't leave the table.

"This is the most I've ever heard you speak," Alexei said a bit pointedly.

"I could say the same for you. I speak when it's important."

Alexei nodded in understanding. "He's important."

"He is."

On that they could agree.

Alexei's impatience knew no bounds, waiting on Jay's arrival. He'd already cleaned his little one-bedroom—he was renting from a man who took cash over checking a credit report and didn't look too closely at government ID—like a madman earlier that morning.

Jay's place had been neat and tidy, and Alexei wanted the little vampire to feel comfortable in his space.

He took a last look around to try to assess for any flaws. Alexei's kitchen was definitely nothing special, but it had a working gas stove and good natural light, and with the counters practically gleaming and all the ingredients laid out, it didn't look so bad.

Even with his expecting it, the doorbell ringing had Alexei's heart in his throat. Jesus, what the fuck was wrong with him?

His nerves were hard to reconcile with the adorable vision that greeted him at the door: Jay in baby-blue fleece pants with little snowflake patterns, the legs of which were just peeking out from under a truly massive orange down coat.

Alexei quirked a brow at the sight. "You've got your own unique style, did you know that?"

"Thank you," Jay answered with full sincerity, clearly taking it as a compliment. "I like to be cozy."

"You're coziness personified, sweetheart." The new term of endearment dropped from Alexei's lips without his permission, but he couldn't really regret it. Even if he'd started out meaning to tease, the beaming smile Jay gave him in return made him happy he'd said it. He stepped back from the door, beckoning in his guest. "Come in from the cold, kotyonok."

"I will, thank you." Jay stomped his boots first, clearly mindful of tracking snow into Alexei's apartment. "It doesn't bother me though. Just so you know. All temperature is more or less the same."

Alexei nodded pointedly to the giant coat. "Well, you're certainly dressed for it."

"It's to blend in," Jay informed him, shrugging off his outerwear.

Alexei processed that information as he was handed the practically neon coat—one of the most hideous things he'd ever seen in his life—and tried his best to keep a straight face, but Jay's focus was already 100 percent elsewhere.

The little vampire bounced onto his toes, doing a strange little skip / dance up to the ingredients on Alexei's kitchen counter—there weren't many in the recipe itself, but Alexei laid out all the toppings as well, to add some flair—and Jay's enthusiasm for something as simple as making Russian pancakes had Alexei grinning like a fool.

He tried to school his face into something less ridiculous, rubbing at the back of his neck, his hair already tied up and out of the way. "I thought we'd just do each step together. I don't have a written recipe or anything."

Jay was turning the block of farmer's cheese over in his hands like he'd never seen anything so fascinating in his life. "Who taught you again? Your mother?"

"No, my grandmother. She'd make them with me the few times we visited Russia, when I was a child." Watching Jay—whose very presence imbued the small kitchen with such sweetness and warmth—Alexei felt compelled to share a truth he didn't give often. "My mother was very…sad when I was growing up. She was kind but not always there, I guess you could say. And then she left when I was quite young. I don't even know where she is now."

His memories of her were at this point a blurry haze of scattered moments, filled with Russian endearments and a softness he hadn't felt since.

Jay set the cheese down, immediately giving Alexei his full attention, his gray eyes empathetic. "That's so sad. That's *too* sad. I'm so sorry."

Alexei cleared his suddenly dry throat, ready to shrug it off, but then another truth was just spilling out of him like poison. "I wouldn't have stayed with my father either."

"Your father the…mobster?" Jay asked hesitantly.

"My father the asshole," Alexei said, with more harshness than he had intended. "He wasn't kind, not like her. He raised my older brother and me with a real 'heir and a spare' mentality. Pitted us against each other, always let Ivan know he was replaceable and me know I was a backup. It was like he thought if we loved each other, supported each other, it would just make us...weak."

Jay made a small sound of distress, and then suddenly he was in Alexei's arms, a warm bundle of comfort, the distance between them gone in the blink of an eye.

Alexei was taken aback by the hug and not only because Jay moved so incredibly fast. Alexei wasn't used to people who...comforted. Not since the last time he'd seen his grandmother, well before he'd even reached puberty.

But he wrapped his arms around Jay's small frame anyway, grateful for the contact. There was a cynical part of him that worried he'd just used his own personal pseudotragedy to imbue closeness between the two of them. But wasn't that just what normal bonding between two people looked like? For people who weren't raised by cold Mafia men where everything was secrets and stoicism and pain?

"Would you like to talk about something less sad now?" Jay mumbled the question into Alexei's sternum after a solid minute of silent hugging.

Alexei tightened his arms one last time before releasing Jay from his hold. "I would love to, kitten. Let me show you what we're working with."

It was an easy enough recipe, probably boring for most people, but Jay was an incredibly enthusiastic student. He hadn't been lying about being good with direction. When told what to do, he followed each step with a perfectionism that was mildly alarming.

When relaxed and happy, he was also apparently a very chatty little thing.

He asked approximately a million questions for such a simple meal—about each and every ingredient, about the chemistry of the process itself—only half of which Alexei had the answers to. But Jay was never dismayed when Alexei told him he didn't know something. The vampire would just beam at him anyway, saying, "Okay, we'll look that up later."

Alexei loved that "we." He absolutely fucking adored that "we."

He noticed other little things about Jay. Like how he seemed oddly...distressed when he made a mess with the excess flour. He seemed upset when he made any mess at all, actually, up until Alexei exaggerated his own clumsiness with the ingredients, telling him, "If you're not making a little bit of a mess, you're not doing it properly."

Then Jay positively *glowed*, telling Alexei once again he was the "nicest human."

Alexei almost felt like that could be true, with that little bundle of sunshine in his apartment, beaming at him at every opportunity. Alexei felt a new sort of contentment growing in him, one he had very little experience with, as Jay sat upon the counter, legs swinging, watching him flip the last of the remaining pancakes.

"I'm sorry your mother was sad and never taught you to make pancakes. But I'm very glad your grandmother did."

"Me too, kitten. And I'm happy to have you here as my assistant. The best pancake assistant there ever was."

Jay flushed deeply, pink all the way down to his neck, and squirmed a little on the counter. "Really?" he asked, voice hopeful.

God, he was so fucking responsive to the least bit of praise. "Really, really," Alexei said, placing the last of the pancakes on a plate and turning off the burner. He sidled up in between the vampire's dangling legs. "You know the only thing that could make you a better assistant right now?"

Jay leaned forward, eager. "What?"

"If you gave me a kiss."

Once again, the speed with which Jay moved was alarming, his arms wrapping around Alexei's neck in an instant, his eager lips on Alexei's mouth before he could blink. But Alexei rolled with the fucking punches, kissing the sweet vampire with enthusiasm, letting it devolve quickly into absolute filth, licking into his mouth and letting Jay explore as much as he wanted in turn.

For such a sweet little thing, Jay kissed Alexei like he wanted to devour him whole, moaning when Alexei pulled him forward by the hips, the counter setting him at the perfect height to grind their cocks together.

When Alexei finally pulled away for air, they were both panting like mad. Jay had been panting the night before as well. "Do you—do you need to breathe?" Alexei asked between his own labored breaths.

Jay blinked dazedly at him, cheeks flushed and lips swollen. "It won't kill me not to, but it's a very uncomfortable reflex to suppress. The body remembers."

That brought up a question that had been lingering in the back of Alexei's mind, but he wasn't sure how to phrase it in a way that wasn't horribly macabre, or just plain offensive. Jay seemed to read it in his face anyway, smiling softly at him, sadness tinging the corners of his mouth. "Beheading or total consumption by fire. That's how to kill us."

"Well, fuck." Alexei had seen men die, yes, but not quite like that. "Did you—have you ever seen that?"

Jay dropped his arms from Alexei's neck. "Beheading, yes."

"That sounds like a story."

"I'm over two hundred years old. I definitely have stories."

It was so easy to forget most of the time. Jay had such a youthful air, to go along with his youthful face. But then there were moments like this one, when something came into his gray eyes: an air of unknowable depths, completely at odds with the enthusiasm he showed for simple things, like making fucking pancakes.

Alexei should leave it alone. But his hunger for Jay extended to *all* of Jay, including his history. "Maybe—maybe a *bad* story?" he pushed.

Jay shoved him back gently then, as if he needed the distance to consider Alexei properly, cocking his head and looking him over. Alexei could only hope he passed the test.

He really wanted to pass the fucking test.

After a moment of that, Jay cleared his throat and folded his hands on his lap, like he was preparing for a recital of some kind. "I was turned to be someone's...companion," he said. "I was raised as a vampire in a den where humans were considered lesser. And even within the den, there was an established hierarchy. If you turned someone, they were yours, to do with as you wished. If it didn't work out, the newer vampire was killed. My companion, Vee—Veronique—she needed me to be neat, and quiet, and obedient. If I was, we got along quite well. If I wasn't, I was...left alone. I'm very good at passing time alone." Jay looked him straight in the eyes then, his gray pair looking positively ancient. "But I don't like it."

Alexei tried to put together the strange pieces of that story, mulling them over in his mind. "You were...owned? And...abused."

Jay shrugged, but the movement came off as anything but casual. "My friend Soren was in the same den. His maker wanted him for sex as well as service, and he—he hurt my friend. A lot. Vee never did that to me. Not physically." He took a deep breath, letting it out in a whoosh. "Ten years ago the lead vampire of the den went feral. He had to be put down, and Vee helped in the effort. She was killed. I was there, but I ran. I'm not—I'm not very brave."

Alexei wasn't sure what to say in the face of all that. Except, "I ran too. From my brother. I'm not very brave either."

"Well, your mortal body *is* very fragile," Jay conceded.

Alexei had never been called fragile in his entire life. "What did you mean, he went feral?"

"It's the natural end for many vampires. A loss of our humanity. Unless we're tethered, mated to another."

Something cold ran through Alexei's veins at the thought. "You're not mated, are you?"

"No." Jay seemed to misunderstand the direction of his question. "But don't worry. If I were ever to have signs of going feral, I would leave Hyde Park. I wouldn't endanger anyone there. I promise."

Alexei wanted to tell him that was the last fucking thing he was worried about. That he was much more terrified of the thought of this sweet vampire losing his mind, being potentially attacked by his own kind. But Jay looked so sad, and it was all Alexei's fault for bringing it up.

"Hey," he said, stepping forward again. "Have I told you yet you're the best pancake-making assistant I've ever had?"

Jay smiled, a tentative thing. "You have. And you're lying, which isn't very nice."

"Never." Alexei pressed a kiss to Jay's cheek. "So sweet." A kiss to his forehead. "So gorgeous." A kiss to the very tip of his button nose. "Perfect."

Jay giggled, that old sorrow seeming to seep from his body, but then looked at the counter, at the specks of floured dough, and his brow furrowed. "We've made a real mess. Everything was so tidy before."

Alexei shrugged. "I'm not really that much of a neat freak. I only straightened up for you."

Jay seemed delighted by that confession, perking up considerably. He reached up to tug Alexei down by his shoulders, stretching up to whisper in his ear, like it was some kind of secret, "I actually *like* things a bit messy."

Alexei arched a brow at the little vampire, wanting to kiss his nose again but figuring he'd already been cheesy enough for one evening. "Yeah? Okay, kotyonok. Let's get messy."

Ten

Jay

"Let's get messy," it turned out, was not a sexual phrase, even though Jay had maybe, kind of, sort of been hoping it was. But what Alexei had them do—after sticking the plate of finished pancakes in the oven to keep them warm—was mess up the living room.

They tugged and tossed the couch pillows until they were in disarray. They set the coffee table on its side up against the wall. It was all silly and ridiculous, but every time Vee's voice threatened to ring out in Jay's head and tell him so, Alexei was speaking up right in front of him instead, encouraging Jay to flip a book onto the floor or kick a corner of the rug up.

The best part was when they traipsed into Alexei's room and tugged all the bedding from his neatly made bed (which had Jay wondering: had Alexei made it so neat for Jay?) and piled it onto the floor, making a sort of nest out of the blankets and pillows.

When the oven beeped at them, Alexei went through all the toppings options with Jay, letting him put on as much whipped cream and syrup as he wanted, stacking them into a sizable tower on a plate for them both. Jay loved that they were sharing a plate; something about that felt cozy and intimate to him.

They climbed back into their nest, and before Jay knew it, he'd eaten almost all the pancakes ("So good! I can't believe we *made* these!").

He looked up to see Alexei eyeing him with brows raised high.

Oops.

Jay had forgotten how much was normal for a human to eat. It had been so long since he'd needed human food that he usually just ate whatever tasted good and was directly in front of him. He'd learned a lot about what was normal for humans from everything he read or watched, but books didn't usually specify amounts, and while on TV, humans always had food in front of them, they rarely seemed to actually be eating it.

Jay wiped a stray crumb from the corner of his mouth. "That wasn't a regular number of pancakes to consume, was it?" he asked sheepishly.

Alexei pulled down the blanket that had been partially covering Jay, looking over his admittedly petite form. "Where does it all *go*?" he asked, a note of wonder in his voice.

Jay patted the soft swell of his belly and handed Alexei the one remaining pancake. "Just...poof. Magically gone, I guess."

"Magically...," Alexei mused, cutting into his pancake.

Jay licked his lips—had he gotten all the crumbs?—noticing that when he did so, Alexei's eyes gained that heated look he'd seen in them the other night. Because Alexei *wanted* Jay. Wasn't that great? Alexei wanted to kiss him and touch him, and maybe if Jay was good, he would even work that big cock inside of him.

Jay squirmed in place on the blankets, thinking his dirty thoughts while he watched Alexei bite into his pancake. Jay wanted more lessons—really, *really* wanted more lessons—but he wasn't quite sure how to get things started. He knew humans could, and often did, flirt with varying degrees of subtlety, but Jay's brain didn't really work that way. Double entendres and coded messages weren't quite his things.

So he went with saying exactly what he was thinking. "I want to try mouth stuff with you."

Alexei sort of choked on the bite of pancake he'd taken, and Jay started pounding him on the back helpfully—although it didn't seem as helpful as they made it look on TV. Maybe Jay was doing it wrong?

Either way, eventually Alexei got control of himself and set his plate aside, clearing his throat. "You want my mouth on you, sweetheart?"

Oh, that "sweetheart" was so nice. Just as nice as "kitten," really. It was kind of...boyfriendly, wasn't it? That Alexei gave him sweet little nicknames? He didn't look like the sort of person who did that with a lot of people. So maybe Jay was special, in that way?

Jay wanted to be special to him.

Alexei made a questioning sound, and it took Jay a moment to realize he'd never answered the question. The thought of Alexei's mouth on him was very, very tempting, but Jay shook his head, nibbling at his lower lip. "I want my mouth on *you*, I think."

"Yes. We can do that." Alexei inhaled sharply, and Jay very much liked that the human was affected by the idea. "We can *definitely* do that."

Jay fiddled with the comforter underneath him. He knew he was supposed to let Alexei teach him, but he had some...opinions. "I also think you should get naked."

Alexei let out a soft, surprised chuckle. "Oh yeah?" He set the empty plate aside and tugged gently at the bottom hem of Jay's shirt. "What if I think *you* should get naked, kotyonok?"

Oh yes. Jay could definitely do that. He bounced up onto his knees, tossing his shirt over his head with enthusiasm and starting on his fleece bottoms immediately. "Yes, let's both be naked." Because Jay liked to be cozy, and what was cozier than naked? Especially with soft blankets and pillows everywhere and everything smelling so good and a human that Jay's little beastie very much wanted to taste, and look at that—Jay's cock was already hard, jutting out against his pale belly, all flushed and pink and eager to be touched.

And oh, Jay *really* liked the way Alexei looked at him when Jay was naked. Those pretty hazel eyes filled with heat, and his wide mouth parted slightly.

He should just always be looking at Jay like that.

"Your turn," Jay prompted, still perched on his knees. He watched, refusing to even blink, as Alexei removed his clothing. His human was so *handsome*. He had lovely definition in his muscles, looking strong but not massive, with a slight padding to his middle that made him seem extra snuggly. Jay thought he was the absolute *perfect* size. Almost as pale as Jay, but his forearms and neck had a more golden coloring. Jay cocked his head, considering. "How do you have tan lines in the winter? Do you sunbathe in the snow or something?"

Alexei paused in the act of removing his underwear, fingers tucked in his waistband, that delicious bulge still covered, and rubbed at the back of his neck. "Ah, no. But I never got to be outdoors much in New York. I've been taking a lot of walks, I guess."

Happiness bubbled in Jay's chest at the realization that they had something else in common. "I *love* nature," he gushed. "I love the outdoors. I like dirt under my toes and the sun on my face and just all of it. Every bit."

Alexei grinned. "Yeah? I bet there're a lot of good camping spots around here. We could go in the summer. I've never really been, but...we could learn together?"

Jay's first reaction was a flood of wonderful, wonderful warmth in his belly. Alexei wanted to explore the outdoors with him. He wanted to spend more time with Jay, as far into the future as the summertime. They could run around barefoot in the woods and swim in streams and—

And just like that, Jay's stomach sank.

He sat back on his heels, dejected.

The summer would be too late. Jay would be gone by then.

It hit him then, for the first time since making his new friend. Leaving Hyde Park would be leaving Alexei.

Worry flashed over Alexei's face as Jay's own expression visibly fell. "Hey, hey. You okay, kitten?"

Jay wasn't, not really. But he wasn't about to let the future ruin the present. Not when he had such a perfect new friend, one who looked like all Jay's secret fantasies and smelled like everything yummy and good.

Didn't Jay deserve some good?

He cleared his throat, forcing a smile onto his face. "I would love to go camping with you." (It wasn't a lie, okay? He wanted nothing more.) "Now please remove your underwear."

Alexei paused for one more moment, searching Jay's face, before lowering his black briefs, and ohhh, there it was. Warmth pooled again in Jay's stomach, replacing that awful cold rush of his reality check. The human's cock was already hard, just as thick and delicious-looking as the first time. Jay wanted to taste. His inner beastie was *ravenous*, and not for blood.

Alexei had meanwhile wrapped a loose fist around his cock, smirking slightly at whatever look was on Jay's face. "How do you want me, kotyonok?"

"Lie back, please." Jay wanted to take his time, and he wanted Alexei to be comfortable for it.

Alexei did as he asked, lying back on the comforter, his hands behind his head, all six feet four of him sprawled out for Jay's pleasure. A tingle ran down Jay's spine at the thought of it. The *power* in it.

He crawled forward and considered his options, ultimately deciding to explore the surrounding area before the main event. He nosed at the curls at the base, darker in color than the golden hair at the top of Alexei's head. Jay breathed in deep there, delighting in the muskier note in Alexei's scent here. He pressed his hands onto Alexei's thighs, loving how firm and muscled they felt under his grip, the little hairs tickling Jay's palms. He pressed a kiss to the soft crease where Alexei's thigh met his hip, the skin so pale there he could see the little blue veins.

Alexei sucked in a breath at the contact. Was he sensitive there? Jay did it again, just to check. Another sharp inhale.

He repeated the process again and again until Alexei let out a strangled laugh. "Sweetheart. You're killing me."

"I am?" Jay peeked up, checking to see if Alexei was angry with him, but the human's eyes were hooded and dark, and he looked just as hungry for Jay as Jay felt for him. Ah, he was teasing.

Jay giggled in response, pressing one last kiss before turning his attention where it so desperately wanted to go—Alexei's hard, jutting cock. Jay grasped it with one hand at the base, bringing it to the correct angle for his purpose. He pulled back the skin at the head and started with a lick, gathering the drops of precum, savoring the salty, bitter flavor of it.

Alexei gasped, then grunted when Jay went in for more, suckling at the head, exploring the weight of it in his mouth. It felt pretty nice, stretching his lips, all warm and smooth, jerking each time Jay's tongue swirled around it.

Alexei made some more grunting noises. Jay liked the sounds—he knew what they were signifying—but he needed....

He lifted his head from his task. "Um...can you...talk to me? Like last time? Tell me if I'm doing a good job?"

He felt himself flush with the request. He knew he was being a little needy, but it had been so nice, the dirty words Alexei had showered him with. Jay wanted more of them.

Alexei's eyes went wide. "Oh, fuck, sweetheart, of course. Your mouth just felt so good my brain short-circuited for a moment. I can give you words if you want them, kitten."

Jay wriggled with happiness ("sweetheart" *and* "kitten," all in one go!) before getting back to business.

Alexei kept his promise as Jay worked him over. "That's perfect, kitten. Your mouth feels so good. Suck the tip again for me. Yes. Fucking perfect. Can you go deeper? Don't strain yourself. Fuck! Just like that. So good."

Jay melted into the praise, a tingling warmth flooding through his chest, through his limbs, through every part of him at Alexei's words. Jay loved knowing he was doing a good job, that he was pleasing Alexei with his mouth. His own arousal was reaching a fever pitch, and he found himself flattening his hips so he could thrust against the blankets, his aching cock searching for any kind of friction.

When he whimpered around the girth in his mouth, Alexei ran a soft hand through his hair. "You trying to come, sweetheart?"

Jay looked up, his lips stretched around Alexei's cock, to find his human propped up on one arm, meeting his eyes again.

Alexei let out a harsh breath. "Fuuuck. Look at you, so gorgeous. You look so good like this, hm? But I think we can do even better."

He tugged gently at Jay's hair, pulling Jay off his cock, laughing affectionately at Jay's whine of protest. "Patience, sweetheart." Then Alexei's hands were on Jay's waist, and he was manhandling him into the reverse position over his supine body. For a human, he was still strong enough to move Jay around bodily, and Jay couldn't help loving that. Such masculine strength.

Alexei maneuvered Jay so he was on all fours above him, Jay's cock aligned with his mouth, his cock aligned with Jay's.

Jay's breath stuttered out of him, and his arms almost gave out when he felt warm, wet heat engulfing his aching cock. "Oh! Oh God."

Cool air hit him as Alexei briefly released him to say, "I won't be able to tell you with my mouth full, but believe me, I'm going to enjoy this, kitten. It's not gonna take long, whatever you want to do."

Jay took a minute—possibly much more than a minute—to appreciate the new sensation, this hot mouth licking over him. And then he eagerly chased Alexei's bobbing cock back into his mouth, figuring he couldn't go wrong just doing his best to copy whatever Alexei did to him, suck for suck, lick for lick.

And Alexei was right—it didn't take long at all for Jay to come, tremors racking through his body at the release. But instead of dropping Alexei from his mouth, he doubled down, finding he quite liked having something in his mouth to suck and swallow as the waves of his orgasm washed over him.

Alexei released him with a wet pop, turning his head and groaning into Jay's thigh. "Oh fuck, baby. Fuck. Keep doing that. So good. So, so good."

Jay bobbed eagerly, barely avoiding choking in surprise when hot spurts of cum started filling his mouth. Alexei's hips jerked under him, and he bit into Jay's thigh with blunt, forceful teeth.

Jay swallowed.

It wasn't until Alexei tapped his hip that Jay released his softened cock, panting slightly, still propped on his hands and knees. "You're such a good teacher, Alexei."

The warm, relaxed laugh Alexei gave from under him was Jay's new favorite sound.

They decided to sleep in their blanket nest instead of a proper bed. Jay hadn't known they'd be having a sleepover—hadn't wanted to presume—but when he'd asked Alexei if sleepovers were part of sex, Alexei had tightened his hold (he'd kept Jay on top of him, tucking him into his chest, and it was maybe the best position in the whole, wide world) and said, "Yes, definitely. You have to stay the night. That's part of it."

But Jay hadn't brought anything with him, so Alexei said he could use his toothbrush.

When Jay had finished in the bathroom, wriggling back into the blanket nest, he commented thoughtfully, "I didn't know how it would taste, but it wasn't bad."

"My toothpaste?" Alexei asked, tugging Jay easily back onto his chest.

Jay snuggled in. "Your cum. You taste very good, Alexei."

Another soft, relaxed laugh. "Oh fuck. So do you, sweetheart. I'll do that anytime, anyplace." He started running his fingers through Jay's hair. "Speaking of taste. I asked Colin about it today. He's okay with me...taking over."

Jay lifted his head to see Alexei watching him with a cautious look in his eyes. "You mean the feedings?"

"Yeah. I meant to tell you earlier, but then you said 'mouth stuff,' and my mind went blank. Do you...do you want to do it now? Are you hungry? I mean, I know you ate like a dozen pancakes, but..."

The thing was Jay *was* hungry. He didn't technically need to feed again so soon, but he'd been taking it easy for so long, trying not to take too much from Colin at one time, that the idea of biting someone twice in one week felt almost impossible to resist.

He was being greedy, but...he wouldn't take too much. *Just a little nibble*, his beastie agreed. "You're sure that would be okay?"

"Definitely. What do you need me to do?"

"Stay just like this." Jay's spent cock actually twitched at the thought of it. They were lying skin to skin, all warm and soft and surrounded by blankets. And neck bites were...intimate. Jay had only done it once that way with Colin; their last time in the alleyway, at Colin's request.

But that was what he wanted again with Alexei. Jay wanted his neck. His beastie did too.

Jay squirmed around until he was back on the blankets and his front was against Alexei's side, Jay's half-hard erection pressing against Alexei's hip.

He brushed aside some strands of Alexei's pretty hair, which he'd let out of its bun for sleep. "Remember, it will only hurt for a moment."

Jay let his beastie out.

It always felt so good, the change. Like stretching after resting in a cramped position for too long. And now? With Alexei's sweet vanilla postsex scent flooding the entire room? Jay didn't even hesitate. He bit in, the rich, warm blood flooding his mouth.

Alexei tensed, just for a moment, but then almost immediately, his muscles relaxed. "Oh. Oh fuck. Why does that feel so good?"

Jay hummed his pleasure around his mouthful of blood, throwing his leg up and over Alexei's hip. He was glad his human was enjoying the bite. Jay gulped, hungry and eager, knowing he was making greedy little moaning noises into Alexei's neck but unable to stop himself.

He just tasted so *good*. Better than the pancakes. Better than anything.

It took all Jay's willpower to force his beastie back in the end, to keep from taking too much. His beastie hadn't wanted to stop, not at all. He'd wanted to keep drinking. He'd wanted to open their own wrist, feed Alexei their own blood, and then drink to the very end.

Jay licked the bite closed. *Bad beastie*, he chastised. *Very bad. No.*

Unaware of Jay's internal admonishments, Alexei laughed, his big body shaking against Jay.

"What's so funny?" Jay asked, a little concerned he'd maybe taken too much and now the human was becoming delirious.

But Alexei waved a hand at his own stomach, where white streaks were now adorning his body. "I fucking came. You just gave me the hottest blow job of my life, and two seconds later, I came all over myself."

Jay absolutely could *not* help preening at that "hottest blow job of my life" bit.

Just one more little taste.

He licked up the cum on Alexei's belly. Oh yes, he did very much like the taste after all. Maybe with enough practice, Jay would become a new kind of vampire, one who could feed on every part of Alexei. His blood, his sweat, his cum.

Was that gross to think about? Maybe Jay would just keep that to himself.

Alexei let out a soft, pleased sigh at Jay's ministrations. "You treat me so well, sweetheart."

"Do I?" Wasn't that just the nicest thing to say?

"Yeah, you really do." Alexei let out a sleepy sigh this time—Jay was learning all his different noises—before yawning widely. "I think I'm fading, kitten. You've worn me out. Little sex demon you're becoming."

Jay giggled at that. "Go to sleep, Alexei. I'll be right here."

In fact, Jay had trouble falling asleep at all. He wanted to treasure every second of this. He had this perfect, lovely human right in front of him; how was he supposed to close his eyes? Because looking at Alexei, his stern face relaxed with sleep, all that golden hair spread over the pillow, Jay really thought he must be the handsomest man in all of existence.

Jay didn't want the night to end. He didn't want Hyde Park to end.

He took a deep breath, grabbing his phone and sending out a single text.

I want to stay.

Eleven

Alexei

A lexei was even more of a hopeless case than he'd thought.

Because one would think, now that he had Jay in his life in a real way—in his house, in his hands, in his fucking mouth—Alexei would be able to stay away from the coffee shop, but apparently no. Not at all.

He'd had one night alone without contact from Jay—no texts, no immediate prospects of seeing him again—and Alexei was once again resorting to stalker behavior.

And not only was he walking through that obnoxiously ringing door, but he was for some reason holding on to a little box, one he felt more than a bit foolish for bringing. But he couldn't seem to help himself.

All in all, the chime of the bell over Death by Coffee's front door sounded out like an accusation.

But Alexei couldn't beat himself up for too long because then there was Jay, looking absurdly adorable in some sort of corduroy overall number over a fuzzy purple sweater, staring off into space over the cash register. The majority of the café's tables had people sitting at them, but there was no line—possibly because Alexei had deliberately chosen a time when he'd been hoping there would be a lull at the café—and it didn't take long for Jay to notice him, breaking out into one of his beaming smiles, waving enthusiastically as Alexei approached. "Alexei! Hello! You're here! How nice."

"Hey, kitten," Alexei said, resisting the urge to grin back at him like a maniac. Still, he was feeling magnanimous enough, now that he had Jay in his sights again, to shoot a nod of acknowledgment at Alicia, manning the espresso machine.

Jay placed his hands first on the counter, then on his register, then fiddled with the clasp on his overalls. "I've missed you, and it's only been a day. Isn't that funny?"

Alexei's heart clenched at Jay's casual admission. Maybe that was why his own words came out easier than he would have expected. "I missed you too, kotyonok."

Jay unclasped and then reclasped the button on his shoulder. "Really?" he asked, an uncharacteristic shyness in his voice.

Alexei noticed then that up close, Jay looked a little...different. Dimmed, somehow, even with the clear delight he felt at Alexei's arrival.

Alexei placed his box on the counter, leaning in. "Hey, are you okay?"

Jay shrugged, still fiddling with the button on his overalls. "I've just been a little stressed. It's been...stressful."

Alexei had no idea what "it" would be regarding. The café? Something with Jay's friends? *Alexei?* "You want to talk about it?"

Jay's brow furrowed, just the slightest bit, and he released his overall strap, instead poking at one of the bags of coffee beans at the counter. What came out of his mouth next was not what Alexei was anticipating. "I think we should have penetrative sex."

The air punched out of Alexei's chest. How was Jay always doing that to him? The admittedly sheltered vampire had next to zero sexual experience, zero flirtation game, yet he was always so easily pulling the rug out from under Alexei, leaving him feeling desperate and wanting like no one ever had.

Instead of answering with the *Fuck yes, we should* thrumming under his skin, Alexei rubbed at the back of his neck, still concerned with the strange nonverbal signals he was getting. "Is that, uh— Is that what's been stressing you out?"

Jay flapped a hand in the air. "Unrelated. But I think we should. We definitely should do that. Soon. Tonight." He punctuated the last statement with a sharp nod before his lips twisted into a thoughtful frown. "Wait...no. I have family dinner tonight. Tomorrow, then." Then he was looking up through his lashes at Alexei, biting his lip. "Unless you don't want to?"

Oh fuck. He *had* to know what he was doing, right? No one was that completely oblivious to their own appeal, were they? Alexei couldn't help it. He leaned forward, wanting to tug that lip between his own teeth, not caring how many customers were in the café or who might see them.

A throat cleared.

Alexei paused, mere inches from Jay's now upturned face. "Hello, Colin."

"Hello yourself, Alex," Colin said, tapping at Jay's shoulder from where he was suddenly looming behind him. "Short stack, you mind going to the storage closet and grabbing some more bags of French roast?"

"Oh, sure." Jay blinked slowly, looking a little dazed, before shaking his head and bouncing off to the back, leaving Alexei with a predictably scowling Colin.

Alexei heaved a sigh, wondering what the source of the seemingly increased hostility was. He'd thought they had things squared away. "What's up your ass today?"

Colin turned toward the back quickly, making sure of Jay's continued absence, before he answered, "Jay's been...off. Since yesterday. Distracted, and not in his usual way. Like, worried. Sad." The glowering intensified noticeably. "What did you do?"

"What do you mean, what did I do? Nothing. He had—we had a date. It went well. We made pancakes." *And somehow, virgin that he is, he still managed to suck my soul out through my cock.* Alexei decided to keep that last part to himself. He rubbed at the back of his neck again, confused. *Had* he fucked up somehow? Made Jay sad? But then why was Jay asking for penetrative sex, as he'd so plainly put it? "I like him a lot," he admitted to Colin, more than a little helpless at the admission.

Colin gave him a skeptical once-over. "Like having your dirty paws all over him, more like."

Alexei bit back the inappropriate urge to laugh. Who the fuck talked like that? "I *like* him, okay? He's weird and funny and sweet, and he's not a raging asshole like ninety percent of the human population."

Jay chose that moment to bounce back over, bags of coffee in his arms. "That's so nice, Alexei. I don't think you're a raging asshole either."

Alexei took a moment to appreciate the sound of Jay's sweet voice saying the word *asshole*. "You heard that, did you?"

"I have excellent hearing." Jay placed his wares down before leaning forward to whisper loud enough for the entire café to hear, "Because of...*you know*."

"I was just telling Colin how much I've enjoyed spending time with you." And then—because he had no idea what had Jay feeling so upset, but he so very much did *not* want it to be because of him—Alexei did what he'd been wanting to do since the moment he'd walked in and seen Jay's smiling face. He leaned in all the way over the counter and planted a kiss on those Cupid's bow lips.

It wasn't a proper kiss unfortunately, not with the café full of strangers and Colin's black cloud of disapproval hovering over them. Just a brief brush of lips. But still a sort of...claiming.

Alexei straightened back up after not nearly enough time, assessing the damage. "Was that okay?"

Jay's cheeks were pink, and he smiled wide, looking brighter and happier than he had a few minutes before. "Very okay. You can kiss me anytime you like, you know."

"I don't think you realize what you're giving me permission for, kotyonok."

Jay cocked his head. "To kiss me. Anytime. Was that unclear? Maybe not too much tongue in public though. You might make my fangs pop out."

"Is that a euphemism?" Alicia called out from the other end of the counter.

They both ignored the question, Jay biting at his lip and looking thoughtful. "Do you—would you want to come to family dinner tonight?"

Someone else's family dinner would normally be Alexei's idea of a waking nightmare. He had barely survived his own relatives; he had no interest in being surrounded by anyone else's. But for Jay? Who asked the question so sincerely, with a vulnerable edge to it even Alexei, completely out of practice with any real emotion or vulnerability, could recognize?

"Of course. I'd be honored." And because he wanted more of relaxed, happy Jay, Alexei pushed the forgotten box on the counter toward him. "Also, this is for you."

"For me?" Jay whispered, his gray eyes shining. Well, fuck. So the little vampire liked gifts? If Alexei had known, he'd have been bringing them from the very beginning. Probably shown up on day two with a goddamn diamond ring.

He held his breath as Jay opened the little box to reveal the bougie vanilla cupcake hiding inside. Alexei had a brief, panicked moment of feeling incredibly foolish again. Had Jay been expecting something more exciting? Something—anything—better than a stupid fucking cupcake?

But Jay was already gasping in delight. "It's so pretty!"

"You think so?"

"Mm. What a beautiful little cupcake you are." Jay directed his words into the box. At the actual cupcake.

And now Alexei was jealous of a baked good. He cleared his throat. "You mention them to me often enough. Thought I'd bring you one."

"The nicest human," Jay whispered. Then he shut the lid on the box. "I'm saving it for my break. To *really* enjoy it."

"That's fine."

Alexei lingered at the counter as long as he could, listening in delight as Jay prattled on about family dinner. How since he was issuing the invitation, he would pick Alexei up but was hoping to take him to his own apartment afterward. How his place was still looking very neat and tidy, but they could mess up all the pillows when Alexei came over. How he had already purchased "supplies" and they didn't need to worry about that. (Alexei had no idea what that might entail, unless Jay was just casually bringing up lube and condoms at the café counter. But then, knowing him, that was probably exactly what he was doing.)

Eventually another customer came in, and Alexei was forced to step to the side.

Alicia, waiting for him at the other end with an Americano, smirked at him. Always smirking, that one. "You've got it so bad," she accused, clearly pleased as fucking punch.

Alexei grunted noncommittally. Not that he was saving much face. He'd brought a goddamn cupcake, after all.

"That was a good move though. The public smooches. You know how many people have tried to give that one their number? That sleazy doctor Monroe was in here earlier, practically salivating." Her smirk only grew as she watched Alexei's muscles tense at the thought of someone else salivating over *his* vampire. "Anyway, good to lock the Jayster down."

Alexei couldn't even pretend to himself that locking Jay down didn't sound like the best idea he'd ever heard.

The house they pulled up to (Alexei had ended up driving, since apparently Jay had a tendency to "terrify people" behind the wheel) was a cute yellow number, backing up to the pine forest surrounding their town. Not too far from the local hospital either. Jay had told Alexei his friend Danny was a nurse.

A vampire nurse, which sounded only slightly terrifying. Not that *Jay* was terrifying in his vampire form. He was gorgeous and sweet in every iteration, fangs or no. More like, it gave off the impression that vampires had infiltrated all these mundane aspects of the human world. They were in hospitals, obviously enough. What about schools? Were there vampire elementary schoolteachers? Politicians?

There was so much Alexei didn't know about Jay's world. He said he'd been raised in a den, but how many dens were out there? Were they all as isolated as his?

Alexei did his best to put it out of his mind, to focus on getting into a socializing mindset. He didn't want Jay to regret inviting him to dinner.

The man who opened the door, a barking cattle dog at his side, answered a question that had been in the back of Alexei's mind: whether all vampires were adorable aliens like Jay.

No. Definitely not.

This guy—almost as tall as Alexei, dressed in a full suit, with blue eyes so cold it seemed like the already frigid evening air dropped by another ten degrees just looking at them—was the furthest thing from adorable. He reminded Alexei much more of the mobsters he'd grown up with than the sweet-natured vampire beside him.

But Jay seemed unfazed by the chilly demeanor. "Roman!" he greeted happily. "I brought my human friend Alexei. I already asked permission from Danny, so I'm not being rude."

Before Roman could respond, Alexei's mouth worked against his will, his earlier conversation with Alicia hovering in the back of his mind. "Boyfriend."

Roman arched a dark brow, his focus shifting from Jay to Alexei. "Pardon me?"

"I'm Alexei, his human *boyfriend*." Alexei glanced down at Jay as he said it, worried maybe he'd misread the meaning behind Jay's blanket permission to kiss in public earlier, but Jay was beaming at him, clearly delighted by the possessive declaration.

Good enough for Alexei. After all, if he was going to stake his claim, why not start with Jay's intimidating vampire friend who looked at Alexei like he was an annoying bug to be squashed under his expensive Italian loafers?

Lucky for all of them, Alexei was used to cold, murderous-looking men sizing him up and finding him wanting. He could handle it well enough with mobsters. He supposed he ought to be able to handle it with vampires as well.

Jay turned that beaming smile to Roman, seemingly undeterred by the cold reception. "Yes, my human boyfriend. Isn't that nice, Roman?"

Alexei could have sworn for a second there was something close to fondness in Roman's gaze as he stared back at Jay, but the next moment, his eyes were cold again, and he turned his attention to the dog at his feet. "Settle, mutt," he ordered the animal, who was wiggling and whining and trying to get Jay's attention. The blue-gray dog immediately sat, muzzle shut obediently.

"That's Ferdy," Jay explained to Alexei. He gestured to the dog. "Ferdy, this is Alexei. My human boyfriend."

Ferdy cocked his head, and Alexei had the momentary, insane thought the dog was actually listening to Jay's words. Roman only stepped aside from the door, sighing a little, like Jay introducing people formally to his pet was an everyday sort of occurrence. "Everyone is in the kitchen."

"Everyone" meant three other people. Vampires all, Jay had told Alexei. There was the strange blond one from the day before; a muscled, all-American-looking guy who towered over him, holding on to his hand; and a third, dark-haired one with pretty brown eyes, who looked vaguely related to the second.

They were each ridiculously good-looking. Maybe there was also a vampire modeling agency somewhere?

Jay gasped in apparent surprise as they entered the kitchen. "Soren. You're here *early*."

Soren grinned that wide, creepy grin. "Didn't want to miss a moment, Jaybird."

Introductions were made, Jay emphasizing the word *boyfriend* three separate times, to Alexei's satisfaction, and then Soren stepped toward Alexei with a goblet—an actual fucking *goblet*—of ruby-red liquid in his hand. "Can I offer you a drink, human?"

Alexei couldn't help it: he hesitated. There was that eerie fucking smile again.

The third guy—Danny, the nurse—made a sound of distress. "Soren. You're being creepy on purpose." He made an apologetic face at Alexei. "It's just red wine, I promise. No blood at the table."

"Me, creepy?" Soren's manic grin fell, and his lower lip pushed out in an exaggerated pout. "Cutie, you wound me. I never get to play it up with humans." He waved a hand in Alexei's direction. "He already *knows*. Let me have my fun."

"Not at the expense of our guest."

The big guy, Gabe, grabbed Soren by the waist, tugging him back against his front. "Come here, brat. Behave." He then looked Alexei over in that way buff guys sometimes did when they realized Alexei was bigger than them and they didn't like that fact one bit.

Alexei did his best not to glower back, trying to keep his face in some semblance of a neutral expression. It wouldn't do to alienate Jay's friends at the very first meeting, not when the word *boyfriend* was being thrown about so wonderfully.

Soren relaxed back in Gabe's arms with a sigh, looking to Alexei, then to Jay, and arching a brow. "I should lend you my heeled boots, Jaybird. Your human is going to get a crick in his neck trying to kiss you."

Alexei huffed a reluctant laugh, but Jay shot Alexei a concerned look, his brow furrowed. "Does it hurt your neck, kissing me?" Before Alexei could even answer, Jay was patting his arm soothingly. "Poor human. Next time, just pick me up." He turned to the rest of the room. "He's very strong for a human. He can toss me around no problem."

A variety of expressions went around the room at that statement: Soren looked delighted, Gabe horrified, Danny embarrassed, and Roman completely neutral.

Alexei shrugged.

There was an awkward silence after that, Alexei doing his very best to hold in the urge to ask everyone to pull out their fangs because—other than Soren's creepy vibes and suspicious goblet—no one was *acting* like a vampire, and that in itself was kind of freaking him out.

Surprisingly, it was Roman who came to his rescue. "I am concerned I perhaps added too much garlic to the sauce for the chicken. Jay tells us you are versed in the culinary arts, Alexei. Perhaps you can try it?"

With those words, it hit Alexei for the first time how good the kitchen smelled. He rubbed a hand on the back of his neck. "Oh. Well, I'm not really. I only know a few Russian recipes. But my palate isn't bad."

When Roman didn't rescind the offer, Alexei tasted the sauce. Fucking delicious. And it was kind of hard to tell, but he thought the vampire seemed pleased enough by his praise when he told him so.

That seemed to set everyone else in motion, Danny pulling Jay into the other room to help set the table while Soren and Gabe let the dog out into the backyard.

Alexei, left alone with the intimidating vampire, cleared his throat, feeling once again unspeakably awkward. "So...garlic?"

Roman shrugged a shoulder. "A myth, of which there are many. Sunlight is irritating to our eyes but not deadly. An invitation to a human's home is not necessary to enter. Mirrors and photos depict us just fine. A stake to the heart would only earn you an enraged vampire at your heels."

"Beheading or fire," Alexei murmured.

Roman turned to Jay, who had come back into the kitchen and was rummaging for glassware in the cabinet. "*Johann.*"

Jay didn't even turn from his search. "What? He's not going to hurt us. Are you, Alexei?"

"*No.* No, of course not."

Gabe—and when had he and the dog come back from the back-yard?—glared at Alexei from his spot at the door. "What *are* your intentions toward Jay?"

Roman scoffed, stirring his sauce. "Did you not hear? He is the *boyfriend.*"

Danny, among them once more because apparently no one could stay out of the kitchen for more than thirty fucking seconds, smiled happily at Roman. "Remember when you were my boyfriend?"

"I prefer husband. Lover. Mate," Roman declared, turning from the stove to kiss him soundly, and from the way Danny looked so flushed and happy afterward, the guy couldn't be made completely of ice.

Alexei's ears perked up. There was that *word* again. "Mate? You two are mates?"

No one answered him right away, but everyone was looking at him with strange intensity. Looking at *them*, Alexei realized, as Jay had come to stand at his side, a stack of glasses in his hands.

"So Jay...told you about those?" Danny finally asked hesitantly.

"You have two mated pairs in this room, mobster," Soren said, that intense grin once more on his face.

Alexei startled a bit at that "mobster," but he couldn't dwell too hard on his past being outed when he had a room full of vampires and a head full of questions. "Oh. Okay. How...I don't understand quite how they work. How do you know you've found your mate?"

Alexei had no fucking clue if this was polite predinner conversation to have with a vampire crew or not, but he wanted to know, and no one seemed about to bare their fangs and tear his throat out in anger or anything.

Jay for his part was now ignoring the conversation completely. He'd set his glasses aside and had his attention focused on the cattle dog at their feet.

"A pull," Roman answered, eyes boring into Alexei's. "An intense, unshakable draw to another. My demon wanted him, and I just...knew."

"Your demon?" Alexei asked. Maybe Roman was—what—some kind of supervamp?

"His beastie," Jay answered from his crouch on the kitchen floor, his voice strangely flat. "The vampire part inside him. The part you see when my fangs are out."

"Ah. Okay." Alexei would come back to that later. "And how are they...chosen? What makes someone mate material?"

Was Alexei's desperation—his fucking obsession with being bound to Jay in whatever way possible—coming through in his questions? Probably. It was hard to care, though, when he was actually getting answers.

"We don't really know," Soren answered, his gaze fixed on Jay and Ferdy. "Fate, they say. Can't really argue with that. Roman and I ended up in Hyde Park, of all places, and our mates were just...here."

Alexei tried to wrap his head around the likelihood of that. "But you've both been alive for centuries? Like Jay?"

Soren and Roman both nodded.

"So the odds of two of you finding your mates here..."

"Oh yes," Soren giggled a little wildly, seemingly at some joke of his own. "*Two* of us."

Danny cleared his throat. "Shall we eat?"

Twelve

Alexei

D inner wasn't nearly as awkward as Alexei had feared.

With the minor inquisition—What are your intentions? Who's mated to fucking who?—out of the way, it seemed like the group was content to proceed with the night as usual, chatting with one another easily.

Jay—seated next to Alexei at the dining room table—was quieter than Alexei had come to expect when it was just the two of them in a room, but he seemed content enough, gazing at his friends happily, eating more food than his small frame should ever be able to accommodate.

No one seemed to expect Alexei to talk much, which suited him just fine, especially with such an incredible meal before him. He couldn't remember the last time he'd eaten so well, weirdly enough (were there vampire cooking show hosts as well?).

Although, Alexei still had...questions.

Mate. Mates. Mated pairs. *Fated* mates.

How did one go from being a boyfriend to being a mate? It was incredibly fucking important that Alexei find out, preferably yesterday. But the fate part of it was throwing him for a loop. Did that mean Jay had a mate out there already? Was Alexei just...filler? Prepping Jay, giving him a taste of sex and romance, only for someone else to take him away permanently further down the line?

Alexei hated the idea, so much so that his generally steel-lined stomach started churning well before they got to dessert. Why the fuck couldn't *he* be Jay's mate? He'd be the most devoted mate there ever was, given the chance.

And no, the irony didn't escape him. The fact that he'd only just recently risked it all, blown up his entire life to be free of family obligation, to avoid a future of permanent fealty to his brother. Only to be ready, less than two months later, to swear eternal devotion to the pint-size barista with a traumatic past and very specific dietary needs.

Alexei couldn't find it in himself to care though. Because Ivan? Ivan was a toxic, power-obsessed asshole of the highest level, molded to be so by their complete dick of a father. And Jay? Jay was everything good and right and wonderful, somehow remaining so even after centuries of horrific influence.

So yes, Alexei would be fucking *thrilled* to be mated to Jay.

But Jay would have told him, wouldn't he, if that were the case? The little guy was an open book, a large-print picture book at that. He didn't exactly seem the type to keep many secrets at all, let alone a massive one like a fated, vampiric bond with each other.

One big question *did* make its way out of Alexei during the first real lull in the conversation, his practical side unable to keep holding it in. "What will you all do ten or twenty years from now? When none of you age?"

It was Danny who answered his question, after sharing a look with Roman. "We'll leave," he said simply. "All together. Find somewhere remote to spend some decades, until enough time has passed to join society again. Somewhere new though, obviously. A different country most likely."

Alexei looked to Jay, who was helping himself to a fifth portion of chicken. "And...you'll go as well?"

Jay flushed, shifting in his chair. "I'm not— Well..."

"Of course you will," Danny protested, his voice infused with a sincere warmth. "You and, um, well...any companions you might have. Luc and Jamie will come too, I think."

Alexei had no idea who those two were, but the other three vampires around the table—Jay excluded—started protesting immediately.

Danny only shook his head, a stubborn set to his features. "They're our friends. We're putting petty differences aside in the future. *For* the future."

"Gabe's broken arm—"

"Your *murder*—"

Alexei took a large sip of wine. Maybe life around vampires was more violent than he had originally thought.

He wondered if Jay had an opinion about the two potential additions to their getaway crew, but Jay ignored the argument, declaring a complete non sequitur instead. "I'd like to make a snow angel, I think."

Everyone stopped talking, all of them looking at him with varying degrees of fond indulgence, but no one was actually stepping the fuck up for his suggestion. So Alexei did. "I'll make one with you, kotyonok."

Even with Alexei's coat on for once, the cold night air was biting, but it was hard to care when Jay was so clearly delighted by the prospect of playing in the thick snow blanketing Danny and Roman's backyard, bouncing on his toes on the deck like it was Christmas morning.

Alexei, slightly more sedate, stood next to him with his hands in his pockets, hoping his lack of gloves wasn't going to lead to his fingers falling off. "Do you know how to make one, or do you want me to show you?"

"Of course I know *how*. You just flop like this—" Jay stepped off the deck and did exactly as he said, flopping onto his back "—and then you move your arms and legs like this—" He stretched his limbs out like a starfish, grinning like a loon all the while.

Alexei's chest ached with a strange sort of pressure at the sight, as if it was too full of emotion for him to even begin to bear. He knew he wasn't much to offer anyone, let alone an immortal being. Alexei was a runaway ghost, without a present or a future. He wasn't particularly kind, or good, or fun, or funny. But in the face of Jay's sweet delight, sprawling about in the snow, Alexei thought maybe he could offer *something* at least. He could be a companion. A witness. To help Jay enjoy the simple pleasures he'd been clearly denied for so long.

Jay loved the outdoors? Alexei would live in a forest cave with him, if he asked. Jay wanted to be around people? Alexei could handle that, if it was for Jay. He'd let Jay do all the talking, all the inadvertent charming, and it wouldn't be so bad. Jay wanted a messy house? They'd make blanket forts, have a million pets, destroy their kitchen with culinary experiments. Alexei could be enough. He could try. He *would* try.

Until Jay's better half came along and ruined it all, at least.

And wasn't that a kick to the fucking gut? But even if they weren't fated, Alexei could stay at Jay's side until then, couldn't he? Until Jay found the right person to tether him. It wasn't like Alexei was going to deny him that, when it came down to it. Not if the alternative was insanity or death for his perfect, sweet vampire.

Jay, seeming to take Alexei's silence as reticence, peered up at him cautiously from his spot on the snowy ground. "Have you ever made one before?"

"No, kotyonok." Alexei made his way off the deck. "I wasn't much for the outdoors when I was a kid. Or maybe I would have been, but I wasn't given much of a chance. Not much of a childhood, really."

Jay nodded solemnly and lifted his gaze to the stars above them. "I had a good childhood, I think. I do remember being very sad when my parents died. But my aunt and uncle had a farm, and they took me in. I liked it. The chores. The animals."

Alexei could picture it so perfectly, sweet Jay tending to the cows, running barefoot in the fields. "And that's where Vee found you?"

"Yes." Jay's face fell. "And then my life was very different."

Out of a desire to bring that joyful smile back to Jay's face more than anything else, Alexei flopped onto his back in the snow and spread his arms and legs about. He looked to the side to see Jay peering up out of his Jay-sized hole in the snow, gray eyes once again lit up with happiness. It took so fucking little to make him smile. "See?" Jay beamed. "Isn't this nice?"

"So nice, kitten." It was miserably fucking cold and wet was what it was, but that didn't make Jay any less right.

"I've always liked the snow," Jay mused, flopping again onto his back. "I wonder what else I might like? It's weird... I've been alive for so long, and we'd move about so often, but it was always to the same kinds of places. Different variations on remote European countrysides. There's so much of the world I haven't seen, except for through books or movies. I went to the desert for the very first time this year. I poked a cactus, just to feel it." Jay held up his pointer finger, as if in demonstration.

"Didn't that hurt?" It was certainly hurting Alexei, this absent-minded confession of all Jay had never been given, never been allowed.

"Oh yes." Jay smiled up at the night sky. "But it was a reminder. That it was...real."

It was suddenly completely unacceptable that Alexei didn't have Jay in his arms. "Hey," he said softly. "I'm a little lonely over here."

"You are?" Jay scrambled up out of his snow angel immediately, clambering on top of Alexei's supine form, settling his round bottom on Alexei's stomach. "Better?"

"Almost." Alexei tapped at his own lips with one ice-cold finger. "Need a kiss, I think."

Jay leaned down eagerly to oblige, his frozen lips still managing to warm Alexei from the inside, out.

Jay released the kiss first for once, darting out of Alexei's reach with a giggle. Then he sighed, but it was a contented sound, full of relaxed pleasure. "I'm very happy when I'm with you, Alexei."

"I'm very happy with you too, kotyonok." Alexei reached up to brush a strand of hair from Jay's rosy cheek. "I didn't have a real childhood. Your adulthood was stolen from you. Do you think together you and I could make one complete person?"

Jay pressed his cheek into Alexei's palm. "Except I'm not a person."

"You *are*." Alexei frowned, confused at Jay's self-assessment. "You mean because you have a"—what had Jay called it?—"a beastie inside you?"

Jay nodded solemnly against Alexei's hand.

Alexei let out a slow breath. "You're a person, Jay. A vampire person, maybe. But still a person." When Jay still looked unconvinced, Alexei pressed on. "Would you tell your friends in there they aren't real people?"

"That's different though. Danny and Gabe...well, they're freshly turned. Practically still human. Roman and Soren... They've *lived*. Out in the world. Soren escaped our den; he experienced humanity all these years. I've only read or watched or heard stories. I'm odd and stunted, and most of the time, I don't even know I'm acting that way. Until someone laughs at me or looks at me strangely."

"If I laugh, it's only ever because you delight me."

Jay smiled softly down at him. "I know that. You look at me differently from other people. I like it very much." He started playing with the loose strands of Alexei's hair. "Why does your brother want to kill you?"

"I deliberately went against orders. I made a business decision that cost him a lot of money. I was...tired, I guess. I wanted to blow it all up. I wasn't brave enough to do it literally, so I went the monetary route."

"You wanted freedom."

"I wanted freedom." *Freedom to find you* was the thought that went through Alexei's head. *Freedom to choose. To find a person worthy to serve. Worthy to love.*

Jay tugged gently at Alexei's hair. "Thank you for playing in the snow with me."

"Anytime, kitten. Literally anytime."

"I read a book once on love languages," Jay mused, a thoughtful expression on his face. "There were five of them, which doesn't seem like nearly enough. I think quality time might be mine."

"Oh yeah?"

"Yes. I like having you with me, at my side. Although, I also very much like physical touch." Jay leaned down, pressing his hands down on Alexei's chest, and smacked a kiss to his lips in apparent demonstration.

"Mm. I noticed. And you've maybe got a bit of a thing for words of affirmation too, don't you, kitten?" Alexei teased, thinking back on how much Jay had wanted to be told he was doing a good job in the bedroom.

Jay flushed, his already rosy cheeks darkening even more. "Maybe."

"And you like to make people comfortable," Alexei said, now thinking about the five blankets and the many glasses of water. "Acts of service."

Jay nodded. "Yes, that. Also, it was very nice when you brought me a cupcake. I liked that. Gift giving."

Alexei couldn't help his laugh, could only hope Jay knew it came from deep affection and not any sort of mockery. "Well, now you've named all five, haven't you?"

Jay's flush deepened, if that was possible. "I guess I have. Is that horribly greedy of me?"

"Maybe, but I don't mind. You're hungry for affection; I'm hungry to give it to you."

Jay beamed down at him. "Have I told you lately you're the nicest human?"

"Only to you."

Because you're special and perfect and I adore you even though we've only been technically dating for a day.

Alexei wondered, staring up at that gorgeous, happy face, if he could make the words come out. He wondered if he even should.

But there wouldn't have been time for it, anyway.

Because the little vampire atop him suddenly cocked his head, the smile dropping from his face as he turned with a start to the yellow house behind them. "We need to go back in, Alexei. And you need to stay behind me."

"Sorry?"

But Jay had somehow already pulled Alexei to standing and was tugging him back to the house by his hand.

Inside, Jay's friends were squared off to the front door. Danny was pushed behind a growling Roman. Soren was in front of Gabe, held tightly to him, as if Gabe was preventing him from leaping forward. And in front of all of them was…well, he sort of looked like the head of a British boarding school, really. A slim man in a brown tweed suit, his light-brown hair slicked back severely.

"I will ask you one more time," Roman warned, and holy shit, that dude could really growl when he wanted to. "Who *are* you?"

The stranger caught sight of Jay and Alexei then, and a cold smile graced his lips, one that didn't reach his flat brown eyes. "Ah, Johann. There you are," he said coolly, his accent very much matching his clothing.

The stranger inclined his head to Roman then, as if he was being introduced at a dinner party rather than two steps away from having four different vampires jump his ass. "My name is Wolfgang. Or Wolfe, should you prefer the simplicity." He met Alexei's eyes. "I'm Johann's fiancé."

Thirteen

Jay

Well, this was just great. So flipping *fantastic*. See? Jay could do sarcasm with the best of them. Sometimes. When the situation warranted it. And this situation most certainly did. Sarcasm and maybe even a few swears.

Jay squeezed Alexei's hand in his, grateful his human hadn't pulled away yet. "Hello, Wolfe," he said despite his annoyance, because really, it would be rude not to greet a friend he hadn't seen in months. But then, because he *was* really actually quite annoyed, he said, "You shouldn't have come without asking."

Because Jay had been texting and calling and generally trying to get a hold of Wolfe for freaking *days*. After Jay's declaration of wanting to stay in Hyde Park, he'd only received a single ominous text: *You're not staying. I'm coming to get you.*

And since that was obviously unacceptable, Jay had done his best to try to stop that from happening, but...nothing. Wolfe hadn't responded to a single message. And now he was just *there*.

Like, what the heck? It was frustrating, and a little scary (because he may have been Jay's friend, but Wolfe was also Wolfe), but mainly it was just freaking *rude*.

Wolfe—clearly intent on being a complete butthead—only arched a brow at him.

Jay dared to steal a glance at Alexei, who had *not* followed directions and was hovering at Jay's side rather than behind him. Jay clearly needed to work on putting more authority into his tone when issuing commands. Not that he wanted to issue a bunch of commands at Alexei all the time or anything, but safety was very important. Although, to be fair, it could also be because Jay hadn't let go of his hand yet.

The point was, though, his human was looking a little green around the gills and seemed to be mouthing the word *fiancé* to himself.

They'd been having such a nice moment outside too. Talking and kissing in the snow like characters in some kind of lovely fairy tale. It just wasn't fair to be interrupted this way.

Soren was a little more vocal than Alexei about his reaction to Wolfe's declaration. "*Fiancé?*" He twisted in Gabe's arms to shoot a wide-eyed look back at Jay. For once, Jay's friend wasn't smiling. "You have a *fiancé?*"

Jay fiddled with the hem of his shirt with his free hand, wishing he could have a moment alone with Alexei without the entire room staring at them. "Well, it's not the word *I* would use..."

"Betrothed?" Wolfe suggested dryly, his hands in his pockets like he was on some sort of afternoon stroll and sounding generally much more amused than he had any right to. "Intended, perhaps?"

Jay glared at him. He could feel his temper, over which he usually had iron control, fraying a bit at the edges. "Stop *doing* that, Wolfgang. You're making it sound like it's something it's not."

Wolfe's answering smile was mean. Because he could do that, somehow. Smile at someone and make it look *mean*. "Soon to be bound together in holy matrimony?"

Jay let out a tiny, muffled scream behind closed lips, just because it felt good to do so. "There's nothing holy about you. You made your big entrance. Now please stop toying with everyone. It's—it's rude. You're being *rude*."

"I don't understand what's happening," Alexei muttered so very quietly. He sounded lost and maybe a little sad, and Jay really wanted to fix it, but everything was such a mess, and he didn't know how yet.

"Join the fucking club," Soren snapped from Gabe's hold.

Well, jeez. Apparently everyone was feeling a little testy, not just Jay. And yes, that was probably Jay's fault. He should have come clean to his friends earlier. Much, much earlier. But that would have made it real, wouldn't it? For them to know. And Jay had wanted to...pretend. Pretend he would be allowed to stay. Pretend he actually belonged.

How silly. How *stupid.* How childish of him.

Wolfe sniffed delicately, eyeing Alexei now with way more interest than Jay was comfortable with. "I see. We have a human in our midst, do we?"

Jay tightened his hold on Alexei's hand and straightened his spine, dropping the hem of his shirt. He didn't like this new expression on Wolfe's face. Jay couldn't show weakness, not right now. For once, he needed to be strong. Firm. "This is my boyfriend, Alexei. Alexei—everyone—this is Wolfe. He's from my den."

As Jay probably could have predicted, that seemed to be the final straw for Soren. He broke out of Gabe's arm prison, rounding on Jay with more fury than Jay had ever had directed at him by his old friend. "You brought someone from that fucking den *here*? To Hyde Park?"

Jay's heart was racing, and his stomach was a hard knot. Because Soren—Soren, who'd been so kind to him, who'd let him *stay*—was angry. So very angry. And while Jay was generally immune to violent reactions or raised voices, after centuries of exposure to temperamental den members, he hated seeing his friends so upset. He swallowed hard and tried his best to explain. "I didn't tell him to come. I've been trying to prevent it."

Wolfe sighed, lifting a hand from his pocket and eyeing his manicured nails like they were vastly more interesting than the chaos he was actively causing. "No, you didn't tell me to come. You told me you were staying. And you know I can't allow that." Wolfe lowered his hand, fixing Jay with a look even Jay could tell was meant to be condescending. "What did you think would happen, Johann?"

His patronizing attitude had Jay feeling a bit petulant. He raised his chin. "You're not actually the boss of me."

"Too true. I'm not," Wolfe conceded with a dip of his head. "But agreements were made. And I'm not the only one with a vested interest in your return."

Roman, still using himself as a body shield to protect Danny from any potential harm, spoke up then. "Although I love indecipherable allusions and veiled threats as much as the next vampire, I must interrupt. Johann, is he an immediate threat to our collective safety?"

That was easy enough to answer. "No. Wolfe is my...friend. Sort of. He's not going to hurt anyone. Are you?" he asked pointedly.

Wolfe dipped his chin again. "I have no such intentions at the moment."

The vagueness of that had Roman bristling again, a low growl leaving his throat, but it was good enough for Jay. He dared another look at Alexei at his side. He wasn't quite so green anymore, but he wasn't exactly flush with health either. What did one give a human after a terrible shock? Water? Blankets? More garlicky French chicken?

Jay should at the very least get him off his feet. So he took a page out of Roman's book. "I think we should all sit down for some tea," he suggested. "Wolfe, Danny here made some really good cookies for dessert tonight. Have you ever had a snickerdoodle?"

"He doesn't get any *cookies* until the two of you explain what the fuck is going on," Soren huffed, clearly still grumpy, but at least he wasn't yelling anymore.

Wolfe's attention zeroed in on Soren. "A beautiful, feisty blond vampire with negative feelings toward our beloved den. Are you perhaps the infamous Soren, Hendrick's former companion?"

Well, jeez freaking Louise. Wolfe could not possibly have said a worse thing if he tried (although, knowing Wolfe, he probably *was* trying to be as antagonistic as possible, just for fun). The room tensed in a way that had the hairs on Jay's arms pricking up, and Gabe looked a moment away from vampicide.

But then Wolfe smiled at Soren in that way he did sometimes, all white teeth and zero warmth in his eyes. "I was pleased to hear of his demise. Hendrick always was insufferable."

Soren sniffed, pursing his lips. "You can have *one* cookie."

Okay, this was all much better. Or at least more civilized, everyone with a hot mug of tea in front of them.

They were crowded around the coffee table in the living room. Alexei was sitting—his brow stern and his muscles tensed—next to Jay on the couch, Danny and Roman squished in beside them. Wolfe had wisely refrained from trying to seat himself next to Jay and was instead resting in an armchair across from the couch. Soren was in the other armchair, at the opposite corner of the coffee table, Gabe standing at his side in a way that made Soren look like a spoiled prince and Gabe his knight errant.

Jay almost giggled at the thought of it, but that wouldn't be appropriate with how unhappy everyone still looked, so he took a sip of tea instead.

While he was sipping, Roman took charge of the situation, clearly tired of all the half answers. "Explain your presence here," he requested from Wolfe, although with his tone of voice, it sounded more like a command.

Wolfe looked to Jay instead of answering.

Jay couldn't tell if he was still just being a butthead or if he was asking Jay's permission to share secrets, but either way, Jay shrugged at him in answer. Jay didn't have any intention of lying to his friends. It was bad enough he hadn't been forthright before now.

He'd somehow assumed, clearly incorrectly, that it all just...wouldn't come up. That eventually it would be time for Jay to go and his friends would be fine with it. They all had their mates, after all.

Jay was the outlier, he knew that.

Wolfe seemed to find the answer he was looking for in Jay's shrug, and he crossed his legs gracefully, ignoring both his tea and the plate of cookies Jay had set before him. "I'm assuming, as his dear friends, you all know Johann's worth?"

There was a moment of confused silence. "Like, as a person?" Danny finally asked hesitantly. "Of course we do. Jay's wonderful."

Wolfe gave an amused hum at that answer, eliciting a growl from Roman, who clearly took it to be mocking (it definitely was). "I mean monetarily," Wolfe clarified. At their blank looks, he sighed, clearly pained beyond belief. "Johann is, to be frank, a billionaire. Several times over."

Wolfe was still ignoring the plate in front of him. Was he really not going to eat a *single* cookie? Jay was starting to feel a little offended on Danny's behalf. He'd made such delicious snickerdoodles for everyone.

"Jaybird? A *billionaire*?" Soren sounded uncharacteristically frazzled. "This Johann right here? That's who you mean?" He waved a hand at Jay, top to bottom, and Jay could only assume Soren was attempting to disparage Jay's dinner outfit, which was maybe a little unfair when Jay had tried so hard to look nice. His fleece pants were a very dignified black tonight, and his sweater was such a pretty pink, the lime-green flowers embroidered on it really making the lovely color pop.

Sure, Jay had found both items used at the thrift store near the café he liked, but that didn't make them any less nice. He'd washed them and everything.

Wolfe chuckled at Soren's disbelief, the jerk. "Mm, yes, the clothes. Jay's really come into his own, fashion-wise, since Veronique's demise."

Jay shifted, wanting to find comfort in holding Alexei's hand again but not sure if that was currently allowed, considering how uncomfortable his poor human looked. It was making Jay's beastie restless—he wanted to soothe, to comfort, not to explain every detail of his sordid financial history.

But he realized explanations needed to come first. So Jay took a bite of cookie instead. "Please talk like I'm actually here," he requested around his mouthful.

Wolfe dipped his chin again, this time in apology. (Over the last decade, Jay had gotten really good at reading the different meanings behind each of Wolfe's stately nods.) "Shall I explain?" Wolfe asked.

Jay gave a nod of his own, possibly less stately considering the mouth full of cookie he had going on.

"Once Veronique passed, her impressive fortune naturally went to Jay, as her surviving companion," Wolfe explained to the group. "But her passing coincided with that of other leaders of the den—Silas and Anton, namely—who, being without companions at the time, had each passed their fortune to the other den leaders in a descending order. Basically, when the legal dust settled, which took a number of years, Jay was left with all of it."

"Holy shit," Soren murmured, grinning widely.

"I don't really understand," Danny said. "Aren't you all pretty wealthy to begin with?"

"There is wealthy, and there is *wealthy*, my love," Roman answered. "We may not want for money, but I do not possess billions."

Danny shifted in his seat, clearly not quite placated with that explanation. "But with compulsion and living on the outskirts of society, what does it matter?"

Exactly what Jay had always thought, but he usually seemed to be the only one.

"Vampires are like anyone else in that regard, I'm afraid," Wolfe explained. "Compulsion is well and good, but when it comes to legal documents, assets, the like...money is still key. It takes a lot of capital to move around an entire den every decade or so. Money is power, frankly. And Jay has quite a lot of it."

And then all eyes were on Jay again. He took a sip of tea, washing down his third cookie in as many minutes. He had Alexei's hand entwined with his—Jay hadn't even realized he'd grabbed it—but his human's broad palm was disconcertingly limp. Jay stole a look, concerned, but Alexei definitely wasn't sleeping, his pretty eyes instead wide and unblinking, focused fixedly on Wolfe.

Should Jay be taking him to the doctor or something?

"And how do you fit into this exactly?" Roman asked Wolfe when he realized Jay had nothing to say.

"There were...concerns...in the den. Jay has been a member for centuries but as a companion, not as a leader. They wanted some assurance he would adhere to...expectations. I have the power and the, shall we say"—a twitch of Wolfe's lips—"ruthlessness to lead, but I'm a much younger vampire in the grand scheme of things. I haven't amassed the wealth or the experience others have." The unspoken words there being that the den didn't trust Wolfe as far as they could throw him. "So an agreement was made. A joining of our houses, so to speak, to put the den at ease."

"Why— Why would you agree to that, Jay?" Danny asked, dismay etched in his features.

Jay shrugged again, feeling more than a little uncomfortable with the continued scrutiny. "It didn't matter to me at the time. I don't care about the money. I just wanted to be left alone. And Wolfe has always been...kind to me. Without his interference, they probably would have just killed me, found a way to transfer the will to someone else."

Soren had an odd glint in his eye, and his smile was nowhere to be found. Jay thought he knew that look: Soren was feeling guilty about leaving him behind again. But it wasn't Soren's fault. It was Jay's, always, for not being brave or strong enough to stand on his own two feet. "All I asked in return was to be given some time. And then...after your phone call...a year to spend in Hyde Park."

"A year," Roman mused. "So you were leaving..."

"In the spring, yes."

"Would you even have told us?" Danny looked wounded at the thought of it.

"Of course I would have!" Jay protested. "I just wanted to...wait a little bit. To pretend, I suppose."

Alexei's hand finally came to life then, his grip tightening in Jay's, and then he spoke for the first time since they'd all sat down in the living room. "Do you love him?"

His words weren't directed at Jay but at Wolfe.

Wolfe cocked his head, a strange half smile on his lips. "No. Of course not. It's a business arrangement."

Alexei's eyes narrowed. "I don't believe you."

Jay patted Alexei's knee, placating. "He can't love me, Alexei."

Alexei turned to him, his brow furrowed, looking as stern as he ever had before he and Jay had gotten to know each other and his eyes had begun turning soft, just for Jay. "Why not?" Alexei asked harshly. "You're perfect. Anyone could love you."

Well, that was...nice. So nice. It made Jay feel all warm and fuzzy inside, as a matter of fact. But still, Alexei was wrong. "Not Wolfe though. He's a psychopath."

Soren giggled. "Harsh thing to say about your friend, Jaybird."

Jay cocked his head, considering. But he didn't think it was harsh to speak the truth. "Well, he's my friend, yes. But he's also a psychopath."

Wolfe raised a hand, looking almost fond of Jay in that moment. "Guilty as charged, I'm afraid."

Jay nodded, vindicated. "It's not his fault though. He was just born that way."

"Wait." Danny looked from Jay to Wolfe and back again. "You mean...literally?"

Jay nodded, then turned to Alexei. "So you see, he can't love me. Not really."

Soren giggled again. "Jesus fucking Christ."

"Not that I don't love this heart-to-heart we're having," Wolfe broke in, obviously growing bored with the minor derailment to his purpose. "But the real issue here is you, Johann. Telling me you've changed your mind."

"So?" Soren scoffed. "Good for him. We want him to stay."

"So I'm afraid it's unrealistic at this time. I really can't allow it."

"How did you even find me?" Jay asked.

"I'm tracking your phone, obviously. Did you think I'd let you flee the country without a way to find you again?"

Jeez, where was the trust? It had Jay feeling petulant again. "I don't *want* to go back." Maybe if he said it enough times, Wolfe would get the picture.

But Wolfe's sharp eyes zeroed in on Jay and Alexei's joined hands. "Is that the problem here?" he asked pointedly, baring his teeth. He somehow made it look scary, even without his fangs. "Easy enough to fix."

Jay's beastie tensed within him, and he had to stop himself from squeezing Alexei's hand hard enough to break bones. "Don't threaten him, Wolfgang."

"A single human in between me and what I want," Wolfe mused, uncrossing his legs and leaning forward in his chair. "What else am I supposed to do, Johann?"

Jay took in a shaky breath, mustering his courage. "If you try to hurt him, you'll have to go through me. And—well, you probably could," he conceded. "I don't know much about fighting. But then I'd be dead and you'd be out of luck anyway. So just...don't."

Jay didn't actually know for sure that was true. There was definitely a possibility Wolfe had made some moves behind the scenes already, in case of Jay's death. But it wasn't very likely he'd managed to arrange to get *everything*, not when Jay's finances were so complicated, so Jay could only bet on the fact that Wolfe needed Jay alive and relatively well to achieve his aims.

The smirk on Wolfe's lips was anything but kind. "Johann, darling. Have you grown a spine since we last met?"

"Don't be mean." Even if Wolfe maybe had a point, it wasn't a very nice thing to say.

Soren cleared his throat. "You wouldn't be fighting just Jay. I really hope you know that."

Wolfe took a moment, studying the room, the five vampires who would be against him in any sort of fight. "Very well." He rose from his chair, smoothing out the lines of his suit. "I'll be in touch, Johann."

He never did try a cookie.

Fourteen

Alexei

It took almost the entire drive back to Jay's apartment for Alexei's near-catatonic state to break, and when it did, it broke into laughter.

Because...fuck. Jay was a billionaire? A billionaire with a goddamn vampire fiancé?

A fiancé.

A fucking *fiancé.*

That word on its own was enough to send Alexei into orbit. Because he'd lived his entire life surrounded by people obsessed with money and power. Gaining it, keeping it, lording it over others. He'd finally—fucking *finally*—run from it all, and where had it led him? To the goddamn heir apparent *billionaire* of some sketchy European vampire den, one who was currently rocking a significant threadbare hole in the left arm of his thrifted sweater.

How could Alexei do anything else *but* laugh at the ridiculousness of it all?

"Um..."

Alexei tore his eyes off the road (and had it really been the best idea to let him drive?) long enough to see Jay staring at him, that pale brow furrowed in visible concern. "Is inappropriate laughter one of the symptoms of shock?" Jay asked.

It was the faint note of real anxiety in his voice that had Alexei's laughter finally quieting down. "Sorry, kitten," he managed to get out, trying to swallow down the last errant chuckles. "I'm just realizing my father might actually have approved of you after all."

He stole another look to see Jay nibbling at his lower lip, face drawn. He looked absolutely miserable. "I didn't ask for the money, Alexei," he said dully. "Vee just wanted to be sure I was taken care of, if anything happened to her."

"Taken care of and then some," Alexei countered, pulling up at the curb in front of Jay's apartment. He didn't know why he said it, why he poked at what was clearly a sore subject for Jay. Maybe he wanted, just for a moment, for Jay to feel bad. Bad for lying to Alexei, for giving him hope for something more—something real—when he had always intended to leave.

He told Wolfe he wanted to stay, argued the more reasonable part of Alexei's brain.

Either way, Jay had no answer to his petty statement, and they made their way into his apartment in strained silence. Jay immediately wandered into the kitchen, and Alexei lowered himself onto the couch, his movements stilted, his mind torn between obsessively focusing on that one not-so-little fact (fiancé, fiancé, *fiancé*) and splintering off into a thousand different, confused directions.

He didn't realize he'd been starting at the wall, eyes unseeing, until Jay's throat clearing broke through his haze. "Okay, I have a big glass of water for you, and then I've eaten most of the stuff in my pantry, but I did have some bread, so I put some butter on it for you. Bread and butter—that's a classic, right? That should be tasty. Right?"

Alexei focused his vision with effort and turned his head to the left to see Jay hovering by the edge of the coffee table, a cup in one hand and a small plate in the other.

Alexei eyed the contents of the plate, and it was almost enough to make him smile for real. "Kotyonok. Did you use the entire stick of butter?"

Jay frowned down at the plate thoughtfully. "No, just, um, half? Why, should I have used the whole thing?"

Alexei shook his head, charmed in spite of himself. Fucking hell, how was anyone supposed to stay mad at this earnest, alien creature? "No, sweetheart, it's perfect. Come here, please. We just got back from dinner. I don't actually need any food right now."

"The water though," Jay insisted, stepping closer and holding the cup out in front of Alexei's face. "You're in shock. You need to hydrate. Right?"

Alexei took the glass from him only to set it down on the coffee table. "I'm not *in* shock, sweetheart. I just *am* shocked. Come here. I'm lonely sitting here all by myself."

Jay set the plate down—carelessly enough to cause quite a bit of noise—and rushed the last few steps over, as if he'd only been waiting for permission to get closer. And maybe he had been. Maybe he'd been worried Alexei would reject him. Alexei knew he'd been in a strange, fuzzy-headed state since the arrival of Wolfe in Danny's home. Processing, in his own way. And he didn't generally speak much when he was processing, which may have thrown Jay for a loop, considering Alexei's uncharacteristic chattiness where the little vampire was concerned.

No wonder Jay thought he was in a state of shock.

Alexei pulled Jay onto his lap immediately, rubbing his nose into Jay's dark hair, letting the refreshing peppermint scent clear his mind as Jay wiggled around to straddle his thighs. "Why are you so into human food, anyhow?" Alexei mumbled into the messy strands.

"Well, I never really got to have it, when Vee was around," Jay mused, wrapping his arms around Alexei's middle. "She thought it was gauche, to eat when we didn't need to. Sometimes we had food for human guests, but I wasn't allowed to take any for myself."

"Jesus." Alexei hated every new little bit he learned about Jay's life with Vee. He'd been turned so young only to have so much of life's pleasures denied him, so many experiences kept out of his reach. He'd been purposefully stunted before he could reach his prime.

Alexei pressed a kiss to Jay's head, aware he was acting like a complete sappy fuck. But Jay clung to him right back, rubbing his head into Alexei's shoulder like the kitten Alexei so often called him. "Are you angry with me?" he asked hesitantly, and fuck did Alexei hate the anxious note to the question.

But that *was* the question, wasn't it? Was he? Alexei knew he should be. However new their relationship with each other may have been, wasn't it basic common decency to tell someone about a fiancé, even an unconventional one?

But for once in Alexei's life, he couldn't muster up the anger—an emotion usually resting just underneath his skin. Not for Jay. Not when he kept dwelling on what Jay had said, back in his friends' living room. *Without his interference, they would have probably just killed me...*

The underlying message behind all Jay and Wolfe's revelations had been that Jay was in danger, by virtue of the inheritance he'd gained. And that thought had a terrifying choke hold on Alexei.

How could anyone—no matter how vicious, how fucking blood-thirsty—want to hurt this sweet vampire? Why had Jay, of all people, had to be pulled into such a brutal world? He could have stayed a happy farmer, content with his family and his connection to the land.

But if Jay's life had never changed direction, if Veronique had never turned him, Alexei would never have met him; their lives would have been separated by centuries. Which meant while Alexei still held a deep, piercing hatred for Veronique, he couldn't fully regret her actions, could he?

And that made him the biggest asshole of them all.

Alexei realized Jay had tensed in his hold. Of course. Because Alexei had never answered his fucking question.

Alexei pressed another kiss or five against Jay's hair, rubbing along his slender back with one hand. "Oh no," he soothed. "I'm not angry with you, kitten. It's just... I wanted to say I'm sorry that you were turned against your will, that you've had to deal with all this mess. But I'd be lying, wouldn't I? I'm glad you've lived long enough for us to meet."

Jay tensed again, releasing his hold on Alexei's middle and struggling against Alexei's arms, and Alexei worried for a moment that he'd fucked up entirely, truly offended his sweet vampire with his complete lack of appropriate empathy.

But Jay was smiling at him, a strange shyness to the expression. "I'm not sorry either," he whispered, like it was a secret confession. "I know— Well, it's not a burden I'd wish on anyone else." There was a pointedness to that statement, his gray eyes incredibly serious, though Alexei couldn't figure out why. "But I've been happy here, in Hyde Park. Even when I was lonely or sad, before we met, I was still happy. Does that make sense?"

Alexei brushed back a strand of Jay's dark hair, tweaking the lobe of his ear. "Sure, kotyonok. That makes sense."

Jay beamed at his understanding for just a moment before his face fell back into appropriate solemnity. "I'm sorry I didn't tell you about Wolfe."

Alexei swallowed hard before shrugging with a misleading casualness. He may not have been angry, but he didn't know quite what to say. Or at least not what to say that wouldn't reveal the depths of the knife he could feel twisting in his gut. "What will you do?" he asked instead.

The unspoken part of that question being, *Will you leave me? Will you run away?*

"I don't know," Jay said. He'd started toying with the hem of Alexei's shirt in the way he often did with his own. "If I could just give the money away, I would. But... I don't trust the den with it. It's a rotten place. They don't deserve that much power. With Wolfe, I could maybe keep a handle on it, but...I don't want to leave. I just want to...exist. For myself. With the people I care about."

A helpless sort of hope filled Alexei at the thought that he could be one of those people. He really, really hoped he counted as one of those people. "Can't you just give it to Wolfe, then?"

Jay had now bunched two handfuls of Alexei's shirt together and seemed to be attempting to tie it all into some sort of weird knot over Alexei's stomach. "He might not take it. Alone, he's more vulnerable. He's too new to the den. There's not enough trust there. It's more convenient to have me on board. And Wolfe is big on what's convenient."

Alexei considered taking his own shirt off and letting Jay tie whatever intricate knots he wanted into it but ultimately decided the move would break Jay's clear concentration. "You said he's a psychopath."

Jay bit at his lower lip, dropping his fistfuls of cloth and busying himself smoothing the wrinkles he'd made back down. "He is." He said it with the same cool acceptance as the first time. "But he's not cruel without purpose. He likes things orderly, under his control. It makes him less erratic than the others, really. Plus, he sort of...saved me."

"And how did he do that?" Alexei asked, trying to keep his voice as calm and level as Jay's even though anything Wolfe-related threatened to send his blood pressure through the fucking roof.

"He kept me fed, after Vee was killed. He compelled humans for me. He convinced the den members to stay back while I regained my strength. I think his support is the only thing that kept me from being put down."

Oh. *Oh.* Alexei grabbed Jay's hands with his own, halting their smoothing efforts, needing that extra contact. He was grateful Wolfe had kept Jay alive—the thought of any other alternative too hideous to bear—but fuck if he didn't hate feeling indebted to the guy. He wished he could have been the one to save Jay, to keep him safe, keep him nourished. He would have offered up every bit of his own blood, down to the last fucking drop, to keep Jay whole.

"I want you to stay." Alexei hardly recognized his own voice, the rough gravel that came out of him in saying the words.

But there it was. The selfish truth of it. He didn't care about the money, about Jay's prior agreement with Wolfe. He didn't care about the den of cretins Jay had left behind. All Alexei cared about was Jay with *him*. He wanted Jay by his side, happy and hale. He just…wanted him.

Jay tilted his head from where he'd been studying their joined hands to smile up at Alexei, so soft and sweet but with a sadness in those gray eyes Alexei absolutely hated.

"Please," Alexei begged. "Please stay."

"It's like I told Wolfe: I want to stay." And because Jay was good and kind and perfect, he added what Alexei had been afraid to. "I want to stay with you."

Alexei's sigh of relief was cut off halfway through because then Jay's mouth was on his, the vampire wrapped back around him in the way he should always be.

Because Jay *should* just always be there, in Alexei's arms. There was no other reality that made sense.

Alexei tried, at first. He really did. They'd just both had something of a shock, and emotions were running high. So he did his best to keep the kiss chaste and sweet, to not give in to his inner greed for more, always *more*.

But soon enough Jay was slipping his tongue into Alexei's mouth, seemingly hungry as ever for every bit of Alexei's touch, and Alexei couldn't resist matching his pace, meeting him hunger for hunger.

So it didn't take long until Jay was writhing in Alexei's lap, rubbing his ass—intentionally or not—up against Alexei's clothed erection.

Alexei groaned his complaint when Jay finally broke the kiss.

"What I said before?" Jay asked, panting and rocking against Alexei's cock, practically riding it. Jesus fucking Christ.

Alexei tried to focus through the fog of his lust to find Jay's meaning. When he did, an electric shock of desire ran through him. "You mean penetrative sex, kitten?"

Jay nodded eagerly, latching onto Alexei's lips again before breaking off, looking ridiculously shy all of a sudden for someone who was humping Alexei's lap like there was no tomorrow. "Um, if you still want me?"

Alexei's answering laugh was strangled. "I can't breathe without wanting you, kitten." The surprised delight on Jay's face almost broke Alexei's heart. Because fucking hell, had Jay really thought Alexei would say *no*? "We're sticking with our after-dinner plans, sweetheart. Most definitely."

Jay moved as if to scramble off Alexei's lap, but Alexei tightened his arms and kept him close, rising off the couch and taking Jay with him, his little vampire fitting so easily into his arms. "I've got you, kotyonok."

Jay beamed up at him and wrapped his legs around Alexei's hips. "So strong for a human."

"Please, kitten. You're light as a feather." Alexei carried Jay in the direction of the bedroom, trying not to lose his mind at the way Jay tucked his head into the crook of Alexei's neck, sniffing at him like Jay could consume him via scent alone.

Jay's room was as neat and tidy as one would expect, other than a stack of drawings scattered haphazardly on his bedside table.

Alexei didn't waste too much time taking in the view, tossing Jay immediately onto the bed, more out of a desire to hear Jay's answering giggle than any willingness to let him out of his arms.

Jay didn't stay put where he landed, instead scrambling over to the bedside table and opening the drawer there—still giggling wildly—and pulled out a bottle of lube and then, much more hesitantly, a package of foil-wrapped condoms. "Um, so as a vampire, I can't give you anything bad, even if it weren't my first time. But if you'd feel better with these...?"

Alexei froze in place, standing there at the foot of the bed, his cock so hard it was becoming painful. Jay was giving him the option to go bare? Fucking *fuck*. "We don't need them," he said, his voice coming out gruffer than he'd intended. But Jay only beamed back at him, clearly pleased at his decision, and shut the condoms back into the drawer before bringing himself and the bottle of lube once more to the middle of the bed.

"So, um, I've looked it up. I know I need to...prepare myself. Stretch myself." Jay looked pointedly at the bulge in Alexei's jeans. "Your penis is quite large, you know."

Alexei bit back his smile at that, trying to keep his face as serious as this moment warranted. He considered the incredible appeal of Jay working himself open, learning to coax his body into accepting Alexei's cock. But ultimately the desire to have his hands on Jay as much as possible won out. "You know what I'd like, kitten?" he asked. "What would make me feel really good?"

"What?" Jay bounced up onto his knees with the question, eager as ever to please.

"If you'd let me do it for you. Just relax back and let me take care of you. I can make it feel so good for you."

"You'd like that?" Jay asked, cocking his head, the skepticism clear in his voice. "Really?"

Oh boy. Alexei's little acts-of-service vampire, so thoroughly trained to meet the needs of others.

"You have no idea how much, kotyonok."

Jay gave him another skeptical head tilt but ultimately nodded shyly before scrambling to get undressed. Alexei followed suit at a slightly more sedate pace. Not because he was any less eager but because his goddamn fingers were *trembling*, he was embarrassed to note.

It was just...to share this first with Jay, to bond them together in this way. Alexei wanted it so fucking much. Probably too much. More than he'd ever wanted anything.

He felt like his gaze left Jay only for a moment, only for enough time to get his shoes and jeans off, and when Alexei focused back on the bed, his breath left him in a rush.

Jay was sprawled on top of the covers on his back, fully nude, hard cock leaking on his stomach, his face looking flushed and unbelievably happy, with his legs held up and back by his head.

He'd literally folded himself in half for Alexei's ministrations, not a drop of coyness in his gorgeous body.

"Look at you, kitten," Alexei groaned, palming his own hard cock. "So good for me. What a fucking gift you are."

Jay squirmed with pleasure at the praise, but he didn't release his hold on his legs. Of course he didn't. Such a good fucking boy for Alexei.

And as much as he wanted to drink in this sight for the rest of eternity, Alexei didn't waste any more time. He crawled up onto the bed and started immediately pressing openmouthed kisses to the exposed undersides of Jay's thighs, unable to resist mouthing at the smooth, pale skin there.

Jay sighed happily at the contact, his legs relaxing back even further. Alexei rewarded him by kissing the tip of his hard, pretty cock, drinking in Jay's little whimper like it was a fine wine, then kissing along Jay's stomach, working his way up to swirling his tongue around Jay's pebbled nipples.

Really, Alexei wanted to map every inch of Jay's skin with his mouth, to taste every bit of this buffet laid out before him.

But he was also an impatient fuck who wanted nothing more than to take advantage of this particular position, this open eagerness. So, because Jay made it so easy for him, displayed so fucking beautifully, Alexei lasted barely any time at all before he was swiping his tongue over Jay's exposed hole.

Jay jerked, his raised ass lifting even higher off the bed. "Oh!" he gasped. " I—I didn't—I thought... Fingers?"

Alexei lifted his head to see Jay gazing down at him, gray eyes wide and startled, cheeks still adorably flushed. "We'll get there, kitten. I promise. You just look so scrumptious." Alexei bit gently at Jay's thigh. "I have to devour you, I'm afraid. I simply have to."

Jay giggled breathlessly at his teasing, but it was cut off by a gasp as Alexei delved once more into the furrow of his cheeks. "Oh my God!"

Alexei worked at his hole, softening it with relentless kissing and probing, letting his saliva pool and then spearing him with his tongue. He kept at it until Jay's whimpers were an ongoing, steady stream of noise and his thighs were trembling so much they finally dropped from his careful hold. "S-Sorry," Jay gasped. "Oh God. I'm sorry, it just felt so good."

Alexei smiled against Jay's skin. "You never need to apologize for your responses to my touch, kitten. Let's get you ready for me, hm?"

"Is that—is that not what you were doing?"

"Oh, sweetheart," Alexei crooned. "That part was just for me."

Alexei grabbed the lube next to him on the bed, drizzling some on Jay's hole before slicking his own finger up.

He went slowly, so slowly. Because Jay, as eager as he may have been in his mind, was...tight. So very tight. And really, two-plus centuries of virginity would do that to a guy. Alexei almost laughed at the thought, but he glanced up to see Jay's gray eyes were staring down at him with such solemnity that he didn't dare. "Does that feel good, sweetheart?" he asked instead.

Jay nodded, eyes wide. "So good."

Alexei explored cautiously, stroking with the one finger, crooking it until he heard the surprised, delighted gasp that meant he'd found Jay's prostate. He soon had Jay whimpering again, but he was hesitant to add the second finger.

Right up until Jay started pleading with him. "More, Alexei. More. Please. I'm not delicate. I can take it. I'm strong, I promise."

Alexei knew Jay was strong, stronger than he thought he was. Alexei hadn't missed the part, back in that living room, where Jay had offered to fight for him. To die for him. No one in Alexei's life—not a one, not ever—had offered to fight for Alexei. Even his mother, his only consistent source of kindness in his childhood, had chosen to leave instead.

But Alexei didn't want thoughts of his family invading this moment. "Is that you asking for another finger, kotyonok?"

"Yes," Jay groaned, impatience lacing through his voice. "*Yes.*"

Well, then. Alexei did as he was told, adding another finger. When he was up to three, Jay tensed. "Oh no."

Alexei paused his movements. Had he hurt him? "What's wrong? Too much?"

Jay whimpered, wiggling against Alexei's invasion. "No. It's just...I'm gonna—um, like this."

Alexei couldn't help grinning when he realized the problem. "Ohh, I see. Are you going to come, sweetheart?" He twisted his fingers inside Jay, causing the vampire to let out a helpless moan. "Go ahead, kitten. We can get you going again, I promise."

Jay positively keened as Alexei pumped his fingers with renewed vigor. Alexei surged over him, sucking the head of Jay's cock into his mouth just in time for Jay's release, swallowing every drop of his cum.

"Oh my goodness. Oh my God. *Oh!*"

Alexei released Jay's cock, rising to meet his vampire in a kiss, losing himself to the heady way Jay met his lips so fucking eagerly, never mind the fact that he'd just come in Alexei's mouth.

Alexei wasn't sure how long it had been when Jay broke the kiss, pushing at Alexei's shoulders. "I'm ready for more now."

"Are you?" Alexei propped himself over Jay on one elbow, working his fingers back into him, just to be sure.

"Alexei!" Jay whined. "Sex. Penis sex. I'm *ready.*"

This time, Alexei really did laugh; he couldn't help it. "My little alien," he crooned, pressing another kiss to Jay's lips, so completely overwhelmed with fondness for this strange creature.

"I'm not an alien," Jay protested, his lips pursing into a pout. "I'm a vampire. Now how do you want me?"

"Just as you are," Alexei said. The words had a much deeper meaning than just physical positioning, but they were true enough for that too.

He wanted to see Jay's face when he entered him for the first time.

Alexei lubed himself up—possibly excessively so, but he didn't want Jay to regret a single second of this—before working more lube into Jay with his fingers.

"*Alexei.*"

Alexei laughed at the frustration in Jay's voice, lining his cock up to the vampire's slick hole. "Hush, kitten. Like I said. I've got you."

He pushed in slowly, his breath catching at the incredible tightness. His eyes wanted to close, but he kept them open, watching Jay's gorgeous face for every change of expression. There was surprise. A twinge of what looked to be discomfort. But then... Jay's tongue darted out to wet his lips, and a slow smile built on his face. "Ohhh, Alexei. I like it. I like it so much. More." He pressed his heels into Alexei's ass, pushing him to move deeper.

And when Alexei bottomed out, Jay's fangs descended, his eyes darkening to that deep black. He was gorgeous, perfect, everything Alexei had ever wanted. Alexei told him so.

And then, because he couldn't help it, Alexei begged once more. "Say you'll stay with me. Say you won't leave me alone." He knew it wasn't fair to ask for promises midcoitus, but he was desperate. Unbelievably desperate.

Jay smiled wide as Alexei's hips began to move almost against his will, those fangs gleaming even in the dim bedroom lighting. "We'll stay. We won't leave."

Alexei froze, the movement of his hips pausing. "Are you... Is this Jay's beastie?"

A pause, and then Jay's fangs receded, his eyes swirling back to gray, the pupils still wider than Alexei had ever seen them before. Jay didn't address the strange slip, instead arching his back, pushing himself up into Alexei's cock. "More, please. I'm ready."

So Alexei gave him what he asked for, kissing Jay as he worked into his vampire with deep, fluid thrusts, searching and finding the right angle to have Jay once again whimpering mindlessly, his hips trying to find a rhythm with Alexei's.

His movements were awkward and unpracticed, but fuck, did they drive Alexei wild. Alexei made sure to tell him so, knowing how much his vampire liked to know when he was doing a good job. "So fucking perfect for me. Taking my cock so well, kitten. You were made for this, baby."

With Jay's apparent hair trigger, it didn't take long until he was warning Alexei once again of his imminent release.

Which, thank fucking God, because Alexei was holding on by a thread, wanting nothing more than to empty himself into Jay, to fill him up with nothing but Alexei.

The second Jay's back arched, his muscles trembling with the force of his orgasm, Alexei hitched Jay's legs higher up onto his hips, pushing into Jay once, twice more, before burying his face into Jay's hair, electricity shooting up and down his spine, his own orgasm leaving him unable to think, unable to move, barely able to even breathe.

Fucking hell.

When Alexei's brain and muscles came back online, he made moves to pull out, but Jay wrapped his legs tighter around Alexei's hips. "Not yet, please. Stay a little longer."

Alexei stayed where he was.

Fifteen

Jay

J ay held his human in place, his legs wrapped tight—not too tight; he knew to be careful not to break him—Alexei's softening cock still inside him.

He knew he was being greedy, not letting Alexei pull out, but he wasn't ready to break their connection just yet. His beastie wasn't ready either, keyed up enough to speak full words for once in Jay's head. *Smells so good. Feels so good. Bite. Bite him.*

Jay resisted the urge with effort. It would have been such a nice end to his first time—a mouth full of warm, coppery blood—but he didn't trust his beastie one bit at the moment. He didn't trust it not to sink its sharp teeth into Alexei and never let go.

"You okay, kitten?"

Alexei was looking down at him with concern in his pretty eyes. He was worried about Jay, worried Jay hadn't had the most perfect first time. He was worried because he was the nicest human in the whole wide world. And he'd just taken Jay's virginity, and it had felt so good that Jay wanted to do it a billion trillion more times.

If Jay had known earlier that sex was like *this*, maybe he would have tried harder to have it before now. But then again, he had a feeling it wouldn't be the same with anyone else. Anyone other than his Alexei.

"I'm okay," he reassured his perfect, nice, wonderful human. "I just like the feel of you."

Alexei smiled down at him, so wide and pleased that Jay wasn't even anxious over him minding Jay's greediness. Because Alexei never seemed to mind how much Jay *wanted*, all the affection he craved every second of every day.

Sometimes Jay felt like he was a bottomless pit of want and need. And he was only just recently realizing how deep it went. He wanted to be held, possibly all the time. He wanted to experience everything he'd ever missed. He wanted to taste every kind of human food. He wanted to meet every kind of person. He wanted to pet every animal in the whole wide world.

He wanted Alexei with him always.

And Alexei made him feel safe with that want. He wouldn't scold Jay over needing too much. He wouldn't judge him harshly for his many missing pieces. Maybe it was because Alexei had missed out on enough in his own life to understand that kind of want.

"I liked—" Jay started to say but stopped when he realized he wasn't sure how to finish the thought.

Alexei stroked his cheek, his weight on top of Jay so delightfully heavy and comforting. "You liked what, sweetheart?"

"Well." Jay bit at his lip, considering. "I liked the other day, when we were both pleasing each other with our mouths? But I liked this too. I liked...relaxing and letting you take care of me, like you said. Is that bad?" Jay kind of felt somehow like it *should* be bad. Like it was selfish of him to like being under Alexei's care so much, to take all that pleasure without giving back.

But Alexei was still smiling at him, stroking Jay's face. "We've got a budding pillow princess on our hands, huh?"

Jay didn't know what that meant, but Alexei's voice was so clearly full of affection when he said it that Jay couldn't help smiling back in response.

The kiss Alexei pressed to Jay's neck had a lovely shiver running down his spine. "I could do that," Alexei murmured, the words rumbling against Jay's skin. "Make you feel good like that—all day, every day for the rest of my life, kotyonok. It's not bad at all that you enjoy it. It's like I said earlier: you're greedy for affection, and I'm greedy to give it to you."

See? Alexei really was the nicest human in the entire world.

The reassurance had Jay finally feeling ready to relax and let Alexei out of his hold. He slackened his legs, and Alexei pulled out of him slowly. It felt...strange.

As did the cum dripping out of Jay's body. Jay peered down at his lower half. "Oh. Goodness."

Alexei was up on his knees above Jay's sprawled body. His hair had come loose from its bun at some point during all the sex stuff, and the strands were wild around his face. He looked so unbelievably handsome. Jay wanted to draw him. "We can use condoms next time, if you'd prefer."

"No!" Jay's response was more vehement than he'd intended. He cleared his throat and softened his voice, folding his hands over his belly. "No. I like this. I like having you in me."

Was that too much to say? But Alexei was still looking down at him with fire in his eyes—the good kind, not the angry kind—so it must have been okay.

"All right, then. Be right back, kitten."

Alexei left the bedroom, and Jay could hear him rummaging around in the bathroom, then the sound of the sink running. He came back quickly with a warm, wet washcloth, and he started cleaning Jay up—first his stomach, since Jay had orgasmed all over himself—and then his...delicate bits.

If Jay could purr—really purr—he would be doing it right about now. His beastie was certainly purring inside him. For a creature with such potentially vicious cravings, it definitely liked having Alexei caring for them so gently. Really, it just liked anything involving Alexei at all.

Hussy, Jay accused. (Not that he was any better.) His beastie only purred louder in response.

Alexei cleaned himself after Jay, then left one more time to toss the washcloth somewhere, and then he was back, still deliciously naked, sitting at the edge of the bed, his broad back tempting Jay to bite at it, even with his blunt teeth.

But the urge left him when Alexei held up one of his drawings, and Jay realized what he'd been looking at. A portrait of Vee.

"Is this...?"

"Veronique," Jay answered, his voice coming out smaller than he'd like.

Alexei studied the picture, his face looking awfully stern, reminding Jay of his early days in the café. "She's beautiful."

Jay rose into a kneeling position, looking at the portrait over Alexei's shoulder, breathing in his yummy vanilla scent. "I know I'm supposed to hate her," he said. "She took me from my human life, molded me to her needs. She never once considered mine. And the virginity—" Alexei's muscles tensed against him "She'd have these parties sometimes. There were always vampire men. I could have... But they always scared me. And she—I knew she would be displeased. She would have considered it a division of my loyalties. So I just kept all my desire to myself. And she let me." Jay sighed, resting his cheek against Alexei's shoulder and closing his eyes, not wanting to look at the drawing any longer. "But she was also my companion. My...friend. I'm not—I'm not brave or strong or tough. I missed her when she died. Sometimes I still miss her. I miss having someone just for me."

Alexei set the portrait down, one of his broad hands reaching back to stroke Jay's hair. That was nice. "It's hard to hate the people who raised you. My father was a bastard of the highest order. But if he suddenly rose from the dead and just—I don't fucking know—told me he loved me? Offered me a fucking hug? I'd probably end up taking it, wouldn't I?"

Jay wrapped his arms around Alexei's chest, tucking his head more firmly into the crook of his neck. "I'll give you hugs, Alexei."

"I know you will, kitten." Alexei maneuvered his head back to give Jay a kiss, one much chaster than their earlier aggressive mouth mating (that was what it felt like sometimes to Jay when they were making out—a mating of their mouths).

"I have a photo. Do you want to see?" Jay felt a little shy suggesting it. But he'd never had anyone else to show. Soren hated any mention of the den, any sign of Jay's lasting loyalty to Vee. And there was no one else who would have cared. But Jay knew Alexei would understand; he wouldn't judge that Jay had held onto it.

Which he proved with his next words. "I'd love to, sweetheart."

"In the drawer," Jay said, unwilling to relinquish his hug.

Alexei pulled out the photo. He had to bend forward slightly to do so, but Jay kept his hold on the human, his body moving with him. The photo showed Vee, dressed in a beautiful, severe gown. And Jay by her side, his hair short and slicked to the sides, dressed in an equally severe suit.

Jay already knew every detail by heart, so he focused on Alexei's face instead. His human looked surprisingly sad. Jay hadn't expected that. "Your clothes..."

"Pretty dapper, huh?"

He could actually hear Alexei's hard swallow. "I like how you dress now better."

Warmth filled Jay's chest at the unexpected compliment. "Me too." He pressed a kiss to Alexei's neck. "I don't miss the clothes. Or the rules and restrictions. But I guess I miss belonging to someone. I know that's bad to say. It's just—I get lonely."

Alexei set the photo down, then covered Jay's hands on his chest with his. "You have me now, if you want."

And Jay did, didn't he? At least for now. And Jay had promised to stay. A promise he meant from the bottom of his heart.

A promise he maybe didn't quite know how to keep.

But Jay didn't want to think about the bad right now. He released his hold on Alexei and flopped onto his back on the bed. "Isn't this the part where we cuddle? You said cuddling was part of sex."

"You're so right, sweetheart," Alexei agreed, nice enough to not point out that they'd technically already been cuddling. "Scootch over."

When Jay only scooted on inch, Alexei manhandled him until he was on his side, facing away from Alexei. And then, to Jay's delight, Alexei latched onto *him*—like a reverse of the position they'd just been in but lying down.

Spooning. That was what it was called.

They lay like that long enough that Jay thought his human must be drifting off. But then Alexei's voice cut through the silence, surprisingly soft. "I get lonely too."

"You do?" Jay asked.

"Not as much, now that I met you." And wasn't that the nicest thing to say? "I can be that person for you, Jay. Someone just for you. Let me be that person."

Jay covered Alexei's broad hands with his own.

He wanted that. More than anything.

"I won't let him take me away from you," Jay vowed. And he was doing it again. Making promises he didn't know how to keep.

He listened carefully to the sounds of Alexei's breath slowing and deepening. Jay hadn't felt such conflicting emotions since...well, since Vee had died. He was on the one hand almost delirious with happiness at the thought that Alexei wanted him to stay, to be his person. But then on the other hand, there was the dread. The horrible dread. Because if Alexei got in Wolfe's way—if he tried to fight for Jay—he'd lose in a heartbeat.

And Jay wanted to fight for himself, he really did, but he'd never been a fighter. Not once in his unnaturally long life.

And more than that, Jay *owed* Wolfe. He didn't want to hurt his friend, even if his friend was being a massive jerk face at the moment.

So what was a vampire to do?

Jay clenched his teeth to stop the chattering as his body became racked once again with shivers.

It felt like his bones might shake out of his body with the force of it. Was that something that could happen? Probably not, he figured, knowing what he did of basic anatomy.

But he'd never gone this long without feeding before. Who could really say?

He figured eventually the shivers must stop; maybe his blood would freeze in his veins, and he'd become some sort of little vampire popsicle.

Jay had never had a popsicle before. They always looked so refreshing on TV. But weren't they really just big flavored ice cubes?

He was vaguely aware—underneath the fuzzy thoughts of popsicles—of a loud banging coming from somewhere, then some crashing noises, and finally a presence in the room with him. Jay should maybe be feeling alarmed right about now? The den members had probably come for him at last.

But his head felt too much like mush to really muster up the proper emotions. Maybe that was better. He wouldn't give them the satisfaction of his fear. Just his shivers.

"Johann."

Oh. Jay knew that voice. Wolfgang was here. Was he the appointed executioner?

Jay debated turning his head to the side to take a look—he was currently sprawled on the incredibly uncomfortable love seat Vee had always said was "more for aesthetic purposes than practical ones"—but he didn't quite feel up to it. "I thought I bolted the front door," he managed to say, his voice coming out quite hoarse, vibrating with his tremors.

"You did. I broke it."

That made Jay laugh a little, but with another bout of shivers going, it came out strange. Like a death rattle.

"You're aware you can't actually die by starvation, aren't you, little one?" Wolfe asked, sounding calm and cool as ever.

"'M aware," Jay mumbled.

"Then what exactly is your goal here? No one's seen you leave this house for more than a month. Have you really not fed for that long?" The sound of Jay's teeth chattering was apparently answer enough, and Wolfe let out a long-suffering sigh. "Look at me, Johann."

As tired as Jay was, disobeying a direct order went against his very nature (or at least, the nature Vee had cultivated so carefully). He painfully turned his head with a series of stuttered, jerky movements.

Yep. That was Wolfe all right. Jay's...sort of friend? He was definitely frightening, in his own way, but he wasn't overtly cruel in the fashion of so many of their den members. That was because he knew the importance of restraint, he'd once told Jay.

Also, he didn't mind when Jay asked him questions about his psychopathy, so that gave him points in Jay's book.

Wolfe clucked his tongue at whatever he found in Jay's face. "You're still wearing your suit, I see. I confess I'm surprised. You always seemed most uncomfortable in the clothes Vee made you wear."

Jay didn't have a response to that. In truth, he'd been wearing this same suit since Vee had died (he didn't want to think about that; about her head ripped off, rolling on the ground), he was pretty sure. He'd lost his grasp on time for a long while, after he'd made it home, and when he'd eventually come back to awareness, he was already so cold, and so hungry.

"Your life is your own now, Johann. You can wear what you like."

"You're wearing a suit," Jay pointed out, narrowing his eyes to try to focus through the shivers. A tweed number, to be exact. Wolfe's outfits often had the effect of making the other vampire look mild and unassuming. A master of disguise, Wolfe was.

Wolfe gave a nod of acknowledgment. "I am. But I like suits. You don't."

"For how long?" Jay asked, his brain turning over Wolfe's earlier words. "For how long is my life my own?"

Wolfe gazed at him for a long time then. Jay wasn't a master of social cues by any means, but Wolfe was harder to read than most.

Especially when Jay's eyes kept closing without his permission.

"I think you and I can help each other," Wolfe finally said. "But first, you need to eat something. I've brought you a meal. He's in the foyer." Wolfe walked back to the doorway of the sitting room. "Enter," he ordered to whoever was out there.

A tall, heavy-set man came into the room, his clothes just this side of threadbare. He looked like he had a lot of blood in his body was all Jay could think. He could hear *it rushing through the man's vasculature, in fact. Jay's beastie—who'd curled up inside him long ago, utterly exhausted from the lack of blood—perked up immediately.*

Hungry.

Wolfe made eye contact with the obviously compelled human. "Stay calm, if you please. We're all friends here." He waved a hand at Jay, beckoning him over. "Come, Johann. Starvation will only make you weaker in their eyes."

In the eyes of the den, he meant. In the eyes of those who were probably already weighing Jay's value with or without his head.

Jay had always been weak. Easy prey. He knew that. What was the point of pretending otherwise?

But with this human in the room, his beastie awakened to a renewed hunger, Jay's body moved without his permission. He was off the love seat and crawling onto the floor in seconds, his teeth sinking into the man's wrist as soon as he was within reach, not quite having the strength to stand.

The man gasped, then moaned. Jay drank. And drank. And drank.

It was Wolfe who finally pulled him off, clucking his tongue again like Jay had done something naughty. "Let's not drain him dry, hm?" Wolfe pressed his open mouth against the man's wrist just long enough to stop the bleeding, then made eye contact with the human again. "Stay quiet and still until we return you home."

Jay panted from his spot on the floor. His shivers had finally stopped, the cold chill leaving his bones for the first time in weeks. "I could have killed him."

"You could have," Wolfe conceded. "I stopped you."

"I don't like compelling humans." Jay wasn't sure if Wolfe would understand the connection between Jay's hang-ups and his lack of feeding, but Wolfe nodded in understanding.

"I know."

Jay cocked his head. "You do?"

"I'm an observant man, Johann." Wolfe always did that: referred to himself as a man, as if vampirism was a condition he lived with rather than an identity.

He was strange that way.

Really, Wolfe was strange in general. He was also cold and unfeeling, no matter how well he pretended at concern.

But he wasn't weak. He was strong, especially for a younger vampire. And Jay knew for a fact the other den members feared him. Jay had overheard quite a bit in his time with Vee.

And Wolfe thought they could help each other?

If Jay needed a companion to survive—and who was he really kidding? Of course he did—why not pick the fiercest one there was?

Wolfe held out his hand. Jay, kneeling on the floor, an ungodly amount of blood smeared all over his face, took it.

He let himself be pulled up.

He let himself try again.

Sixteen

Jay

J ay woke to Alexei's lips on his, then Alexei's lips on Jay's cock, and then a long, hot shower.

Jay didn't usually think of showers as sexy occasions, but Alexei managed to make it one, lathering Jay up and doing that thing he apparently did now where he didn't expect Jay to do anything at all except receive pleasure from Alexei's hands.

Was that a human thing, maybe? Because it was really very nice. Like, so nice.

And Jay couldn't even feel properly guilty about it because Alexei seemed to enjoy it so much. He even hummed as he rinsed Jay off. *Hummed.*

But then Alexei's landlord called him about a burst pipe, and Alexei had to leave, and Jay was left on his own.

He didn't know how many hours had passed when his doorbell rang.

Oh, dang it. He'd lost time again. He hadn't meant to. He'd only been thinking, trying to figure out the right next steps. Because Jay had told Alexei he'd stay. But he'd also first promised Wolfe a particular arrangement.

Jay had even considered a pros and cons list about leaving with Wolfe.

Pro: I'd be keeping the promise I made once. Con: I'll be miserable and lonely for the rest of eternity. Double con: I'll miss Alexei more than I can stomach. More than should be possible.

And then had followed the pros and cons of staying.

Pro: I've found true happiness in Hyde Park. I could have Alexei by my side for the rest of his days. Con: Wolfe and the den might get angry and try to murder everyone I love.

Jay knew what he was supposed to do, what Vee would have told him to do: honor his prior commitments and go back with Wolfe. It didn't matter what he *wanted*, only what had to be done.

But Vee's voice wasn't in Jay's head anymore, and Jay had so many people he didn't want to leave. But then again, he shouldn't risk bringing any unwanted drama or violence into his friends' lives, should he? That wasn't why he'd come here.

It was all making his head hurt. He wished Alexei were with him. It would be nice to be held right now, to be told again that he wasn't alone anymore. That he had a person just for him.

Jay jumped as the doorbell rang again. Oh, right.

He found Soren waiting for him on the other side, arching a judgmental brow. "You didn't even check who it was before opening the door, did you?"

Jay shrugged. "No."

Soren placed a (judgmental) hand on his hip. "And what if it had been Wolfe?"

Jay shrugged again. "I would have invited him in, I suppose."

Soren scoffed at that, breezing past Jay into the house, making his way into the living room in his heeled boots. "Big mistake, Jaybird."

Jay closed the door carefully and followed after him. "He's not my enemy, Soren."

"He wants you to leave Hyde Park. That makes him *my* enemy."

Warmth pulsed in Jay's chest even as dismay filled him at the thought of two of his friends being enemies. Really, he'd had no idea Soren wanted him to stay so badly, that he hadn't minded Jay sticking around for so long after an unexpected arrival.

Not that Jay thought Soren had *hated* it. But there was a big difference between tolerating an inconvenience and declaring enmity over Jay's potential removal.

Jay wanted to hug him. He was going to hug him.

But Soren spun around before Jay could fully enter the room, crossing his arms and scowling fiercely. He looked beautiful even when he scowled. He was like Alexei in that way. "Don't look at me like that," Soren warned.

"Like what?" Jay asked, trying to figure out if he should lower his hug-ready arms or just play it off like he'd been stretching.

"Like I just professed my undying devotion and then gave you a solid-gold handbag."

Jay cocked his head, deciding on lowering his arms after all. "Is a solid-gold handbag something someone would want?"

Soren huffed. "We've all just gotten used to having you here is all. Plus, I haven't had a proper chance to fix your horrible fashion sense. Now that I know you have billions? The sky's the limit, baby. We're talking designer. Couture. " Soren spun again and made his way over to the couch, the heels of his boots clacking pleasantly on the wood floors. Did he ever try to tap-dance with those shoes on? Jay bet he could do it. Soren could do anything. Clickety-clack. Clickety-clack.

Soren flopped back against the couch cushions, arms spread wide. "Jay."

Jay shook the mental image of Soren tap-dancing out of his mind. "I'm sorry. Shall I get you a drink?"

"No."

"Tea? Water?"

"No."

"A strawberry Pop-Tart, perhaps?"

"Jaybird. Jesus Christ. Sit down."

Jay sat next to him on the couch, careful to keep an appropriate distance between them. Soren repositioned himself quickly, twisting to face Jay completely, one leg curled up under him.

Jay did his best not to fidget as Soren studied him, but Soren still didn't seem to like what he saw. "You can't be thinking of going with him, Jaybird."

Jay wasn't, not really, but that didn't stop him from pointing out that he should. "It's the right thing to do though."

"And what about your mobster?"

Jay didn't have an answer to that. If he did end up having to go with Wolfe, he couldn't very well take Alexei with him. Jay couldn't stomach the thought of his wonderful human having to put up with the den and all its cruelty.

Soren gave a heavy sigh. "Jaybird. I know you don't have a lot of...experience. But with the scent thing...the instant attraction..." Soren trailed off as Jay cocked his head. Then, exasperation roughening his usually melodic voice, he said, "Well, Jesus. Haven't you considered he could be your mate?"

Ah. This.

"Oh. Yes, I know he's my mate." Jay couldn't help but frown a little at his friend, as much as he loved him. "I'm not stupid, you know."

"I—what? No, you *aren't*," Soren agreed with a fierceness that had Jay smiling, just a little. "It's just— Well, okay. Christ. Aren't you going to do anything about it?"

Jay frowned in confusion. "Like what?"

"Like *turn* him."

"Oh no." Jay shook his head fervently. "I wouldn't do that."

Soren threw up his hands. Jay had to admire how expressive he always was. "Why the fuck not?"

"But why would I?"

"Why. Wouldn't. You?" Soren bit the words out, clearly doing his best not to give in to the impulse to yell, an effort Jay very much appreciated. "He's your mate. Your tether."

Jay took a moment to gather his thoughts. What he was going to say next wasn't something he'd ever voiced aloud to his friends, or to anyone else for that matter. "Well, I can see how it would help *me*, yes. But what about Alexei? Have you ever considered that we need our mates but they don't need us?" Jay held up a finger when it seemed like Soren was going to interrupt him. "Not if they're still human when we find them, that is. Alexei is completely, gloriously human. He doesn't need a tether. He doesn't need me. It would be selfish of me to take his humanity away to serve my own purpose."

"And what does your beastie have to say about all that?"

Jay shifted in his seat. "Oh, well...he'd very much like to turn Alexei." Even now, it was hard to focus with how much his beastie was clamoring for their mate. But Jay wasn't one to give in to the beastie's urges without reason, not when it could hurt other people.

"I—" Soren's words seemed to fail him, and for a while, he just sat and stared at Jay. He didn't seem to know what to say, and Jay didn't want to rush him, so he busied himself straightening the coasters on the coffee table while Soren figured it out. If Alexei were there, Jay could just scatter them on the floor, and they'd both laugh about it. Jay smiled a little at the thought.

A good while after the coasters were all straightened, Soren finally spoke. "What about Gabe, then? You turned him for me."

"He asked me to," Jay answered simply. "And you were in immediate peril, Soren. It was sort of extenuating circumstances."

"And you think, if there hadn't been... You think it would have been wrong to turn him," Soren mused.

Jay shrugged, uncomfortable. He didn't have an easy answer, not when he was so pleased for his friend to have found happiness with his mate.

Soren seemed to consider that for another moment, and then he straightened in his seat, fixing Jay with a surprisingly tender look. "You're wrong, you know. And maybe even a few years ago, I might have agreed. But Gabe does need me. He *did* need me, even as a human. People need love, Jay. Most do, anyway. They need connection. They need to be seen and understood and accepted. I gave that to Gabe. I'll keep giving that to Gabe."

That was such a nice sentiment Jay was tempted to try to hug Soren again.

But Soren was already continuing his speech. "And no, you're not stupid, Jaybird—not at all—but you *are* inexperienced. You tend to put humans on a pedestal. You think their mortality gives them something vital, something maybe you lack. But you know what?"

Jay shook his head when Soren paused to look at him because no, he didn't know. He had no idea.

Soren sighed. "I've been around humans. Some are great. Truly great, I'll give you that. But a lot of them are just...sad. And numb. And their eventual demise doesn't make them wise or deep or anything else you seem to think. It just makes them scared and mean. And you know what I see when Alexei looks at you?"

"What?"

"I see a man who was one of those numb, sad, scared people, who has since seen the fucking light. *You're* the fucking light, Jay. Anyone can see it, the way he looks at you. You really don't think he loves you?"

"Oh, I think he loves me." Jay could feel it, whenever he was with his human. The care. The consideration. The desire and the acceptance. He'd seen it in Alexei's eyes the night before, when he was entering Jay for the very first time.

Jay might not have had much experience with love, but he had plenty of experience with its absence. He could tell the difference.

Soren rubbed at his forehead. Was he getting a headache too? Maybe they were going around. "Then...I don't understand, Jay-bird."

"I may know it, but he hasn't told me so. I don't know if he's ready to. We've only known each other a little bit, barely a few weeks. That's fast, for a human. And if he's not ready to even say the words, he's definitely not ready for eternal commitment. Even if he were...I don't take turning someone lightly. I never will."

Soren's face was a strange mix of sad and amused. "Oh, Jaybird. You just— Okay. All right then. Go at your own pace."

Jay smiled at him. See? Soren had such a big heart, underneath all that snark. Jay had always known so.

They sat in comfortable silence for a while before Soren broke it. "I used to envy you, you know."

"Because Vee was so much nicer than Hendrick?"

Soren waved a dismissive hand at the mention of their makers. "Because *you* were so much nicer than *me*. Because you managed to stay so sweet and kind, even in that toxic atmosphere."

Jay hadn't had any idea Soren felt that way. The thought that there was any part of him enviable to Soren was almost laughable. "You don't think that makes me weak?"

"I think it makes you anything but weak."

"I've lost other things though. Other parts of myself." Like Soren had said, Jay was lacking in life experience of all kinds. Stunted.

"I know you have, Jaybird."

"I've always envied *you*. Your bravery. Your boldness."

Soren laughed airily. "Oh, I've got plenty of other faults to make up for it."

"But Gabe loves you as you are."

"Yes, he does," Soren said softly, his expression turning serious once again. "And he doesn't regret turning. I know that for a fact, through the bond if nothing else. What he's gained means more to him than what he lost."

Jay knew that was probably true. But Gabe had only been a vampire for less than a year. How would he feel after two hundred more?

What was right, what was wrong, and what was just a matter of choice?

Jay wished someone could tell him for sure.

Seventeen

Alexei

The burst pipe was...well, it was what it was.

The incident had apparently occurred in the attic, and water had flooded through a crack in the ceiling to Alexei's bedroom, ruining his bedding and a good portion of his clothes. None of that bothered Alexei. What he did check—more frantic than he would have thought—was the little cabinet in his bedside table, which was already warped on the outside but blessedly dry on the inside.

He dug out the contents with care. It wasn't much, just a few photos of his mother, of his brothers, even one of his father he hadn't had the guts to burn yet.

It's hard to hate the people who raised you.

It wasn't exactly true. Maybe for Jay, who was good and kind and pure, all the things Alexei really wasn't (no matter how often Jay may call him the nicest human). But for Alexei, the struggle was keeping that hatred *pure*. The love kept creeping in against his will, built out of tiny, inconsequential moments. The time his father had taken him—only him, not Ivan or Sascha—to a baseball game (Alexei had later found out his father was there for business more than anything else, disappearing for a good hour and leaving Alexei alone with his hot dog). Seeing his father dancing with his mother in the kitchen (Alexei had always wondered how he had wooed her, in the beginning. By pretending to have a heart? How had she possibly been fooled?). The strange, almost proud look in his father's eyes every time Alexei grew another inch (and wasn't that the kicker: the only part of Alexei his father approved of was the thing over which he had no control).

As if summoned by his thoughts, by his proximity to the photos, a familiar number lit up Alexei's phone. Alexei debated leaving it. He should have switched out phones days ago. Should have changed it out the second after he'd hung up the last time, in point of fact.

Still, he pressed the little green button. "Sascha."

"You haven't changed your number yet. That's quite sloppy of you, Alyosha."

That cold, monotone recital definitely wasn't Sascha's voice.

"Vanya," Alexei greeted, using the diminutive of his brother's name in turn—just to be an asshole—while simultaneously cursing himself for picking up the phone.

"You really pissed me off, Alexei, you know that? That was an important deal you fucked up."

Alexei stared at the picture in his hand, the one of the three of them, all standing careful inches apart, Sascha the only one smiling. "That's good. I meant to."

A long silence. Alexei was almost positive Ivan was picturing the many ways he'd like to kill him.

Alexei got bored of the quiet after about ten seconds. "Are you coming for me, then?"

"I don't know where you are, I'm afraid. Stay on this call long enough and I might be able to find out."

The pointed warning—so out of character for Ivan—could mean one of two things: either Ivan already knew where Alexei was and thus didn't give a fuck if Alexei hung up too soon, or he wasn't coming for Alexei at all. He was actually letting him go.

How stupid would Alexei have to be to believe it to be the latter? And yet he really hoped it was, that they could just...be free of each other. "I didn't figure you to be so sentimental, Vanya."

"Maybe you're just not worth my time."

"Maybe not. Always was second best."

"Idiot. Sascha's second best. I don't know what *you* are." When Alexei didn't rise to the bait, Ivan paused for only a moment before continuing on. "Aren't you going to miss the money, Alyosha? You haven't exactly stashed much away. You haven't been withdrawing from your accounts either."

Alexei had already assumed Ivan was monitoring his bank activity, so that little dig wasn't any sort of surprise. Looking at the pictures in his hand, Alexei realized he needed one of Jay. One where Jay didn't look so horribly stiff and uncomfortable, dressed in a suit Alexei just knew he must have hated. "Would you believe me if I said I'm hooking up with a billionaire?"

"No, I really wouldn't. Too high-profile for you, if nothing else."

"This one's...underground."

Another pause, then dark, taunting laughter from Ivan's side of the line. "Oh, Alyosha. Are you telling me you went to all the trouble of burning your bridges, leaving your family in the soot and the wreckage, only to plunge yourself into new criminal activity? That's adorable."

Ivan wasn't exactly wrong. Alexei thought about what would happen if Jay couldn't stay in Hyde Park after all. If he asked Alexei to go back to the den with him (Alexei could only hope Jay would ask him—he was too big to stow away in one of Jay's suitcases), one with cruel vampires, strange power plays, and blood money soaking through its roots.

And yet Alexei would go, no question. In whatever capacity Jay would have him.

If Jay asked to be his master, the way Vee had been to Jay, Alexei would serve him gladly. Grateful for the chance to stay close.

The irony didn't escape Alexei; it was the kind of devotion his brother had always wanted from him and Alexei had never been willing to give.

He sighed, tucking the photos into his back pocket. "Just know, if you *are* tracing this and you send someone after me, they won't survive the encounter."

"Like I said, adorable." It was clear Ivan didn't believe Alexei's threat. Fine by Alexei. Ivan would learn soon enough, if he decided to test it. In the meantime, Alexei wanted out of this conversation. He would keep the photos, but his flesh-and-blood brother was staying behind him. "Take care of Sascha for me, Vanya."

There was only silence in response. Alexei hung up. He'd probably stayed on the phone for too long after all, but it was hard to care. He and Jay had bigger, stronger, immortal fish to fry.

Alexei gathered up what meager belongings he cared to—mostly a few articles of clothing—and placed them in a duffel, sending a text to Jay.

You've got a stray coming your way, kitten.

He opened the door, feeling surprisingly light for all the insanity of the past twenty-four hours.

That was until he saw the bigger fish in question standing at his doorstep, wearing another tweed fucking suit, smirking at the shock on Alexei's face.

Decades of experience remaining calm in potentially life-threatening situations had Alexei's voice staying even as he greeted his unwelcome guest. "Wolfgang. What a surprise."

"Is it?" The way Wolfe cocked his head with the question reminded Alexei so much of Jay, and the reminder in that moment—a moment where odds were quite high Alexei wouldn't survive—physically hurt, like a fist slamming into his sternum. "You see," Wolfe drawled. "As far as I can tell, you're the only thing standing between myself and what I want. It would be perfectly reasonable for me to snap your neck right now."

Alexei let out a slow breath. "I suppose it would be."

It had been a long, long time since Alexei had been afraid to die—possibly since he was too young to remember—a character trait his father had worked so hard to instill in him. And Alexei had to hand it to the bastard: that lack of fear was how he'd survived so long in the toxic environment in which he'd been raised, how he'd been able to do something as fundamentally stupid as cost Ivan a massive amount of money and flee into the night. Alexei hadn't cared enough about his life to weigh the consequences with any seriousness, hadn't honestly cared much whether he'd succeed or get caught.

Only instinct—that deep, wretched animal part of his brain that wanted to survive at all costs—had led to him trying as hard as he had to lie low.

But he cared now. And with that caring came fear, more over-whelming than he remembered it to be. Alexei's next breath was stuttered, the fear tightening his throat, but his voice somehow still came out even enough. "Is that what you're going to do?" he asked when Wolfe said nothing more. "Snap my neck?"

"I've been quite seriously considering it," Wolfe mused, letting out a heavy sigh. "But I fear it would make our Johann even more difficult to handle in the end. The loss of a mate can make a vampire so...unpredictable. Too hard to control the outcome."

"The loss of—excuse me?" Oh fuck. There was that fist to the sternum again. Because Alexei could have sworn Wolfe was implying...

What was he implying?

Wolfe's lips twisted into a half smile. "Tell me you're not that stupid," he said, false pity lacing his tone.

Which was maybe fair. Because apparently Alexei *was* that stupid. Or maybe just blind? Or possibly simply confused.

Was Wolfe really saying Alexei was Jay's mate?

And really, if he was Jay's mate, why the fuck hadn't Jay *said* anything? For someone so wide open with all his emotions—Alexei had once overheard Jay telling someone's *dog* that he was feeling a little sad that morning—Jay had been holding a lot of cards awfully close to his chest.

"If I'd known sending Johann to Hyde Park would have such consequences, I never would have allowed it." Wolfe tutted. "I wonder though. If I allowed you to accompany us back, would you interfere?"

Alexei did his best to keep up with the turn in the conversation, despite the way his head was spinning with the fucking bomb Wolfe had so casually dropped. "You mean with the marriage part?"

Wolfe tipped his chin as if to say, *Obviously the marriage, you fucking moron.*

Alexei considered it—considered how much he truly fucking hated the idea—but he ultimately shrugged, rubbing at the back of his neck. "If it's what Jay really wants...if it's what's necessary to keep him safe...then I don't care about that." He narrowed his eyes at the smug look on Wolfe's face. "As long as you have no plans to consummate, that is." Alexei honestly had no idea if consummating a marriage was still a fucking thing, but he wasn't taking any chances with this archaic den and its archaic arrangements. "You sure you're not in love with him?" he asked again.

"Even if I were capable of such an emotion, he's most assuredly not my type. That kind of sweetness leaves an unbearably saccharine taste in my mouth, I'm afraid."

Anger bubbled in Alexei's chest. "He's the most perfect vampire to ever exist in the fucking universe, asshole. You would *be* so lucky."

Wolfe's gaze hardened. "I'll forgive the rudeness, just this once. Clearly emotions are running high."

Despite his words, Wolfe stalked a few steps closer to the door, and it took everything in Alexei not to take a step back in return. More than any of the other vampires he'd met so far—Soren and his creepy grin included—Wolfe had the primal, animal part of Alexei's brain signaling, *Dangerous. Predator. Stay back.*

"You would have to join us as a companion, of course. We wouldn't be informing the den about the mate bond. Mate trumps husband, in vampire circles, and I might end up left out in the cold. I can't allow that."

"You really care an awful lot about leading this vampire den." Alexei had the brief, possibly stress-induced thought that Wolfe and Ivan would probably get along like a goddamn house on fire.

Wolfe shrugged, somehow making the gesture look classy as hell. "I care about quality of life. *My* quality of life. When looking toward an eternity of living, one has to plan ahead. It's not as easy these days, to acquire wealth the old-fashioned way." At Alexei's questioning look, Wolfe waved a hand. "Killing a rich victim and taking their money, for instance. Compelling someone, or many someones. There are too many electronic trails, too much surveillance. And with that kind of technology, with facial recognition software, for example, how long before vampires are outed? There is strength in numbers, even if those numbers may be...odious."

So not just a power-hungry vampire psychopath. A power-hungry, *conspiracy theorist* vampire psychopath? Jay really knew how to pick his friends.

But what it came down to, as it ever did, was that Alexei would do anything to stay by Jay's side. Alexei didn't care about his title, the legalities of their arrangement (or okay, he did care but not enough to make it the deal breaker that kept him and Jay apart). So he nodded like Wolfe was making sense. "Okay. Yes, I'll be Jay's companion, if that's what he wants."

"What Jay wants...," Wolfe mused, taking another step closer. "You see, I'm afraid that's the thing. After many years of friendship"—Wolfe managed to make the word sound ironic—"I know how Johann thinks. And I fear he may...dillydally, you could say. Because of your humanity. He would fear bringing you to the den in your fragile condition. Likewise, he would be afraid to turn you and take away that which makes you so precious in his mind. And while killing you would invoke grief I'm not equipped to deal with, *turning* you, on the other hand..."

Now Alexei did step back. He knew running into the house would be a stupid fucking move, but there was a back door to the apartment. If he could just get there in time.

But of course he couldn't. *Didn't.*

Because Wolfe moved just as fast as Jay did when Jay was trying to get closer to Alexei. And what was so charming in his sweet little vampire was fucking terrifying in Wolfe.

Alexei was on his back in an instant, the breath knocked clean out of him, Wolfe straddling his thighs, pinning Alexei with an ease that would have been insulting had he not been supernatural.

"You know," Wolfe said softly, squeezing Alexei's wrists to the point of pain. "*You'd* really be much more my type, under ordinary circumstances. How *big* you are. With all those delightfully complex emotions hiding in that fragile little skull. Lucky for you I have no interest in someone so devoted to another, hm? Now, wrist or neck?"

Alexei didn't waste time pleading. He could tell it wouldn't do any good and might, for that matter, serve to aggravate Wolfe instead. All Alexei could do was hope Wolfe was speaking truly about his intentions. That he would turn Alexei, not drain him dry and leave him for dead.

"My wrist," Alexei said, voice like gravel.

His neck was for Jay. Only ever for Jay.

Wolfe grimaced. "How predictable." But he did as Alexei asked, raising Alexei's right wrist as his fangs dropped down, those flat brown eyes turning black. "You smell strangely sweet. I wonder if your blood will match."

He bit down.

Wolfe drank quickly, much more quickly than Jay ever had. Alexei only felt a momentary spike of unwanted pleasure before he was already drowsy, fading, barely able to swallow the drops of warm liquid he felt dribbling into his mouth.

And then everything was fire.

Eighteen

Jay

Jay got a little concerned when Alexei didn't show up more than an hour after his text.

Not *too* concerned, because Jay wasn't quite sure what he had meant by bringing home a stray, and maybe Alexei was stopping to pick up an *actual* stray, like a puppy or something? A task like that could cause all kinds of delays.

But that was probably too much to hope for; a week of dating was too soon in the puppy-giving timeline, Jay was pretty sure. Roman had waited almost a year before he'd gotten Ferdy for Danny, after all. Although, Roman was a vampire, not a human, so maybe that was different?

Also, Jay's apartment didn't allow dogs. Should he text Alexei and warn him about that?

But then Jay got more than a little concerned when it had been two hours with no sign of either Alexei or a puppy and Alexei wasn't answering his calls.

And then he got *very* concerned when he received a text from Wolfe instead.

It might be wise to check up on your human right about now.

That was not a good text. That could very well be classified as a bad text. His beastie's hackles rose in response, a new, fearful sort of tension flooding his body.

What had Wolfe done?

The trip to Alexei's apartment passed in a blur. Jay didn't have a car yet—he'd been told by his friends he had to be 70 percent less of a menace on the road before he could consider one—so he was traveling on foot and probably moving more quickly than was wise for blending in with humans. But it was cold enough there weren't many people out on the streets, so hopefully no one noticed.

Alexei's car was in front of the apartment, and his door was unlocked.

"Alexei!" Jay called, rushing inside, hoping to find—well, he didn't know what he was hoping to find other than Alexei safe and whole and happy to see him.

But the next sound out of Jay's mouth was a broken wail, coming from somewhere deep in his chest, from a place he hadn't known could hurt this badly.

Because Alexei's glorious form was sprawled out on the couch, and he was still—much too still—with no audible heartbeat at all, the coppery smell of blood in the air matching the red streaking his too-pale wrist.

"No, no, no." Jay felt sick. He felt hot. He felt...he didn't know. He didn't *know*.

He moved toward the couch cautiously. He wasn't sure why; it wasn't as if approaching too quickly was going to startle anyone. Maybe he was hoping to delay confirming...whatever he would be confirming.

It hurt to swallow. This was all his fault. He'd brought Alexei into contact with vampires, and now his human was *clearly not breathing*, and any minute, Jay's beastie was going to rip out and—and—

Jay paused a foot from the couch, his vision cloudy with tears he hadn't known he was shedding. His beastie was oddly...fine. It was alert but no longer clamoring for Alexei in the way it had been. More like his beastie was...expectant. Waiting for something.

Jay sniffed, wiped his eyes, and looked closer at the scene in front of him.

Blood was on Alexei's wrist, yes, but it wasn't actively bleed-ing—whatever bite had been there was already healed. There was no heartbeat, not yet, but Alexei's chest, once Jay dared to touch it, was warm.

Oh. *Oh.*

Jay had seen this process before.

Turning, Jay's beastie said, smugness radiating from its words. *Our mate is turning.*

Jay was tempted to yell at his beastie for its self-satisfaction. They weren't allowed to be happy about this. This wasn't how it was supposed to go.

He sat down gingerly on the coffee table, facing Alexei, clasping his hands to keep them from shaking, and did his best to reconcile this new reality with the pain he'd felt thinking his human had been killed. It took a long time for his tremors to stop, but he didn't lose time, at least. He couldn't afford to be so careless with reality right now.

Alexei's heart may not have been beating at the moment, but it *would*. And after those first few beats would come awareness. He'd need Jay then. He'd need reassurance, guidance...

And blood. Alexei would need blood.

Jay took a few slow, deep breaths, pleased when his fingers didn't even tremble taking his phone out of his pocket. He pressed on Soren's name in his contacts.

"Jaybird! What's up?" Soren answered in a casual drawl. "Con-fessed your undying love to the human yet?"

Jay cleared his throat, hoping his voice would match the steadi-ness of his hands. Nobody needed his weakness, not right now. "Wolfe's...done something." Okay. Well, his voice was clear enough, so that was good, but it was still sort of a pathetic attempt, when Jay couldn't even say the words out loud.

He took another deep breath. "He's turned Alexei, Soren."

"Jesus fucking Christ." There was no more lazy drawl in Soren's voice. "How's Alexei taking it? How are *you* taking it? When do we kill Wolfe?"

Jay didn't know what to do with the last question, but still, how lucky he was to have such a fierce friend on his side. "He's not awake yet. I need to stay with him. Do you think Gabe could bring some blood from the hospital? Just this once."

Danny had lectured Jay before on the importance of not stealing bags of donated blood from humans who needed it, and Jay had taken that very much to heart. But for Alexei...

Soren tsked. "We'll bring as many bags as you need. I don't have Danny's moral code against blood stealing; I'll empty out the whole hospital if you ask me."

"Um." Jay couldn't tell if Soren was joking or not. "I don't think that will be necessary."

"And Wolfe?" Soren's voice held a dangerous edge.

"Leave him be."

"*Jay.*"

Jay sighed. "This isn't me being too nice or too naive or too anything else you want to call me. He knows I know he did it—he's the one who told me Alexei was...hurt. He'll defend himself against any attack. And I don't want anyone *else* hurt. And—and he could have killed Alexei, if he wanted to. He didn't."

"He still needs to be dealt with. This is some Lucien-level fuckery."

"And Lucien is still very much alive, isn't he?" Jay countered, feeling a little pleased with himself for coming up with it. "But...I know. We need to have a— Um, a sit-down. Somewhere public. Neutral ground. So none of our people are in danger of getting hit."

"Jaybird." Now it sounded like Soren was holding back a laugh, which was a little unkind, considering Jay was coming up with some really great ideas. "Have you been watching mobster movies by chance?"

Jay was grateful Soren couldn't see his flush over the phone. "Um. When Alexei told me about his past, I wanted to do some research."

Soren didn't quite hold the laugh back this time. Jay didn't mind all that much, really. They'd both been exposed to so much trauma and violence in the den, and Jay knew Soren was skilled at getting his laughs in where he could (even if Jay thought he'd acted totally reasonably). "What did you choose for your *research*?"

"I started with *The Sopranos*, but I didn't get very far. Tony wasn't very nice to his wife."

"That's the *Italian* Maf— You know what, not important right now. We'll bring the blood. See you soon."

After Soren hung up, Jay leaned forward to smooth Alexei's pretty hair back from his handsome face. He pressed a kiss to Alexei's cheek. He grabbed onto his human's cold hand.

And he waited.

The first beats of Alexei's heart sent Jay's own hammering.

It was happening. It was *happening*.

Jay tightened his grip on Alexei's hand, his beastie alert and watchful.

Soren had told Jay bonded mates could feel each other's emotions. How would Alexei feel when he woke up? Scared? Regretful? Resentful, even? It was Jay's fault this had happened. Maybe Alexei would never want to speak to Jay ever again. And Jay would respect that. He *would*.

He stilled himself for the onslaught, not daring even to breathe, his entire being focused on Alexei's face.

But the only thing Jay felt through the bond when Alexei opened those pretty multicolored eyes was…relief. Followed by affection. Desire. And a mix of the two that felt an awful lot like love.

Jay's breath left him in a rush. Oh, it was there all right. Jay had been right before. Alexei had so much love for Jay.

"You're here." Alexei's voice was raspy, like he'd just woken up from a long sleep. Which Jay supposed he had.

Jay squeezed Alexei's hand. "Of course I am. Alexei, I'm so, so sorr—"

"My mate," Alexei said, his gravelly voice so full of satisfaction that Jay could recognize it even without the added help of the bond.

Jay bit at his lip. "I'm sorry I didn't tell—" His words were cut off in a gasp as, in one smooth motion, Alexei rose into a seated position and pulled Jay onto his lap, curling forward to nuzzle his head into Jay's neck like a big blond puppy.

"Smell so good," he murmured, nosing at Jay's skin.

It was Alexei who smelled so good, but Jay didn't feel like arguing the point. Instead, he dealt with his frazzled nerves by petting Alexei's lovely hair, untangling all the messy bits with his fingers while Alexei nuzzled at him.

Alexei sighed with pleasure at the contact. "I don't regret it." He spoke the words into Jay's neck, and they came out slightly muffled. "Don't be sorry, kotyonok."

Jay worked his fingers through the soft strands for a few long moments as he considered what to say. "I would have done it differently is all."

That wasn't all, not when Jay wasn't sure he would have done it in the first place—taken away Alexei's humanity—but he didn't think Alexei would appreciate all his doubts and hesitations at the moment.

Alexei lifted his head and straightened to his full seated height, a half smile on his lips as he met Jay's eyes. "Oh yeah? How would you have done it?"

Jay took a moment to think, playing with the ends of Alexei's hair now. "Candles" was what he came up with. He'd seen enough romantic movies to know that was the very thing when trying to set a scene. "Lots of candles. Like a million of them. No overhead lighting at all, just soft, flickering candlelight."

Alexei's half smile deepened. "Candles."

"And flowers!" Jay exclaimed, accidentally tugging on Alexei's hair with his enthusiasm as he got into the idea. "Big bouquets everywhere. With red rose petals on the bed."

"You do watch a lot of movies, don't you, kitten?"

Jay flushed at the dig but stuck to his guns anyway. "It should have been romantic," he argued, afraid he was coming dangerously close to pouting. "It should have been *me*. It was—it was—" He struggled to find the right words "—it was so *rude* of Wolfgang, to do that without asking."

Alexei's smile grew tender, his eyes unbelievably soft as he stroked Jay's cheek. "He said he thought it would make you a little less...conflicted, if the deed was done."

"But now I'm angry!" Jay scowled in demonstration, pointing a finger at his furrowed brow. "And I hate being angry. He's not going to bully us into going."

"I'll go with you to the den, Jay. If it's necessary. I don't mind, even if we have to pretend..."

"No," Jay said firmly. "Taking your human life away is one thing. I'm not letting him take it and then drag you into such a terrible place." He twisted a strand of Alexei's hair around two fingers. "I want to give you...goodness, Alexei. My friends here are *good*. We deserve to stay with them. We deserve good things. We deserve a life of our choosing." He gave the hair a gentle tug. "No more— No more meanies."

Alexei hugged him closer. "All right, kitten. No more meanies."

He nuzzled at Jay's neck again, his warm breath tickling Jay's skin enough to have Jay squirming. "Hungry," Alexei groaned.

"Oh." Jay moved to get up, to fetch his supplies, but Alexei's arms tightened into a cage. Jay tapped at Alexei's shoulder. "Gabe brought us some blood. Let me go and I'll grab it."

"Not hungry for blood," Alexei murmured, nosing along Jay's jawline. "Hungry for *you*."

"Oh. *Oh*."

Danny had told Jay about this once: the heightened craving he'd had for Roman in the beginning (and still had, as far as Jay could tell). Was Alexei feeling that same pull?

Jay's beastie started purring, immensely pleased with this turn of events.

Alexei lifted his head from Jay's neck, his pretty eyes looking dazed and heavy-lidded already, like with the serious discussion out of the way, his need for Jay had gone from zero to a hundred. "Where's your lube, sweetheart? Need to open you up, baby. Need to be inside you."

Yes, definitely zero to a hundred.

The dirty words sent a rush of heat through Jay's body, mixing strangely with the lust he could now feel radiating off Alexei through the bond.

"Um." Jay tried to focus on something besides his own hardening erection. Lube. Lube? He had a bag on the floor, from when he'd bought supplies before, still not put away because he was trying to embrace casual messiness. Jay pointed at it, since Alexei didn't seem inclined to release his hold, and Alexei folded over with Jay still in his arms, grabbing hold of the lube and settling them both back onto the couch.

"Naked," Alexei grunted.

Jay rushed to comply, but the act of getting undressed without letting go of each other—because Alexei still seemed completely unwilling to release Jay for even a moment—had Jay giggling. That soon turned to gasping when Alexei's thick, impatient, talented fingers got to work opening him up.

He didn't treat Jay like glass this time. Jay wasn't sure if that was because it wasn't his first time or because Alexei could sense through the bond how eager he was or just that Alexei was *that* hungry for him that he couldn't go slow.

Either way, it wasn't long before he was lining that big cock up to Jay's entrance, and then Jay was sinking down slowly.

Oh God. He was full. So very, very full. *Perfectly* full.

When he was seated all the way, his bottom brushing against the soft hairs on Alexei's strong thighs, Alexei stroked his cheek, looking awed. "Want to try it, kotyonok? Try moving your hips for me."

Oh, right. Because Jay was on top.

But Alexei helped in the beginning, guiding Jay's movements with his hands on Jay's hips. "Perfect," he praised, as if Jay was doing it all on his own. Even in his newly turned state, Alexei was so nice to Jay. The nicest in the world. "My perfect vampire," he crooned. "My perfect kitten. My perfect mate."

Jay watched in fascination as his own cock bobbed with every move of his hips. He angled himself so the leaking tip brushed against Alexei's warm stomach instead. Oh goodness, that was nice. He did it again and again, even as Alexei's hands traveled from his hips to stroke Jay's back, his neck, his nipples.

Jay could feel this deep, almost obsessive satisfaction coming from Alexei, at filling Jay up, at being connected in this way. It pulsed with each one of Jay's whimpers, his little moans.

And Jay loved that he was making them both feel so good, but he wanted...he wanted something else. "Take over?" he pleaded breathlessly.

He worried for a second that Alexei would be disappointed in him, but his mate's eyes only darkened further—not all the way black, not yet—and he let out this sexy, growly-type sound that was new. "You want me to help you move, sweetheart? You want to relax and let me do all the work, hm?"

Jay nodded frantically, not even embarrassed because he could *feel* how hot Alexei found it. Alexei's hands moved back down to Jay's hips, squeezing there, and then he was pressing Jay down at the same time Alexei's hips pumped up, hitting that one wonderful spot, and ohhh. That was nice.

That was good. That was so good.

Jay's body went limp with pleasure as he moaned, and he wrapped his arms around Alexei's neck, slumping against Alexei's broad chest. He tucked his head into the crook of Alexei's shoulder, inhaling that wonderful vanilla scent, and let his mate move them both.

He lost himself a little then, feeling so wonderfully loose and pliant and a little unmoored, overwhelmed with the intensity of their combined emotions flooding through him, but Jay was brought back to awareness with a start as sharp teeth sank into his neck.

Oh. *Oh.* Alexei was biting Jay. He was drinking from him.

"Oh God. Oh my goodness," Jay moaned, waves of dark pleasure rocking through him.

He came, startling himself with the force of it, throbbing and shaking and barely in control of his own muscles. *Which is fine*, Jay thought dreamily, *because Alexei is moving my muscles for me.*

Alexei groaned into Jay's neck—a low, growly sound—and slammed Jay's body once, twice, three times more before Jay felt the warmth of Alexei's release flooding into him.

He twitched with the sensation. Jay loved it. He loved being filled by Alexei. He loved this physical connection.

And he loved Alexei. So, so much.

"I love you too," Alexei murmured, licking at Jay's neck, at the bite he'd left there.

Had Jay said that out loud?

"I can feel it," Alexei told him, still apparently reading Jay's mind. "I can feel your love for me."

Jay made an incoherent mumbling sound in response.

Alexei pressed a kiss to his neck. "Was—was that okay, sweetheart?"

"Sex is always okay," Jay sighed happily. "I think I want to do it all the time."

Alexei's answering chuckle made his chest vibrate against Jay's body. "No, kotyonok. The bite."

"Oh." Jay somehow found the strength to lean back and make eye contact, a little sad to see Alexei's face had already returned to its human form. Jay would really like to meet Alexei's beastie. "Very okay. It's...um..." He could feel himself flushing. "Biting is a form of intimacy between vampires."

Alexei smiled at him, the tiniest spot of blood—Jay's blood—still lingering at the corner of his lips. "My cock is still inside you and you're blushing over a bite?"

Now Jay's cheeks were absolutely on fire. "I'm just— It's another...first. For me."

That intense sense of satisfaction pulsed through the bond again. "Good thing too. You taste so delicious no vampire would give you up after a bite."

Jay squirmed with pleasure at the nice words, and Alexei hissed, raising Jay by the hips and moving him off his softening cock.

Jay tried not to pout, but he wasn't quite successful. "I wasn't ready yet."

Alexei laughed lightly, but there was a new tension in his brow. "Sorry, kitten. But I think I might need that blood now."

Right. Because it may have been intimate, but vampire blood wasn't going to give Alexei the nourishment he needed.

So Jay fetched him the blood and watched his newly turned mate feed. Alexei's beastie was just as pretty as Alexei himself, even if the black covered all the multicolored goodness of his eyes. Jay found himself wishing they had time to stay in this apartment for the next month or so, to learn these new sides of each other and explore this bond.

But they had plans to make. People to call.

Meanies to chastise.

Nineteen

Alexei

They chose one of the fancier, quieter bars in town for the meeting with Wolfe.

Alexei wasn't quite sure why Jay was so convinced his psycho-pathic intended wouldn't start a fight with humans around—it wasn't like Wolfe had been the picture of restraint so far—but Jay had told him assuredly that Wolfe was practical, avoidant of "scenes," and incredibly wary of being outed for what they were by the human population.

So a quiet yet populated bar. One with leather-clad booths, dim lighting, and cocktail prices more suited for a big city than an outdoorsy tourist town.

One where Alexei could smell the overwhelming scent of human blood, pulsing away beneath each patron's skin. It was his first time out in public since turning, and there had been brief concern from the others he wouldn't be able to focus. And yes, his "beastie" was on high alert, but its focus was—as Alexei's had been from the very first moment in the café—zeroed in on Jay. On his scent (which, now that Alexei had turned, he could tell had a strange metallic edge under the peppermint); on his mood (an intoxicating blend of nerves, anger, and residual lust); on trying to figure out the quickest viable way to be touching him again (skin on skin, cock to cock, filling him up and making him keen). Its mantra at all times was to touch Jay, taste Jay, claim Jay, love Jay.

It made Alexei almost wonder if that obsessive pull to Jay from the very beginning had always been his beastie, lying dormant, waiting only to be awoken.

The human blood in this bar, in contrast, was only the most minor distraction. Alexei had fed on blood bags just an hour before; he wasn't hungry.

But he was realizing that counting on Wolfe not to resort to violence might have only been half the equation. What would this new beast in Alexei not do, when it came to Jay? What did it care for witnesses, innocent bystanders, destruction of property?

Behave, he chastised preemptively. It rumbled its pained disapproval in return.

Wolfe was already waiting for them, an open bottle of wine on the table, when Jay and Alexei walked in, Soren and Gabe right behind them. Jay had told the others to stay behind ("we don't want it to feel like an ambush").

"Alexei," Wolfe purred once they reached the table, the ghost of a smile on his lips. "You're looking quite well."

Jay frowned, halting their little group's forward momentum with one hand, a surprisingly imperious gesture. "Before we sit," he said primly. "Wolfgang, what you did was very rude."

Wolfe swirled his glass of red wine without lifting it from the table, in that way old-money people sometimes did. "Some might say I did you a favor, Johann."

Jay folded his arms across his chest. "Some might, but *I* don't." He raised his chin. "I request a formal apology."

There was a brief stare-down between the two, Alexei's beast ready to do violence at the smallest sign Jay wasn't appeased, and then Wolfe tipped his own chin in conciliation. "I apologize, Johann. For taking something from you I cannot return."

"Thank you," Jay answered solemnly.

And just like that, Alexei felt some of the uncharacteristic anger that had been simmering in his mate, palpable through their bond, recede. And that seemed to be it, for Jay. He took a seat next to

Wolfe, reaching for the drink menu with enthusiasm, as if they were at the bar solely for cocktails rather than a strategy meeting. "I've never had a daiquiri," he said brightly. "Do you think they'd make me one here?"

"Not that kind of place, Jaybird," Soren answered, taking his own seat and pulling Gabe down next to him. "Maybe try a White Russian." A wink to Alexei with that little comment. "I think that would suit your tastes."

Alexei took his own seat next to Jay, unable to keep himself from sitting close enough for their arms to brush. Drinks were duly ordered, and a strange, calm silence blanketed the table after the waiter left.

Alexei observed his companions: Wolfe and Jay both looked placidly peaceful, Soren mildly touched in the head, and Gabe supremely uncomfortable. Alexei had no idea what his own face was currently showing; he had decades of experience keeping it unreadable, but having this new creature inside him changed the game a bit. It kept wanting to pop out at inopportune times—mostly whenever they caught a whiff of Jay's peppermint scent and the mindless thing demanded they be joined to their mate immediately, in whatever way possible.

Because if Alexei thought he'd been obsessed with Jay before...well, goddamn. The intensity was...alarming. Or at least, it should have been. Perhaps when he had more time to process it all, it would be. As it was, all he'd been able to muster was immense relief Jay didn't have another mate out there after all, threatening to tear them apart the moment that mate came into the picture.

Jay felt so *much* all the time, his emotions zipping around like fish in a pond. Most of it was positive, which Alexei found a bit shocking, considering Jay's relatively traumatic past. But aside from the anger at Wolfe and the undercurrent of worry over Alexei's new state, it was mostly little bolts of delight and pleasure at the strangest things: a cat's paw prints in the snow, his landlord out on the porch in his robe, the White Russian he now held in his hands.

Alexei was getting a firsthand look into that alien mind, and it was only making him love Jay more, making him want to tuck his perfect mate into his pocket and never let him out again.

Maybe he should see a vampire therapist, when all this was over and done with.

It was Wolfe who broke the silence, apparently unconcerned with the potential power play of letting one's opponent speak first. "So was the point of this meeting simple chastisement, or are we planning out your return? I could book us three tickets as soon as you like."

Jay set down his already half-empty drink and folded his hands. "I want to discuss what it would take for you to let me stay."

"I'm afraid that's not poss—" Wolfe's words cut off with a start, his impeccable posture stiffening even further. He turned in his seat, a wary cast to his gaze, and watched a new party entering the bar. A party of three, one of whom—a tall, blond, sturdy-looking guy somewhere in his thirties—caught a glimpse of them and waved at their table.

"King!" the blond human shouted boisterously. "Fancy seeing you here."

Gabe gave him a grimace and a half-hearted wave back, and the man didn't come any closer, only briefly smirking at Soren, glancing curiously at Alexei, and shooting a wink at Jay (which, holy fuck, Alexei's new beast didn't like one bit).

Wolfe had sunk back into the shadows at the corner of their table, escaping the human's notice altogether. After a moment, as the new trio was directed to a table at the other end of the room, he picked up his wine glass, swirling the ruby liquid there in a much less graceful fashion than before. "Who was that man?"

Soren arched an inquisitive brow but answered the question. "Dr. Monroe. He's not one of us; you don't have to worry about him."

Wolfe took a small swallow of his wine, set his glass down, and tapped one index finger against the table. It was another long moment before he spoke again. Maybe he was as paranoid about humans as Jay had suggested. Finally, he cleared his throat genteelly. "What would be the terms of your staying, Johann?"

If anyone else was shocked by the sudden change from stubborn opposition to careful consideration, they didn't show it in their faces.

"I'd give you half," Jay said, ignoring Soren's immediate protest. "Without the marriage component, of course. You can take it back to the den or keep it all for yourself. I don't care anymore."

Wolfe pursed his lips, thoughtful. "The den wouldn't trust me alone, not without your reputation backing me. That was the point of the whole arrangement."

Jay shrugged, sneaking another sip of his cocktail. "Well, they'd just have to, if they wanted that money to benefit them."

Wolfe considered that, swirling his glass once more. Alexei was tempted to take the damn thing and throw it off the table, but he supposed that would be considered rude. "It's still too much money they'd be losing. They'd come for you; I'm sure of it. They've probably already sent someone. That whole lack of trust in me, you see."

"Well, that's easy," Soren interjected, a broad grin on his face. "We'd kill anyone who tried to take Jay without his consent. The last person who tried to kidnap one of our family is now a pile of ash in the forest."

Alexei felt a strong surge of surprised joy coming from Jay at that word *family* and Jay's implied inclusion in it. Alexei turned to study his face, but Jay was still staring placidly at Wolfe.

Wolfe took a moment to think that over, his gaze wandering the room, catching briefly at the table where the blond doctor now sat with his friends. "I have a different proposal."

"Nothing where Jay leaves," Soren insisted.

Alexei could feel another surge of pleasure run through Jay at Soren's defense. As if he hadn't known before just how important he was to these friends he'd found a home with until that home was threatened.

"It will be tiresome for you all to fight off individual attacks from the den. One of you could get hurt, possibly killed. I could...run interference, in a way. Pass along the message that you've formed your own den, Johann. One with capable protectors. I could even give you my allegiance. Then it's no longer a matter of one run-away companion but a war between two dens. A much more daunting matter for them to consider."

Gabe cleared his throat. "Why can't Jay just tell them that?"

Wolfe shrugged one shoulder. "I doubt they'd believe him, for one. Not without corroboration."

"For half the money?" Jay asked, cocking his head.

"Half the money." Wolfe took a considering sip of his wine. "And I want the doctor."

Soren's grin grew even wider, but his pale eyes turned to ice. "I guess it'll be *two* piles of ash in the forest."

Wolfe waved a dismissive hand at him. "Not *your* doctor. I want the other one. Monroe."

"Well, um... He's not ours to give," Jay pointed out, his brow furrowing in confusion.

At the same time, Gabe scoffed. "Him? Why would you want *him*?"

Soren placed a placating hand on his mate's arm. "Jealousy doesn't suit you, Highness. You know I didn't *actually* sleep with him."

Gabe snorted, but he looked slightly mollified. "You like jealousy on me, brat," he mumbled. "It makes you preen."

Jay cleared his throat, catching both Soren's and Gabe's eyes and tilting his head not so subtly at Wolfe, who was looking quite pained at the interaction. The duo fell silent, but Alexei couldn't help but notice that Soren *was* preening, just the slightest.

"We won't be that kind of den," Jay told Wolfe firmly. "We can't just give you a human from the town."

Wolfe's brow furrowed the tiniest bit in annoyance before he smoothed out his expression quickly. "Fine. Half the money."

"Why?" Alexei asked, speaking up for the first time. "Why change sides like this?"

Wolfe met his eyes, and Alexei hated the little frisson of fear that ran through him at remembering the pain of turning, his worry that he wouldn't wake up again. "I want the stability and protection of a den," Wolfe said, his lips twitching as if he could sense Alexei's fear. He probably could, the creep. "I want funds to live comfortably. I don't particularly need to have loyalty to *that* den in particular. It was convenient at the time. It isn't any longer."

Alexei couldn't shake the suspicion there was more to the story, but Jay giggled. "This is why they don't trust you, you know."

"Yes, well..." Wolfe splayed his hands as if to say, *What can you do?*

"And that's it?" Soren asked, clearly as skeptical as Alexei felt. "Half the money for your...what exactly? Aid? Protection?"

Wolfe let out a dry laugh. "What do you mean, that's it? You act as if it's a paltry sum." He pushed his glass back and rose from the table. "It obviously means I'll need to stay in Hyde Park for a while longer. I have some real estate to peruse, if you don't mind."

And then he walked out. As if the matter had been decided, despite the fact that Jay had never technically agreed.

Alexei turned to Jay, who didn't seem at all surprised by the sudden departure but who nonetheless had an uneasy look on his face. "That was strange," he mused.

"That he gave in so easily?" Alexei asked.

"That he asked for Dr. Monroe as one of his conditions. The companion aspect of the den was never one that appealed to him." Jay frowned. "It was part of why I always liked him."

"You did say he was a psychopath," Soren pointed out.

Jay nodded, but Alexei could still feel tendrils of nervousness coming from him.

Twenty

Jay

The next week of waiting—waiting for news from Wolfe, waiting for potential threats from the den—should have been stressful. And it was. Kind of. Because it would be weird *not* to be stressed about it, right?

But also, it was really, really nice.

Jay had a *mate*. A person just for him. And he was living in Jay's apartment, wanting him all the time.

How could that be anything but the nicest?

And if Jay was being honest, he had to admit he'd always been a little scared of the mate bond. It had always sounded magical, yes, but he'd also imagined how painful it could be for someone to feel every time their partner was angry at or disappointed in them. How badly it would hurt *his* feelings to know for sure he was letting his mate down.

But it was turning out Jay didn't have to fear that at all with Alexei. Or at least not over the little things that had once made Vee so angry.

If Jay was messy, or too talkative, or emotionally needy, or wanted to be held all the time, all he felt from Alexei were these warm, delightful washes of affection. It was the nicest, most comforting thing Jay had ever experienced in all his life.

Who knew love could feel so good? Who knew it didn't have to hurt? That you didn't have to push down parts of yourself just to be accepted?

He'd seen it, of course, with his friends and their mates—he'd technically seen what acceptance could look like—but it was different being inside it. A warm cocoon where Jay felt safe to grow and explore and feel all the things he'd never gotten to before.

And then sometimes it was almost...sharp, Alexei's love for Jay. A little dark, a little possessive, a little obsessive, even. But that felt just as good as the warm, soft love. To know he inspired that kind of devotion in Alexei...Jay couldn't help but be pleased. Because Jay really was an endless pit of need, and he was realizing for the first time how truthful Alexei had been, when he'd said he was hungry to give Jay affection.

Nonetheless, sitting down to their first movie together, Jay felt it best to warn Alexei what was coming. He queued up the movie they'd selected—Alexei had described it as sci-fi horror, and wasn't that an exciting concept?—and turned to Alexei, who was sprawled back on the couch. "Um, I can be a little...loud."

Alexei gave him a lazy, heated look. "Mm. I know, kotyonok. You moan with the best of them."

Jay's cheeks grew warm. "I'm not talking about *that*. Watching movies. I had to stop going to the theaters because I kept getting shushed by everyone." Jay hadn't even known how loud he was being until the other audience members got mad at him. He'd been afraid to go back after that.

Jay could feel a pulse of anger coming from his mate, but Alexei's face didn't show it. Instead, he cocked his head. "You think I'd mind? You can talk through the entire movie if you like, sweetheart. You can yodel for all I care."

Jay giggled at that. "Why would I yodel?"

Alexei shrugged, a small smile playing on his lips. "I'm just saying. I'll enjoy myself because I'm with you."

"You're the nicest hum—" Jay paused, feeling unaccountably horrified. "Oh my God. Alexei. I can't—I can't call you the nicest human anymore."

"Why not?" Alexei teased. "Finally changed your mind?"

"But...you're a *vampire* now."

"You can still call me that if you want, kitten. I'm afraid it was never a very accurate moniker anyway. I hate to break it to you, but I've never been very nice. Not before I met you."

Jay huffed, pressing play on the movie. For all his experience, sometimes Alexei really had no idea what he was talking about. He *was* the nicest human. Nicest vampire. Nicest mate.

Jay settled in on the couch, close enough that his and Alexei's thighs were touching. And then, because Jay and his beastie both agreed that sitting next to each other wasn't actually close enough, he lifted Alexei's arm to tuck himself under. He waited a moment for potential admonishment (such as, *Can't you sit by yourself for one movie, Johann?*), but there was only warm satisfaction pulsing through the bond, so he snuggled in closer, draping himself over Alexei's chest.

That was better.

Jay still tried, at first, to keep his thoughts and exclamations to himself. But he had so *many* of them. They were watching a movie called *Alien*, and the premise alone brought up so many questions that Jay's brain was overflowing with them.

The alien creature was clearly much stronger than the humans, but would it still be stronger than a vampire? How would one of their kind fare against a creature with acid for blood? If a vampire was jettisoned into space, would they still live forever, just floating into the abyss?

Jay couldn't help voicing the questions out loud, which he knew had to be annoying.

But it was like everything else with Alexei. There was no annoyance, no frisson of irritation through the bond. There was only amusement (the nice kind), acceptance, love.

Jay didn't care what Alexei said. He was the nicest human in the world.

So Jay let go of his hesitations and allowed himself to enjoy the movie like he would if he were alone. Except it was all *better* than when he was alone because he was tucked under Alexei's arm, feeling so warm and cozy and safe, and also Alexei had brought them both so many types of candy (even though Jay seemed to be the only one eating it) and Jay wasn't losing any time at all (hadn't lost a moment of time since Alexei had turned, as a matter of fact).

But just over midway into the movie, Jay began to have a different kind of problem.

He was *trying* to stay focused. He really was. But the thing was his beastie was all keyed up at the thought of fighting an alien (his beastie was convinced they could win against one, even if Jay wasn't), and there was Alexei, smelling so freaking amazing.

And so Jay maybe got a little squirmy and horny and also maybe started to have a hard time keeping his breaths regular. And even without the bond, Alexei probably would have noticed, but with the bond, it was only a few minutes before he was watching Jay more than the movie, and Jay could feel amusement (still the nice kind) and lust both pulsing through their connection.

"Getting a little distracted, are we?" Alexei murmured into Jay's hair. And oh, it wasn't fair when he made his voice all low and rumbly and teasing like that. "Do eight-feet-tall exoskeleton alien monsters turn you on, kotyonok?"

Jay's cheeks burned with horny embarrassment. He hadn't even known before Alexei that horny embarrassment was a thing. But it was. It really was. Jay kept his eyes on the TV though. "No, they don't."

"Oh? Then why can I smell desire on you, sweetheart?"

Jay shivered as Alexei nosed at his neck. "You can't *smell* it," he protested. "You're just—you're cheating." Jay wasn't sure if reading his desire through the bond counted as cheating, but he felt like it did. He could have pretended to still be focused on the movie otherwise. Maybe. Probably not.

Alexei huffed a laugh, and his warm breath on Jay's neck had another shiver rushing down his spine. "You still want to finish your movie, kotyonok?"

"Um. Yes." Jay wasn't sure he did, but the whole thing had been his idea, and Alexei had gone through all the trouble with the snacks, so he should, shouldn't he?

Alexei's breath was hot on Jay's ear now. "Well, would you like to finish the movie with my mouth on your cock?"

Before Jay's brain could even process the question, he was scrambling out from under Alexei's arm and plopping onto his back on the couch because yes, yes, he did want that. Very, very much. He *always* wanted Alexei to be touching him, and maybe he'd find it in himself to be even more hornily embarrassed about that fact if Alexei didn't seem to want that very same thing. If Alexei didn't seem to like nothing more than just...loving on Jay. Kissing and stroking and teasing him until he was an absolute puddle of goo.

Jay watched with wide eyes as Alexei tugged down his sweats, revealing Jay's bobbing erection. His mate was so handsome, especially with those pretty eyes all heavy-lidded and intense, looking at Jay's cock like it was a piece of delicious candy.

And then Alexei was looming over him, gently turning Jay's head to the side with two fingers so that he was facing the TV again. "Watch your movie, sweetheart."

Jay tried. He really did. He was even sort of successful at first because Alexei took it kind of easy on him. He started with licking and nibbling at the skin along Jay's hips, which had Jay giggling a little because it sort of tickled. He then turned his attention to the inside of Jay's thighs, a place he'd bitten and drunk from more than once.

Jay expected Alexei to do the same now, but he kept going with those gentle nibbles and warm kisses, not a hint of fangs.

It was...maddening. But also, Jay kept his eyes open and was vaguely aware of movie things happening, and that meant he was being good and following Alexei's request, right? Alexei confirmed it with his words, pouring out praise between presses of his lips on Jay's tender skin. "So good for me, sweetheart. Look at you, trembling like a little leaf. And still so focused. How perfect you are."

And that wasn't quite fair because Alexei knew how much being told he was good turned Jay on. And Jay's cock was jerking and leaking without Alexei even touching it with his mouth yet.

But then it was even more unfair because of course all that was just the warm-up. And apparently Alexei was done teasing. Jay's back arched up off the couch with a breathless gasp as Alexei just *gulped* him down, sucking hard and mercilessly. "Oh God. Oh fu—goodness."

And then it was really, really unfair because Jay could hear the sounds of Alexei stroking himself, even with the movie playing. When had Alexei taken off his pants? Had he somehow gotten naked without Jay knowing? Was Jay missing an opportunity to ogle him?

That was when Jay lost the battle. He turned his head away from the TV.

Alexei, cheeks hollowed around Jay's aching cock, raised a brow as he noticed the shift in Jay's attention. He popped his mouth off, and Jay felt a rush of cool air on his member. "What about your movie, sweetheart?"

Jay was too turned on to feel properly embarrassed for not being able to focus on the movie. "You're so handsome" was all he managed to say in defense.

He really was. Even though Alexei wasn't naked. He'd only tugged his own sweatpants down enough to jerk his cock. And somehow, in the moment, that was even hotter? Like he'd been so turned on just putting his mouth on Jay that he'd had to take himself in hand without even getting undressed.

Alexei grinned at him, proving Jay's point about the handsomeness, and then he put his full attention back into turning Jay into a mindless, panting mess.

And Alexei's mouth was too full for praise now, but he kept making these approving hums and moans and little growls that had the same effect on Jay, so it really didn't take long for Jay to erupt in Alexei's mouth with a howl and for Alexei to quickly follow suit with a moan.

And then they were both mindless, panting, sticky messes.

But Alexei didn't insist they clean up or shower or anything like that. He just scooted up the couch and spooned Jay from behind, turning them so they were facing the TV again.

Jay sighed happily as they watched the alien tear apart another crew member. "I hope the cat survives."

But Jay didn't get to find out. Because two minutes later, Danny was calling him.

"We have a situation."

"Why would Wolfe want to turn Dr. Monroe so badly?" Alexei asked, not for the first time, as they pulled up to an impressively large Victorian home at the edge of town.

Jay stared out the passenger side window, biting at his lip. He didn't have an answer. It was so unlike Wolfe, who, for all his faults, had never seemed interested in the vampire-companion dynamic. It had been a big part of Jay's trust in him, and now that had been shattered. Again.

Had Wolfe suggested forming a den of their own—doing his part to protect them—just so he could continue the old den's toxic dynamic in a new locale? Why? What was the point?

Jay spotted Danny and Roman waiting for them at the edge of the house's front lawn. Roman looked furious, like he had that one time he'd held Jay up against a wall by his neck. Danny looked worried.

Guilt rushed through Jay as he exited the passenger seat. It was his fault they were feeling so upset. His fault for bringing Wolfe here. He should have left earlier. He should have told them the truth. He should have—

He was brought out of his guilt spiral by the feel of Alexei's warm hand taking his. Jay looked up; he hadn't even realized his mate was at his side. He took comfort in the contact, taking a deep breath of Alexei's scent while he was at it.

They joined Danny and Roman. "They're in there?" Jay asked.

Roman nodded. "Yes. Wolfe and Monroe both."

Jay stared at the house, then back at Roman. "Um, if you don't mind me asking—how did you even find out what happened?"

It was Danny who answered. "Roman's been feeling a little...protective—"

"Suspicious," Roman corrected.

"—ever since Wolfe came into town. He may have been...monitoring the situation a bit."

Roman huffed at his mate. "And is it not a good thing I was?"

"Yes, yes. You did very well to stalk the stranger, my love." Danny's tone was sarcastic, even Jay could tell that, but Roman's eyes softened at the praise away. Jay could relate. It was always nice to be told you'd done a good job. "Anyway," Danny continued with an eye roll. "He saw Wolfe carrying in a very limp-looking Dr. Monroe."

"I believed it to be a corpse at first," Roman said, not sounding too upset by that fact. "But he claims he has found his mate and we must leave him be. He became quite aggressive about it."

Jay twisted the hem of his shirt.

A mate.

Well, that would change things a little, wouldn't it? Turning some good-looking human to be a subservient companion was one thing, but turning a mate...most vampires would find that acceptable.

Except Wolfe had only been in town a freaking week. Had he really found his mate and convinced him to turn so quickly?

Jay glanced up to find Alexei studying him. "What's the plan, kotyonok?"

Jay shrugged and dropped the fabric from his hands, flushing a little at the implication he was leading this particular mission. "I guess we knock."

In the end, Jay was the one who knocked.

Danny, Roman, and Alexei remained at the edge of the property. Jay figured if Wolfe was feeling overprotective of his new mate, four vampires at his door probably wouldn't be the best idea. It took more than a little convincing for Alexei to stay behind, but Jay wasn't afraid of being hurt by Wolfe.

Wolfe had never once considered Jay a threat.

It took a full minute of knocking, but eventually Wolfe answered the door, looking surprisingly dressed down in soft-looking black pants and a long-sleeved black shirt.

He was more disheveled than Jay had ever seen him. Which wasn't saying very much, to be fair. But his always perfectly styled hair was mussed, his uncharacteristic clothing rumpled.

Still, his expression was serene as ever as he looked first at Jay, then at the vampires waiting beyond him. "Johann," he greeted, managing to sound only mildly surprised, as if this was a social visit he hadn't been expecting. "How may I help you?"

"Wolfgang," Jay chastised.

Wolfe's lips flattened. "I'd invite you in, but I'm afraid now's not the best time."

"I thought I told you we wouldn't be that kind of den."

"I beg your pardon?" The polite confusion on Wolfe's face was ridiculous.

Jay crossed his arms. "I'll leave you out in the cold, Wolfe. No money. No den. No nothing. I don't like liars."

Wolfe kept up the polite confusion charade for another moment, and then his posture slumped slightly as he let out a drawn-out sigh, as if Jay was being incredibly unreasonable. "It was not...intentional, Johann."

"Explain, please."

"I only wanted a little taste. The blood of a mate is supposed to be especially sweet. I tried to compel him. My beast would not...cooperate." Wolfe ran a hand through his mussed hair. "So I did what had to be done."

Jay couldn't help but frown. It sounded like Wolfe had tried to feed from the doctor, the doctor had panicked, and Wolfe's reaction to that panic had been...turning him? Jay had never thought he could be that impulsive. "And what are you going to do with him now?"

Wolfe straightened his stance once more. "He'll stay with me, of course."

"But that's not your decision."

A flash of pure rage crossed Wolfe's face, the most expression Jay had ever seen on him. "He's *mine*."

Jay fought back the chill Wolfe's anger sent down his spine, determined to stay strong. "That's his choice, Wolfe. You know that."

"He'll choose me," Wolfe said, sounding completely assured of that outcome.

"I can't trust you on that, not after you've turned two people already. Let us see him. Let us see that he's okay. Let him tell us he wants to stay."

That brief glimpse of rage again, but Wolfe didn't growl, didn't glare, didn't let his beast out to challenge Jay. He just...stared. Maybe it was the prospect of the money that kept his temper in check.

Or maybe he just really was that cold-blooded.

Jay waited him out easily. He could do this all day, stand in place on this porch until they both turned into vampire popsicles.

Eventually, Wolfe tipped his chin in assent. "When he awakens, one of you may speak with him."

Jay beamed, resisting the urge to do a little celebratory hop at his success in reasoning with him. "I'll do it," he offered.

"No. You're too tainted by trauma. You'll frighten him unnecessarily."

Well, that was rude. "Alexei?"

"Too new. A veritable babe in the woods. He won't be helpful at all." Wolfe leaned slightly out the door, ignoring Jay's frown at his assessment of Alexei and studying the three waiting vampires. "Your nurse friend with the lovely eyes. When the good doctor awakens, they may speak. Will that appease you?"

Jay cocked his head. " And you'll tell us when he wakes up?"

"But of course."

Jay hesitated. He used to be fairly certain Wolfe didn't lie to him, *wouldn't* lie to him. It was something he liked very much about his friend. Even Wolfe turning Alexei hadn't necessarily broken that assumption. It wasn't like Wolfe had tried to hide it from him. But he was getting the feeling now that Wolfe's priorities had shifted.

A psychopath with a newly turned mate. What wouldn't he do to keep him?

"We'll be back in the morning," Jay eventually said, proud of how firm he sounded in the declaration. "If he's not awake by then, we'll wait it out."

After another long moment, Wolfe inclined his head in agreement, but his eyes were cold. "Now if you'll excuse me," he said, already shutting the door in Jay's face. "I have some preparations to make."

Jay ran back to his friends and recounted the conversation.

"I'll do it," Danny agreed readily.

Jay beamed at him. Of course Danny would. He was kind and considerate and tenderhearted. Maybe Jay would have been less scared, if someone like Danny had been around when he'd been turned.

"This town will soon have more of our kind than its human population," Roman mused.

"For what it's worth, I don't think he'll turn anyone else. He doesn't act without reason. At least, not usually."

Roman's icy gaze met Jay's. "For someone who is theoretically on our side, he has caused an awful lot of trouble. Are you certain we need him?"

Jay wasn't certain of any of it. He was causing his friends so much trouble.

When would they decide enough was enough? When would they want Jay gone?

Twenty-One

Alexei

A lexei felt bad for this doctor he'd never met. He really did. From what Jay had said, it sounded like Monroe hadn't been given much of a choice on his new condition.

And to be mated to Wolfe? That had to be...brutal.

But it was hard to focus on that little shred of empathy because more than anything, Alexei was pissed at how upset this all had Jay. He could feel the little jolts of anxiety, of worry and stress, coming from his sweet vampire since the day before.

It had Alexei's inner beast unsettled, restless, even. It didn't like for their mate to be discontent in any way.

But the frustrating part was, even with the bond, Alexei couldn't tell exactly *why* Jay felt so anxious. Was he feeling responsible for the doctor? Worried Wolfe would turn others?

When Alexei had asked, Jay had mumbled something about all the trouble he was putting his friends through. Which...all right, Alexei could understand feeling guilty a little about that, if he were in Jay's shoes. But why so anxious? Did Jay really think his friends wouldn't have his back? This group of vampires that so clearly adored him?

Was Jay really so unsure of his own place here?

So Alexei was more than a little on edge when they made their way back to Wolfe's mansion.

Surprisingly, the vampire let the three of them—Jay, Alexei, and Roman—wait in the sitting room with him while Danny went to check on Monroe upstairs.

Still, Wolfe remained standing, posture ramrod straight as they waited on Danny's verdict. A verdict Alexei had serious doubts about Wolfe honoring, were it to go any way other than what he so clearly wanted—Monroe remaining at his side.

Roman glowered from his spot in an ostentatious armchair clearly meant more for aesthetics than comfort, looking a moment away from leaping up and following Danny up the stairs. "Have you passed your message on to the den? That Jay has protectors? That he is not to be trifled with?"

Wolfe tipped his chin, his head cocked and gaze distant, half his attention clearly on trying to make out the discussion upstairs. "I did. I made some phone calls yesterday."

Roman's glower deepened. "And why did it take you a full week to make a few phone calls?"

Wolfe shot him a look, face placid. "It didn't. My attentions were focused elsewhere, I'm afraid. I could apologize, if you like, but it would be terribly insincere."

Roman waved an irritated hand, brushing off the nonapology with some vaguely French sound of disapproval.

"And that's it?" Alexei clarified, when neither of his companions seemed eager to speak up. "Jay's free from them?"

Wolfe shrugged genteelly. "I've done what I can. I alerted them Jay had found himself a mate and a den. I may also have intimated that said mate had ties to...Eastern shores." Alexei startled at that. He hadn't realized his Mafia ties would be any sort of deterrent to a rival vampire den. "I also dropped hints of Hendrick's fate. If they're smart, they won't try to provoke a war. They'll either disband or start building up their own resources. I'm sure they've managed to siphon at least some of Johann's funds off him already."

Alexei looked to Jay, who was plucking at the tassels on one of the couch pillows, seemingly entirely unconcerned by the prospect of his money being slowly stolen away.

"And if they come anyway?" Alexei asked Wolfe.

"Then we'll go," Jay said softly, eyes on his pillow, even as Alexei felt threads of sadness leak through the bond. "You and me. We won't put anyone in danger."

Roman stiffened at his words, a grumble of protest leaving his lips, and even Wolfe gave Jay a pained look. "Really, Johann. After I've gone to all the trouble of changing my loyalties..."

But it was Danny's voice that cut in the sharpest. "You *won't*."

Alexei tore his gaze reluctantly off Jay to see Danny standing in the doorway to the sitting room. "You won't go, Jay," Danny repeated. "If they come, we'll fight."

"At least, *some* of us will," Roman interjected, giving Danny a pointed look. Alexei had a feeling it wasn't Roman who wanted to abstain from the fight himself but that he was reluctant to let his mate join the fray.

"We all will," Danny insisted, his cheeks pink with heightened emotion. "Soren and Gabe have already agreed. You're family, Jay. Or, um, our den mate, if that's what you prefer to call it."

"No... Family is good. I like family." Jay's voice came out breathless, his gaze now firmly fixed on Danny, and Alexei could feel how overwhelmed he was. Alexei realized fully for the first time just how many doubts Jay really had been having about his place here in Hyde Park, the cause of his recent anxiety.

Alexei wished once again that Vee would come back to life so he could rip her head off himself, for ever giving Jay cause to doubt how lovable he was.

"How extraordinarily touching," Wolfe remarked dryly, clearly bored of these pledges of devotion. He raised a brow at Danny. "And my mate?"

Danny's pleasure at Jay's agreement dimmed visibly. "He says he'll stay with you," he muttered, clearly uncomfortable with the idea.

Wolfe's eyes shone, their light brown seeming for a moment to almost glow red. Alexei had another moment of pity for the poor doctor fated to be his mate and a surge of gratitude for the vampire fate had chosen for him instead.

"Excellent," Wolfe breathed. "Then as long as he wants to remain here, I'm at your beck and call. Any aid the 'family' needs."

Danny scowled at him. "I thought you were doing that anyway."

Wolfe was already turning toward the stairs, but he waved an airy hand behind his back. "Call it extra incentive to do my part, then."

Leaving the house, Alexei went to grab Jay's hand only to realize his mate was busy twisting his pair anxiously. Alexei became aware of an odd mix of relief, insecurity, and doubt radiating off him.

"So much trouble," Jay mumbled. "I've caused so much trouble."

Alexei's poor, traumatized little alien. How much reassurance would he need before he recognized love coming from someone other than Alexei?

Before Alexei could try to fix it, Danny halted their forward momentum, turning to place his hands on Jay's shoulders, encouraging Jay to look him in the eye. "Jay, sweetie, do you trust me?"

"Of course," Jay answered immediately. "You're the nicest vampire I know." He shot Alexei an almost apologetic look. "Because we're still calling you the nicest human," he explained.

Alexei bit back his answering smile. "Of course."

Danny shook Jay's shoulders gently. "Then trust me when I say I'm *happy* you came to us. And I mean that in a completely selfish way. Eternity is—I still can't fathom it, really. And I'm not like Roman. I can't be a lone wolf. I need people, connections. And not just...surface-level friendships. It'll be unsettling and scary, in its own way, moving from place to place. I want a community. And I want you to be a part of it." A brief glance at Alexei. "The both of you."

Jay seemed to take a minute to absorb those words. Then he shot a shy look over Danny's shoulder to Roman, who was looking with obvious love and pride at his mate. "And you—you don't mind either?"

Roman cleared his throat. "I heard a phrase recently that resonated with me. 'Happy wife, happy life.' If Danny is content, so am I."

Danny scoffed, wrapping Jay up in a hug. "He's being cagey, sweetie. He's very fond of you."

"And I'm very fond of you both." Jay's words were muffled by Danny's shoulder, but Alexei could feel some of that doubt and insecurity finally melt off him.

If he didn't think Roman would punch his lights out, Alexei could have kissed Danny on the fucking mouth.

Nicest vampire indeed.

An hour or so after parting ways with Danny and Roman, Alexei and Jay strolled through Jay's neighborhood, hand in hand.

Jay had professed a need for fresh air, and Alexei had suggested the woods, but Jay had wanted to look at all the different houses. Alexei wondered if he was thinking of actually using some of his billions and upgrading them from his duplex apartment.

They stopped in front of a Victorian number that reminded Alexei of Wolfe's pseudomansion. "Do you think Wolfe really bought that house already?"

"Probably," Jay answered, swinging their joined hands as they stood in place. "Wolfe always liked nice things."

"I thought the whole point was he needed your money to *have* those nice things."

"I think he has some funds. Just not as much as he'd like." Jay waited a beat, as if considering his words. For someone who often spoke in a sort of stream of consciousness way (at least, at home with Alexei), as if there were no filter between his brain and his mouth, he could be very particular about what he said when he wanted to be. "I think what Wolfe said about the den siphoning off some of my money... He's probably done that as well. Only he wants the security of *more*."

Before Alexei could feel indignant on Jay's behalf, Jay tugged him along from the house. "I don't mind. I definitely don't need all of it. I'd actually like to— If you're okay with it..." He peered up at Alexei as they walked along, looking suddenly shy. "Do you *want* to be super rich? Like, super-duper rich?"

Alexei bit back a grin at the wording of the question. "No, I don't need to be 'super-duper rich,' kotyonok."

Jay beamed back at him. "Then I'd like to give some of it away. Maybe even a lot of it?" He paused to gauge Alexei's reaction—there wasn't much of one, not when Alexei had never cared about Jay's funds—then rushed on. "Not all of it, of course. I want to be able to contribute to the—the family."

Alexei's chest tightened with unbearable affection at the little thrill he could feel go through Jay with that word. Family.

"What were you thinking?" he asked, not caring either way. If Jay told Alexei he wanted to dump it all in the river, Alexei would drive them to the nearest body of water.

But Jay, not being an apathetic asshole like Alexei, had a different idea. "Maybe we can brainstorm together? You can help me decide? I want it to be of use somewhere."

"Of course, kitten."

They had time, an awful lot of it.

Warmth filled Alexei's veins as he thought of how satisfying it was going to be, having Jay to himself after all this drama was put aside. He still felt bad for Wolfe's mate but also...grateful. Because now there was someone else to occupy the psycho's time and attention, to keep his focus off Jay, to give him a reason not to double-cross them.

It was selfish and callous of Alexei to think that way, but then he'd always been those things, hadn't he? He was the "nicest human" only for Jay. Because Jay deserved everything good and nice in this world, and Alexei wanted to be the one to give it to him.

Everyone else could go to hell.

But the foreseen lack of drama only lasted for a few blocks, when Alexei and Jay turned the corner to find a man leaning against a chain-link fence surrounding an abandoned, grassy lot.

He was of an average height and build and generally nothing much to look at. Alexei might not have noticed him at all if it weren't for the way Jay immediately stiffened next to him.

Alexei's inner beast went on full alert, but Alexei waited for Jay to let him know exactly how much trouble they might be in.

"Tobias," Jay greeted the stranger flatly. "I thought Wolfe had passed on the message already."

Tobias stepped forward from the fence. "He did. But I was already on my way. It was decided I might as well check things out, in case the two of you were just running off together, trying to scare us away." He ran a long look over Alexei and at his hand joined with Jay's. "Although, maybe the mate part is true after all."

"It's all true. We're starting our own den, and we'd like to be left in peace."

And this was why Jay should be in charge of talking. That was a much nicer way of saying "fuck off forever or we'll break your face in half."

But Tobias didn't seem to appreciate the magnanimous olive branch being waved in front of him. "Of course you would," he sneered. "Our little pacifist."

And fuck, Alexei did not like that tone. Not when Jay was being nothing but pleasant to this undead mouth-breathing motherfucker. Before Alexei knew it, his beast was pushing out, and a strange growl he'd never heard before was coming out of his own mouth.

It was a little embarrassing, to be honest. So much for schooling his reactions to posturing assholes.

"Oh no. Did I upset your pet?" Tobias sniffed at the air. "He smells awfully fresh. You know the thing about baby vamps, Johann. So easy to put down."

Alexei snarled at that, ready to tug Jay back and make a break for it.

But he found himself grasping air, as Jay's hand had left his in that split second of distraction. Out of nowhere, Tobias was knocked flat on his back on the ground, and Jay was straddling him, pinning his arms as well as his legs.

Alexei gawked. Jay's face was still human, and he looked oddly peaceful, as if he'd just happened to find himself in that position, nonchalantly holding the larger vampire down.

"I don't like fighting," Jay said evenly as Tobias struggled. "And I'm probably not very good at it. But I *am* stronger than you. And I don't like you threatening my mate." He frowned down at Tobias. "It's rude."

Alexei fought the inappropriate urge to laugh as he pushed his beast back inside. He was worried Jay might think he was laughing at him, when really it was immensely satisfying watching this intruder try and fail to wiggle out of Jay's hold.

After a few more minutes of pathetic attempts, Jay never looking even remotely strained by the effort, Tobias's head fell back, a sneer still on his face. He resorted back to taunting. "Of course you don't like fighting. You've never been a very good vampire, have you, Johann? Weak. Cowardly."

Jay's face remained as placid as ever, even as Alexei could feel a twinge of old hurt run through him. "Yes, I suppose that's true," Jay agreed. "But my friends are very different from me."

"Too true, Jaybird," Soren drawled, stepping out of the fucking shadows like a movie villain, Gabe a step behind him.

What the actual fuck? Alexei hadn't even known they were there. He'd have to ask Jay about honing his vampire senses; he clearly had a lot to learn.

Soren crouched next to the pair on the ground, that creepy grin he'd once used to intimidate Alexei firmly in place. "You see, unfortunate stranger, we're not nearly as nice as our sweet Johann here." He wrinkled his nose as he sniffed at Tobias. "Thought I smelled a stranger in town. Don't recognize you, so you must be a new addition to the den. You ever meet Hendrick, by chance?"

Tobias nodded warily. Soren's shark's grin widened.

"Perfect. Then you'll be delighted to hear the story of how he perished. By my hands." Soren tilted his head thoughtfully. "Well, by my shotgun to multiple parts of his body, actually. Then burned down to ash by flames, and poof—" Soren made jazz hands, waving them in front of Tobias's face. "No more asshole. And let's see...what else do we have on our group résumé? Our friend Roman just ripped the head off a feral vamp a few months ago. Really wish I'd been there to see that. I don't know if you've heard of Lucien Volaire either, but he's a truly unhinged piece of work, not afraid to leave bodies left and right, and he's been pushing his way into our crew, despite my protests. And then Alexei here—" Soren shot Alexei a sly wink. "With his ties to the Russian mob. Lots of fun weapons to explore there. So no, Jay's friends aren't very nice. Now, can you remember that all on your own, or do we need to leave some permanent reminders?" Still crouched on one knee, Soren turned fully to Alexei. "What would your dear brother take as a message, Alexei? A finger?"

Alexei cleared his throat. "Coming into our territory uninvited, threatening our family? I'd say a hand, at the very least."

Soren looked absolutely delighted at his cooperation. He turned his manic expression back to Tobias. "Did you hear that, stranger? A hand. Now tell me, are you a righty or a lefty?"

Tobias, thickheaded as he was, finally looked properly cowed. He shook his head frantically, rubbing gravel into his own hair in the process. "Un—unnecessary. I'll pass on the message. Really. I was just here to check things out. Not threatening. No threatening here."

Truly pathetic. But it seemed to be enough for Jay, who finally rose from his restraining position, allowing Tobias to run off into the distance at an incredibly unnatural speed.

Soren sighed happily, rising from his own crouch. "That was fun." His grin dropped as he seemed to realize Jay wasn't quite as enthused. "What's wrong, Jaybird? You get his cooties on you?"

Jay twisted at the hem of his shirt. "I brought another den member here."

Soren cocked his head. "And we scared him off."

"But you—"

Soren sighed, not happily this time, and ran his hand through his coiffed blond hair. "I told Danny he was in charge of the mushy stuff," he complained. "And I know he's already gone over this—our...feelings about you. Don't make me say it again."

Alexei, absolutely loving the idea of every single person in Jay's life reassuring him of his place there, spoke up. "Jay's love language is words of affirmation."

Jay nodded solemnly. "And also all the other ones."

Soren looked pained for a moment, then threw his hands up dramatically. "Fine. You're *ours*, Jay. You and your big Russian. There's not a day goes by I'm not happy you came here, even if I didn't know what I was doing when I invited you. And most days, I *still* feel guilty for leaving you in that place for as long as I did. And I'm looking forward to the future, when I don't have to think about any of it, and it's just an accepted truth that we have one another's backs for the rest of time. Good?" Soren gave Jay a sharp look, relaxing when Jay nodded. "Good. Highness?"

Gabe, who'd been leaning against the fence, clearly delighted by Soren's discomfort, looked confused. "What?"

Soren gestured to Jay. "Where are your words of affirmation?"

Gabe straightened in place, giving Soren a panicked look. When he found no sympathy there, he smiled tentatively at Jay. "Oh. Um. I think you're great, little guy."

Jay's answering beaming smile was the most beautiful thing Alexei had ever seen.

Twenty-Two

Alexei

T he next two weeks passed peacefully enough. There was no
further word from the den. No more strange visitors, no
more threats.

Alexei still couldn't help feeling like he was waiting for the other
shoe to drop.

Which didn't mean that the past two weeks weren't the happiest
in Alexei's life (not that there was much competition in that regard,
at least not before arriving in Hyde Park).

They had been, most of all, a revelation in all things Jay. Or
maybe an...intensification.

Because it wasn't until Jay's barriers relaxed that Alexei realized
how many there had been, how terrified his vampire had been of
judgment and rejection.

It was as if Alexei's turning, now topped with the new assurance
that Jay would be able to stay in Hyde Park as long as he wanted,
had taken down the final barrier in Jay's mind about the two of
them, the last layer of insecurity about his perceived weaknesses.

Jay no longer pretended he didn't hate being alone.

He was open about the fact that he wanted Alexei around him
all the time, if possible. He was clear about exactly how much he
wanted to be touched. To be held, really. He was constantly tucking
himself under Alexei's arm, or throwing himself onto Alexei's back.
When they were alone at home, he would jump onto his tiptoes,

wrap his arms around Alexei's neck, and insist on being carried around the house.

He'd been adorably shy about it the first time, but the rush of Alexei's satisfaction through the bond quickly reassured him, and now Jay never hesitated in initiating touch of any kind. Because that was the thing Jay was clearly beginning to realize: Jay may have been codependent, but Alexei was just as bad. He reveled in Jay's need for him, in their constant physical contact. His beast...hungered...always, for Jay.

And that led, often, to more intimate forms of touch. Faced with Alexei's monstrous appetite for him, Jay had become more comfortable in asking for what he'd started calling "loving time," in which he laid back and let Alexei worship his body, take him apart piece by piece while telling him all the while how perfect, how gorgeous, how good he was.

It was Alexei's favorite fucking pastime.

Or was that watching movies, when Jay talked through every scene, his reactions loud and sincere and ridiculous? Or was it just every single moment he was allowed to stay by Jay's side?

So now Alexei found himself at Death by Coffee, waiting on his vampire, content to be there for Jay to wave and smile at between customers, accepting Colin's sardonic raised brows at his choice of reading material (*Jane Eyre*, at Jay's insistence).

And then, as Alexei turned another page of his ridiculous book, a stocky dark-haired man walked in, stomping the snow off his boots at the door, and there it was—the other shoe.

Sergei Kalchik, formerly his father's right-hand man, now his brother's.

Observing the familiar form take in the café, seeing one of the exact people he'd been dreading having follow him finally there...it was surprisingly anticlimactic.

Alexei was a fucking vampire now. What the hell were any small-time mobsters actually going to be able to do to him?

He watched as Jay waved at the newcomer with his usual full enthusiasm. "Welcome to Death by Coffee!"

Sergei grunted back at him before his attention zoomed instantly in on Alexei in the corner; he must have already seen him through the window.

Alexei grinned broadly in greeting, placing his book carefully on the table, and that reaction had even the ever-stoic Sergei blinking in surprise. Meanwhile, Alexei could feel his inner beast perking up in interest at the potential for violence. The greedy thing was usually content enough, as long as they were near their mate (touching their mate, tasting their mate, fucking their mate), but it clearly wouldn't mind reveling in a little bloodshed now and then.

Sergei pulled out the chair across from Alexei, taking a seat without a word of greeting.

"You here to kill me, Sergei?" Alexei asked, unconcerned with the answer either way.

Sergei removed his gloves, working each finger off methodically, before answering, his Russian accent subtle but achingly familiar. "You can't think very highly of Ivan, if you think he'd send me here to off his own brother."

An amazingly typical nonanswer. Alexei wasn't having any of it. "Well, did he?"

Sergei paused to smirk before shaking his head. "I'm here to take you home. Ivan thinks you've had enough fun, Alyosha."

Alexei couldn't help another broad grin. "Oh, my fun's just getting started."

As if in demonstration, a plate of coffee cake appeared on the table, and Sergei shifted slightly to see Jay standing over them, a shy smile on his face. "Hello. You didn't come to the counter, but this is Alexei's favorite from the bakery. You should try it; it's very delicious."

Sergei didn't make a move toward the cake, his gaze traveling over Jay slowly. "Cute," he finally said.

"Yes," Jay agreed easily. He cocked his head, possibly clocking the accent even from that one word. "Are you here to try to kill Alexei?"

Another blink of surprise from Sergei. That was two in one encounter. Possibly a record.

Alexei took a sip of his Americano. "He's here to take me home, kotyonok."

It was such a wonderful thing, to see that cold, protective glint form in Jay's gray eyes, especially when they were always so warm and open to anyone *not* threatening Alexei. "Then there's been a misunderstanding. Alexei *is* home. Well, he doesn't live in the coffee shop," Jay conceded. "But close by. In Hyde Park, definitely."

Sergei turned dismissively away from Jay, looking to Alexei instead, an almost pitying expression on his face. "You're going to get this little one hurt, Alyosha, letting him butt his nose into family business."

Alexei shrugged. "I'm afraid I have a new family now."

He cocked a brow at Jay, who nodded, a mischievous little smile on his face. "Go ahead. I'm blocking you."

So Alexei let the beast come out.

It felt good, almost a rush of relief, like cricking his neck after being slumped down for too long. But it felt even better watching Sergei's face pale as he took in Alexei's new fangs, the all-black eyes. "What the fuck?"

Alexei leaned across the table, making sure Sergei could take in every last detail of his transformation. "I'm afraid I won't be going with you, Sergei. But you can tell my brother something for me. It doesn't matter how many men he sends. There are bigger monsters than him here. And we're not afraid to bite."

Alexei pushed the beast back, ignoring its whining disappointment that they weren't actually going to feed in that moment. He'd have to go hunting tonight. Soren was teaching him how to compel his prey so Alexei could manage for both himself and Jay moving forward.

Sergei stared at Alexei, at his once again human face. After a moment his stunned gaze traveled back to Jay, who was beaming at him. Then back to Alexei. "What the *fuck*?" he repeated. Alexei could practically smell the confused fear coming off him. It was wonderful.

Was it childish for him to be so delighted by confounding and terrifying this once daunting figure from his past? Someone both his father and brother had used to intimidate Alexei into staying in line? Probably. But Alexei could still remember the sharp pain of his ring finger snapping in Sergei's hands under his father's command. What Alexei's supposed teen transgression had been he couldn't even remember anymore.

So maybe he should be lauded for his restraint instead.

He caught Sergei's eyes once more, flashing the beast out and back in an instant, just for the hell of it. "I don't care if you tell Ivan what you saw or you make something up. But the next person he sends isn't making it back. Got it?"

Jay cooed sympathetically at the frozen fear on Sergei's face. "Would you like to take your coffee cake to go?"

As soon as they entered their apartment, Jay was on his tiptoes, his arms around Alexei's neck, and Alexei hoisted him up, wrapping Jay's legs around his waist. He carried his little vampire into the kitchen, for no other reason than the counter there was the perfect height to set Jay down and still have him within kissing reach.

Alexei delved into his mouth, hungry. Always hungry for him, for his taste, for the sweet little noises he made when Alexei had him at his mercy.

Alexei could feel the thrums of happiness, the swirls of early desire coming from Jay, but underneath was a certain...disquiet. Alexei broke off the kiss, ignoring Jay's exaggerated pout of protest.

"Did that scare you, kitten?" he asked, brushing a lock of Jay's dark hair away from his eyes. "Sergei's visit?"

Jay shook his head, nibbling on his lip in that way he did when he was considering how to say something. "It didn't scare me. I just don't like the thought that...if we hadn't met, they might have taken you back there. Where you were so unhappy."

Ah. Alexei's sweet, tender mate, worried over a hypothetical reality where a hypothetical Alexei might have been hypothetically sad.

The real truth was if they hadn't met, it probably would have gone one of two ways: Alexei would have stayed numb and apathetic enough to let himself be caught and put down much earlier, or he would have gotten himself together and been much more diligent in hiding his tracks from his brother in the first place and wouldn't have been taken back at all.

But that was beside the point, so Alexei didn't voice it. Instead, he focused on what really mattered. "Lucky I met you, then, isn't it?"

Jay fisted his hands in Alexei's shirt. "You really think so?"

"Mm. I do. Because there I was, the nicest human, without anyone to be nice to."

"And you like being nice to me?" Jay asked, almost coy.

"Nothing in the world makes me happier, kotyonok."

Jay wriggled in place on the counter, clearly pleased with the reassurance. Alexei pressed a kiss to his temple, taking a moment to inhale that lovely peppermint smell while he was there. "How many ways have I told you I love you today?" he murmured.

It was a little game they played these days. A way to assuage Jay's bottomless need for reassurance and affection and Alexei's matching, bottomless need to give them to him. Alexei tried to get each love language in at least once every day. He usually succeeded many times over.

Jay scrunched his brows in thought, nibbling at his bottom lip again. "Well, you told me this morning how much you love me.

And also that I was—" He paused, cheeks flushing with adorable embarrassment.

"Yes?" Alexei encouraged, pressing a kiss to his ear, watching the delicate shell turn a light pink in response.

"That I was perfect and gorgeous," Jay mumbled, wriggling again.

Words of affirmation.

Alexei kissed Jay's pink cheek. "And?"

Jay giggled. "You carried me to the coffee shop on your back because I thought it was funny."

An act of service, even if it was a silly one.

"Mm. So I did." Alexei pressed a kiss to the tip of Jay's nose. "And?"

"And you gave me candy at work." Jay grinned at the memory of it.

"A little gift for my little love."

"And you waited for me at the coffee shop for hours, just so I could talk to you when it was slow," Jay continued, unprompted.

Quality time. That was an easy one, as they were pretty much always together. Maybe at some point, Alexei would get a proper job, but at the moment, he was knee-deep in trying to figure out Jay's massive, complicated finances for him, which he could do on his own time, in Jay's presence.

Alexei pressed a kiss to Jay's chin. Jay hummed happily. "And now you're kissing and touching me. And you'll probably touch me even more?"

"Mm. Definitely more." Alexei kissed Jay's neck lightly, keeping it chaste for the moment. "And what should we do for the rest of the evening?"

He liked asking because even though Jay was happy with most things—always eager to go with the flow, as long as he was with people he cared for—Alexei liked giving him practice saying what he really wanted. He hadn't had nearly enough of that in his life.

Jay tilted his head in thought, and also clearly in a not-so-subtle effort to encourage Alexei to kiss his neck some more. "Well, I think we should be naked," he declared, almost immediately.

"How shocking," Alexei murmured dryly, obliging Jay's silent request and kissing the other side of his elongated neck.

It was anything *but* surprising. Jay couldn't get enough of what he liked to deem "cozy nudity."

"I'd like to maybe draw later. Oh! Oh!" Jay tugged at Alexei's shirt. "I could draw you naked. I haven't done that yet. It'll be just like that scene in *Titanic* where Jack sketches Rose but without all the tragedy afterward."

Jesus. *Titanic*. Which was now on the forbidden list of movies, ever since it had made Jay cry for what felt like hours afterward. If Alexei could murder a movie, he'd murder that one.

But if Jay wanted to sketch him like one of his French girls, that was fine with Alexei. "You can draw me however you like, sweetheart."

Jay's gray eyes lit up with excitement. "And maybe we could learn a new recipe together?"

"Most definitely."

"But maybe before all that..." Jay shimmied his hips in place again. Alexei knew what was coming—he could feel the lust swirling in his sweet mate's belly, as well as the visible bulge of Jay's burgeoning erection—but he liked hearing the words anyway. Loved that Jay felt empowered enough to voice them. "Maybe you'll love up on me a bit?" Jay peered up at him through his lashes with the question. Had Soren been teaching him how to flirt?

Alexei let out a slow, ragged exhale, unbelievably turned on by the thought of Jay trying to seduce him. "Oh, kitten. I'm going to be doing that no matter what."

He started tugging at the stretchy waistband of Jay's dark-blue sweatpants, ready to have them out of the way. But then he paused, feeling at the fabric between two fingers. It was oddly thick, almost luxurious, and incredibly soft on the inside.

Alexei took a step back, ignoring Jay's whine of disappointment, and looked over Jay's outfit with new eyes, the matching pants and sweatshirt. "Are you wearing...a designer sweatsuit right now?"

"Oh!" Jay peered down at his clothes, smoothing down the fabric and nodding shyly. "Yes. It was a compromise with Soren."

"My little fashionista." Alexei tugged them off anyway, tossing them onto the kitchen floor.

He paused there again, looming over Jay, now naked on the counter, taking in all the smooth, creamy skin on display. It didn't matter how often Jay exposed him to cozy nudity; Alexei would never not be ravenous at the sight of it.

Alexei wrapped his hands around the backs of Jay's thighs, lifting them and encouraging Jay to lean back on his elbows.

Jay's breath hitched as he complied. "Here?"

"Mm. Right here, kitten. We're absolutely starving for you."

Alexei proceeded to eat Jay out thoroughly, mercilessly. Devouring his hole, drinking in the whimpers and sighs and high-pitched cries, making sure to praise his perfect vampire for being so good for him.

"I'm not—I'm not doing anything though," Jay protested at one point, as he always did when Alexei praised him for pillow princess behavior. Another one of their little games.

Alexei speared him with his tongue, getting distracted and sloppy with it, before remembering to answer. "Oh, but you are. You're letting me please you, letting me love on you. And you're doing it perfectly, kitten. So greedy and desperate. You taste so good, sweetheart."

Alexei reveled in the surge of heightened pleasure he could feel rush through Jay at his words, the way Jay's muscles relaxed in his hands.

Normally Alexei could—and did—do this part for hours. Taking Jay to the brink again and again before searching for any relief for himself. But there was a frantic edge underneath his own desire this time. Jay was right; Sergei's visit had brought a reminder that Alexei's life could have been so different. If he hadn't come to Hyde Park. If he hadn't walked into Death by Coffee that day.

He reared back, grabbing the lube out of the cabinet drawer (he'd learned to always be prepared when it came to Jay). "Need to be inside you now, baby."

Jay held his own legs back now, folding himself in half, because he was just that perfect. "Yes. Yes. Always, Alexei."

Alexei sank into his mate, into that perfect heat, and it felt like it always did—like coming home.

He hooked Jay's legs around his waist, leaning over fully to press their foreheads together as he buried himself fully to the hilt. "I love you. So much."

He could feel Jay's answering smile against his lips. "Love you, Alexei."

Alexei and his beast were both soothed by that, and he set an easier rhythm than he'd been expecting, rolling his hips in long, slow, deep strokes, taking pleasure in the soft, happy sighs Jay breathed into his mouth, the slight hitch in his breath every time Alexei bottomed out.

But Jay was a greedy little thing at heart, and eventually he tugged at Alexei's hips with his legs, urging him to pick up the pace. "Please?"

"Oh, my perfect, needy mate."

Alexei gave him what he wanted, losing himself in shorter, faster, almost frantic thrusts, rocking their bodies together on the counter. He palmed the back of Jay's head, bringing his mouth to Alexei's neck. "Come on, kitten. Let those fangs out."

Alexei craved this sometimes. Him and his beast both. To be consumed by Jay, an echo of the thrill of those early feedings, when Alexei's blood had the power to nourish him.

Jay sank his teeth in with a little growl, and fresh heat shot down Alexei's spine at the contact. He stroked Jay's hair, murmuring his pleasure at every gulp of blood.

It wasn't long before Jay broke off with a gasp. "Touch me, please, Alexei. Gonna come. Gonna—"

Alexei grasped Jay's leaking cock with one hand, stroking it to the same rhythm as his hips, helping his perfect, beautiful mate find his release, willing his own to hold back until then.

Jay cried out, head thrown back. With the first spurt of wetness against his fist, Alexei groaned low, hips stuttering as he bit into Jay's taut neck, drinking his own reward in turn.

Alexei stayed in place afterward, having learned his lesson about withdrawing his softened cock from Jay too soon (and it was always up to Jay to declare what constituted too soon). They passed the time with long, thorough kisses, each of them licking the taste of the other out of their mouths, until there was nothing left but saliva, not a speck of coppery deliciousness to be found.

"What should we do first, of all your plans?" Alexei murmured against Jay's lips.

Jay tightened his hold, his legs still wrapped around Alexei's hips. "Let's just hold each other for a while longer. Does that sound okay?"

"That sounds perfect, kotyonok. Absolutely perfect."

Epilogue

Jay

J ay was filthy. Truly filthy.

And it felt *wonderful*.

Especially with the car window rolled down, the warm summer sun shining on his face, and Alexei's delicious scent filling the vehicle. Wasn't Jay just the luckiest?

He looked to his mate behind the wheel. Alexei had dirt on his nose and pine needles sticking out of his pretty hair. He looked as wonderful as Jay felt.

"I think camping is just the best," Jay declared. "Super-duper fun."

Alexei's eyes briefly left the road as he gave Jay a warm smile. "So you've said, kitten."

Oops. Jay *had* said that. Probably about a hundred times already. But it was true. Camping was super-duper fun. And it turned out camping as a vampire was maybe even *extra* fun: they'd been able to hike out super far, miles away from any other living soul; they hadn't needed to bring real food, so Alexei had filled Jay's pack up with tons of different candies instead; and the cold nights couldn't bother them, so it hadn't even mattered when Jay had accidentally snapped the tentpoles in his excitement—they'd just slept on their mats outside instead. Alexei had even claimed it was actually better that way because they'd been able to fully see the stars.

And then they'd gotten to have sex. Outside. In the *dirt*.

Well, Alexei had suggested they put a blanket down ("let's not get dirt packed in anywhere it's not supposed to be"), but they'd still been surrounded by nature and sunlight, and Jay had gotten so into it he'd even taken charge for once, rolling Alexei onto his broad back and bouncing on his cock like some kind of...some kind of *porn star* or something.

Alexei had looked up at him like he was an angel, or maybe an incubus, surprisingly speechless considering his usual sultry words of encouragement and praise, and Jay had felt so full and beautiful and powerful. He was determined to do it again. But also maybe to still do lots of loving time because he really couldn't resist having Alexei's full attention and talents focused 100 percent on Jay.

But! The point was...camping was awesome.

Jay reached a hand out the car window to feel the wind rushing by. "Do you think we could get the family to go camping with us sometime?"

Alexei seemed to think that over for a minute, tapping the steering wheel with his fingers. "Danny, definitely," he said after a moment. "Which means Roman too. Soren you might have to bribe."

Jay wiggled his fingers in the wind, thinking it over. "I could share my camping candy with him."

Alexei made a skeptical sound. "I'm thinking more like letting him talk you into buying some diamond-encrusted designer blouse or something."

What a weird thought. Jay looked down at his filthy, torn T-shirt. "To wear camping?"

Alexei's laugh was deep and rich. "Sure, sweetheart. To wear camping."

Jay really thought that sounded kind of silly and uncomfortable, but he hummed happily anyway, enamored with the idea of a family camping trip. He wondered if Jamie and Luc had ever been camping together. Could someone go camping in the desert? That would be so fun, with cacti all around them. Although, then they'd need to be a little more careful rolling around during sexy times. Although, then again, if they were on a family camping trip, maybe there wouldn't be any sexy times anyway.

Unless...

Jay brought his hand back into the car, settling it on his lap and turning to face Alexei. "Have you ever been part of an orgy?"

Alexei's strangled, "Excuse me?" was about an octave higher than usual.

Or maybe *orgy* wasn't quite the right word. Jay didn't want to actually have sex with anyone other than Alexei. Just maybe at the same time, in the same location, as someone other than Alexei? So that no one had to miss out on sexy times when camping?

What exactly did an orgy entail? He'd need to look it up later.

Alexei cleared his throat, and his eyes kept darting away from the road, which probably wasn't very safe. "Jay..."

But Jay was distracted from clarifying by a blur running across said road. "Oh!" he yelled out. "Stop the car, please."

Alexei stopped immediately, not even asking why Jay was making them pull over. They both hopped out, and Jay hustled over to where he'd last seen the fuzzy-looking blur run to: a row of bushes lining a gas station lot.

There was a kitten cowering against the shrubbery.

"Hello, kitten," Jay said, bending over at the waist to wave at the little ball of fur. "What are you doing out here all by yourself?"

But the little bitty thing kept cowering under the bush, hissing when Jay tried to move closer.

Jay sighed, feeling more than a little dejected. "It's scared of me," he complained to Alexei, who'd crept up behind him. "Dogs I can usually win over with a biscuit or a walk. But I can never get cats to like me. And I like them so much!"

Alexei settled his warm hand on the back of Jay's neck, squeezing encouragingly. "Cats aren't like dogs, sweetheart. They're a little warier. You need to let them come to you."

And then he crouched, motioning for Jay to do the same. They waited there, just like that, for a long while, still and silent, and eventually—in tiny, slow movements—the little kitten inched closer.

"There you go," Alexei murmured, scooping the kitten up in one broad hand. He lowered his head so he and the kitten were nose to nose. "Where did you come from, little thing?"

"From in here," Jay answered from where he'd crawled forward, peering deeper into the bush. He tried to keep still and quiet, even though excitement had him wanting to wiggle around. "There're two more here," he whisper-shouted, crawling back out to rest on his knees. "What should we do?"

"Oh!" Jay startled as Alexei plopped the kitten into Jay's hand.

"You stay here," Alexei said. "I'll ask for a box from the gas station."

Jay stared at the fuzzy creature in his palms. It was black and white, like it was dressed in a little kitten tuxedo. Jay couldn't help but think Soren would approve. The kitten stared back at him, yellow eyes wide and barely blinking. "Hello, kitten," Jay said for the second time, keeping his voice soft, gentle. "I'm Jay."

The kitten started purring.

#

Jay hummed happily as Alexei's strong fingers worked shampoo into his hair, kneading at Jay's scalp in a way that had all his muscles loose and relaxed and melty.

"Why are you so good at that?" he asked in a mumble, leaning back more firmly against Alexei's broad chest and stretching his legs out into the bath.

Jay already knew the answer. Alexei's favorite answer anytime he asked something like that, about why they matched so well.

Alexei didn't disappoint. "Because I was made for you, kotyonok."

Jay was learning that Alexei took the concept of fated mates very seriously. He said that logically, the only conclusion that could be made from the whole thing was that Alexei was literally born to love Jay. That Jay was the reason for his existence.

Jay thought maybe it was all a little more nuanced than that, but he loved to hear it anyway. Because wasn't that just the nicest thought?

He listened in the ensuing silence for any sounds of mewling, but their new houseguests must have still been sleeping.

They'd tried taking the kittens to the shelter, but they'd been told by the harried-looking volunteer that there was no room for them. So they'd picked up extra blankets, wet food, and a heat lamp (the last one being Alexei's suggestion). The kittens had curled up in the box together immediately on arriving in the new home, the lamp making it look like they were all in a little kitten sauna.

"Lean your head back."

Jay complied, and warm water poured over his head and down the back of his neck. He sighed with pleasure.

He loved that Alexei liked taking baths with him (although this time, he'd insisted they both rinse off the dirt in the shower before they got in the tub). He loved that even though they'd just spent the past seventy-two hours solely in each other's company, Alexei was in no hurry to leave his side. That he craved the same closeness Jay did.

Damaged in the same way, Alexei liked to say, when he was feeling saucy.

But Jay didn't think of it as damage anymore. Some of their shared traits may have stemmed from trauma, yes, but he liked to think of it as...a gift. That he and his mate were so well matched. Made to love each other. Maybe that was naive of him. But he didn't care.

"What would you like to do after this?" Alexei asked, working conditioner into the ends of Jay's hair.

Alexei always asked. Because he loved Jay. And even if his love was sometimes sharply obsessive, it was also kind. Thoughtful.

Warm and accepting. Jay didn't care what Alexei said to the contrary; Alexei would always be the nicest human in his mind.

And because Alexei *did* always ask, and never made Jay regret answering honestly, Jay said exactly what he was feeling right now. "I want to keep the kittens."

Jay felt the vibration of Alexei's soft chuckle against his back. "I thought as much."

Jay tilted his head back to meet Alexei's pretty eyes. "You don't mind?"

"As long as you don't mind no longer being the only kitten in town." Alexei pressed a kiss to his nose. "Whatever makes you happy, kotyonok."

"You make me happy," Jay answered easily, turning his head back so Alexei could rinse out the conditioner. "But kittens would be nice too."

Alexei smoothed Jay's hair back with gentle fingers. "Then we'll have kittens."

"And I think I know how I want to give away the first of my money." Jay had been having trouble deciding, these past months. There were so many ways it could be spent, so many worthy causes. How did one choose?

"You want to start your own pet shelter?" Alexei guessed, tugging at one of Jay's earlobes.

Jay froze for a moment, startled. He'd meant giving the money to the other shelter, the one they'd stopped at. Which he could still do, definitely. But he could do more, right? He thought of the small, cramped building they'd seen, the too-small cages without any doors to the outside. They could buy a plot of land, build a bigger building.

He hesitated. "I wouldn't know how."

Alexei wrapped his arms around Jay's chest, and Jay leaned back into his warm comfort. "I would help you," Alexei said. "I mean, I don't know how either. But we could find someone who does. We could learn together."

Jay wiggled out of Alexei's hold and turned around, splashing water onto the bathroom floor as he did so, but that was okay because Alexei never minded a mess, never got angry at Jay for being careless or clumsy or overexcited. So Jay launched himself at his mate in the water, wrapping his arms around his neck, kissing him with full enthusiasm. "That sounds so nice! So, so nice. And we'll hire smart, lovely humans. So when it's time to go, we have someone to hand it over to."

And then he kissed Alexei some more. Just because.

Eventually Jay turned around again and settled back into position, so Alexei could pour more warm water over his head. Not because there was any conditioner left in it. Just because it felt good.

"Do you think we'll always be this happy?" Jay asked, once he was settled back against Alexei's chest.

Alexei pressed a soft kiss to Jay's temple. "I do."

Jay smiled. "You don't think that's too optimistic of us? Or naive?"

"I've never in my life been accused of being either of those things, kotyonok. It's just a fact. We will."

Jay sighed happily. "Because you were made for me?"

"Exactly."

"And I was made for you."

"Made for each other," Alexei agreed.

How perfect that was. How lucky. How nice.

* * *

The End.

Author's Note

Thank you so much for reading book four! I hope you enjoyed seeing Jay find his much needed happy ever after as much as I loved writing it.

Oof, my sweet Jaybird. It's always been such a treat already, writing him from an outside perspective in previous books, but I absolutely *loved* getting into his head properly this time. I can't get enough of the way he sees the world, the little bits of happiness he finds for himself, the importance he puts on people and connection. And poor, smitten Alexei; that man never stood a chance against our bite-y cinnamon roll. I just adored how these two people who haven't been shown nearly enough sweetness or kindness manifested those things for each other. All the love languages all the time!

What's Next?

Book five will be (surprise, surprise) Wolfe and Dr. Monroe! I'm excited to do a bit of a tonal shift, and to explore a fledgling mating bond taking place *before* the two of them even get a chance to get to know each other. And so many questions to be answered: Do Wolfe's psychopathic tendencies really mean he can't love? How will Dr. Monroe handle being mated to such a stone cold fuddy-duddy? Does Dr. Monroe even have a first name?? Only time will tell!

If you want to stay in the know, you can sign up for my newsletter for updates and news on upcoming releases. And I can always be reached by email if you just want to say howdy. I love, love, love hearing from my readers!

graebryanauthor@gmail.com

I also now have a FB reader group: Grae Bryan's Reader Den
Join us for updates, teasers, and first looks at covers and character art!

Thank you all for reading and please consider reviewing if you enjoyed yourself! Your support means the world.

About the Author

Grae Bryan has been reading romance since she was far too young to know any better. Her love for love stories spans all genres, and while her current series is of the paranormal variety, she knows she'll be exploring other worlds further down the line.

She lives in Arizona with her husband, who graciously shares space with all the imaginary men in her head. When not writing, she can generally be found reading more than is healthy, walking her monster-dog, or cuddling her demon-cat.

Find her online: graebryan.com
Join her Facebook reader group: Grae Bryan's Reader Den
Facebook: @graebryanauthor
Instagram: @authorgraebryan
Sign up for her newsletter: graebryan.com/contact

www.ingramcontent.com/pod-product-compliance
Lightning Source LLC
Chambersburg PA
CBHW022040240626
47154CB00007B/2495